MW01173911

"Thank you, Captain.

"You and your men are to stand guard at the entrances to this hall. Do not enter until Sir Loveress lets you in. If that takes longer than a full day and night... inform Duke Elsevier that he is to support King Jason in all ways."

Sir Tim was shocked. "Damien... my King... you can't be serious..."

"You have your orders, Captain Ancellius," Adam Loveress growled.

"Yes, sir!" Sir Tim responded automatically to his former Captain.

As the echo of the doors closing faded away, Adam turned to. "So, you think none of us are going to make it out of here alive?"

"No," Genevieve said firmly, "exactly the opposite."

"So, what am I here for then?" Adam demanded.

"This..." the king held out a gem on a slender chain to Adam, "will end what life is left in my body that remains."

Adam, in the act of reaching for the proffered jewel, froze. *"What?"*

Damien swallowed. "I need to access the Realm at a deeper level than I have since the very first time it Bound me. And it nearly consumed me then. Our people don't need a breathing body of a king withering away without a soul. The jewel will stop my heart without leaving any external marks. No one will know what you did."

"And you just carry this thing around all the time just in case?" Adam muttered, staring at the now-ominous-looking faceted red stone.

Damien glanced back at him. "No. I altered that pendant_on the way here from the Council chamber."

He put his arms around his silent wife. "I'm sorry," he whispered to her, then turned to Adam.

"This is why you have to be in here, Adam. There's no one else I trust for this. But the part about you not coming out – that was just to scare Tim into moving.

"Nothing should happen to you."

THE PIRATE-KING

Book Three of the Chronicles of Ilseador

MANGALA MCNAMARA

Also available in eBook and paperback editions.
McNamara, Mangala
The Pirate-King/ by Mangala McNamara Indiana: Rising Dragon Books, 2024
206 pages, 2 maps
(McNamara, Mangala. Chronicles of Ilseador; bk. 3)
Summary: The wedding and coronation are over – just in time for King Damien to fight off a devastating ice-storm, pirate-raid, and evil sorceress who threaten to destroy his Realm.
ISBN 978-1-960160-32-4 (pbk)
1. Kings and rulers - Fiction. 2. Wizards and Magic - Fiction
ISBN 978-1-960160-33-1 (hc); ISBN 978-1-960160-29-4 (eBook)

ISBN: 78-1-960160-33-1
First Print Edition: April 2024
10 9 8 7 6 5 4 3 2 1

For my husband, always.

And for Piers Anthony, who inspired and encouraged me to write the stories that I needed to.

A note to sensitive souls:
Ilseador is a land that has been misruled for eighty-three years by a tyrant who was also an evil sorcerer in every sense of the word. Up to four generations cannot remember a time before the old king assumed the throne... and the morals (or lack thereof) of a country often develop - intentionally or not - from the example at the top. This is particularly true of the upper echelons of society, which this story focuses on. The result is that it's basically an entire nation of traumatized people who have seen that greed and cruelty and o'erweening ambition are rewarded. The old king's Apprentice is still around to cause trouble as well...

Five years into King Damien's more compassionate reign, there are still far too many scars...

Proceed with caution...

CONTENTS

MANGALA MCNAMARA

PROLOGUE

a few months earlier

"YOU'RE GOING TO TELL ME to wait, *again,*" the huge man growled.

The small, slim, slip of a girl shook her head, her knee-length fall of white-blonde hair waving slowly behind her as she did.

"No. You've waited long enough. *I've* waited long enough. I'm not dependent anymore on the caution – or whims – of old men to get what I want."

The large man glowered down at her, briefly unsure whether she was including *him* in that statement. He was easily old enough to be her father – not quite old enough to have *sired* her father.

But no, the pale, little sorceress was still seething about how her former master had held back her ambitions. It had nothing to do with himself.

And thank the Gods for that. The old sorcerer had disappeared entirely as far as he could tell and it was only reasonable to assume that it was the work of his jealous Apprentice – this wisp of a maiden who looked barely old enough to wed. This ruthless creature residing in the skin of a pretty maiden with manners as fine as any princess.

She made the man's blood run cold and his balls shrivel along with.

If there were any other way to retrieve what he'd been promised – and then had ripped from him so cruelly, so very long ago. The girl he should have married. The son that should have been his to raise and love. Vengeance on his grandfather and the woman the old man had *forced* him to wed at far

1

too young of an age. Vengeance on the cousins who had promised to aid and then left him to suffer his fate.

Oh, aye, he'd do something about all of that.

Though it was too late for vengeance on his grandfather – he was one of the old men the pale little sorceress had referred to.

And the cousins who had betrayed him – they were gone, too. But they'd left a son, and he'd be a fit target. After all, that son had the *other* thing the man lusted for, nearly as much as he lusted for his girl and the love of his son.

So, aye, he'd work with this dangerous slip of a girl for now.

And if the rumors were true, once he had all the things he wanted, he'd have the Power to break with her then. The Power his grandfather had wielded well enough to keep her and her old master at bay for so long, delaying and delaying and delaying…

"So, all your pieces are in place now?" he demanded.

Her smile was the spontaneous, happy expression of the girl she should've been. "The duke is ready to move, yes. And I've had confirmation from my colleagues in Deltheren. They are beginning their part and it should be well-set on its way by the time we're in position. The day after the wedding, if all goes according to plan."

Ah, yes, the *wedding*.

"I'd rather it were the day *before*," he complained.

For all that the day would recognize his son in the position to which he had been born, did anyone but know it. The *wedding* would make it exceedingly difficult to continue on the dynasty.

And given his own hurtful history, it was impossible to believe that this wasn't all being done in despite of his son's wishes. Likely in despite of his groveling and begging for freedom.

His fists tightened. He'd free his son from the bondage. A king could declare a marriage null and void, couldn't he? And he'd be twice a king.

"Evan, my dear, we can't have *everything* our way, now can we?" the girl – or was she really a demon in girl-form? – said with a chuckle. "The news we've gotten is that the king is going to tax his abilities greatly on some frivolous displays. He'll be much more vulnerable after that, as I've told you before."

She smiled. "I will remove the Sorcerer-King from his throne and see that you have your lady in your arms. You can take it from there, I trust."

Evan growled unhappy assent. Better to do it right and win – and *then* fix things for his son – than to make the attempt and have to retreat with his tail between his legs. He was putting all his political capitol into this venture... he'd never be able to manage it again, White Witch of the South at his side or not.

The girl nodded. "Go prepare your fleet. I will join you before we make the assault. And remember..."

Her beautiful, silky, chilling voice caught the man as he began to turn away.

"...I can see you wherever you are, Evan. I am helping you with this so that I get what *I* want and I will not interfere with your quest to retrieve your *'lost love'* and the son you've never met and the crown you covet. But do not seek to betray me in this."

He gave her a curt nod before exiting the black-and-blood-red elegance of her audience chamber. The audience chamber where he had begun meeting with her now-vanished master not all that long ago.

She had said nothing about not betraying *him*, the man noted.

Not so far away, in the city of Emeralsee in Ilseador, King Damien wrestled with his conscience.

To save his beloved, soul-bound Queen and to continue to be able to rebuild his Realm after the damage his grandfather, the Evil Wizard-Tyrant Reginald the Ruthless, had wreaked upon it for eighty-three years, he was having to compromise everything else he held dear:

The honesty that he had always offered his subjects and vassals.

His relationship with the friends who had rescued him, taught him, and placed him on the throne.

His own sense of honor.

It was worth it, he told himself over and over again. The Realm deserved only the best that he could give it, the Healing that only a monarch of the Alsterling line could provide to resolve the damage done by another such. *Genevieve* deserved everything and anything he could give her.

He'd find a way to make it up to Adam and Jason, Ciriis and Lord Aldred.

Making it possible for Adam and Jason to marry – at so long last – was perhaps a start. Though Naming Jason his Heir and Crown Prince was perhaps a step in the wrong direction, since his Champion wanted no such role. Though whom else could he so name, when Jason would secretly be the father of Damien and Genevieve's first child? King and Queen might still not survive the magickal demands of the Realm compounded with the soul-bond and Genevieve's weakness after so many miscarriages. There had to be an obvious and unquestioned Regent waiting to support – and rear – the newborn princess.

Giving Jason and Adam the child they – or at least Adam – so desperately wanted was another positive step… even if that came with secrecy and more emotional complications than Damien could really bear to contemplate. Most men – as even Jason had noted, ironically, that first night – usually outgrew their boyhood infatuations.

He had no idea yet how to mend things with Lord Aldred and Ciriis. His father-in-law, banished now from Court for daring to sire a child on Damien's first lover… another potential claimant to the Throne to set against the child that Damien and Genevieve didn't yet have. Aldred was too savvy not to have known better – he was risking another civil war in a Realm not yet a quarter Healed from the last one… which Aldred had also led, though with what must have been a clearer conscience, given that it had been Reginald the Ruthless against whom he had been rebelling.

How could *trying* so hard to do the right thing by Realm, vassals, people, and soul-bound spouse have turned out so badly in just five short years?

Chapter ONE

Anticipation

"**Y**ou've... looked better, Damien," Rosa said with concern as the king wandered out into the Great Hall late the next morning.

He gave her a distracted nod. "Probably."

She frowned, then handed baby Betha to her husband, and took Damien by the elbow. The former Rebel Countess – and current Duchess of Dalziallest – steered him out of the Great Hall, hopefully before any of the *rest* of his Court that were gathered there noticed.

A number of alarmed-looking young people – members of the Secret Cadre that Rosa hadn't yet been introduced to, presumably – trailed them out of the room in a disorganized-looking flock. They were ahead of the Royal Guards at least, in tracking down their wayward royal charge... but then again, the uniformed knights of the Royal Guard were likely aware that if *they* looked alarmed as they moved rapidly through the castle it might start a general panic. The whole point of the Secret Cadre – more publicly known as Her Majesty's ladies-in-waiting and His Majesty's gentlemen-of-the-chamber – was to ensure that the royal pair *could* be guarded at all times and in all contexts, even those where greater discretion was required.

Exactly *how* Damien had managed to escape his careful (and more than slightly, if justifiably, paranoid) guards of *both* groups simultaneously...

was a mystery. He was usually careful *not* to do exactly that, being more than slightly (and justifiably) paranoid himself.

"Is Her Majesty awake then?" the clever Lady Alanna managed to get in front of Rosa and the king and sank down in a deep curtsy. Rosa stopped, but Damien – still looking half-asleep – might have tripped over her if Rosa hadn't pulled him to a halt.

"Hmmn?" The king seemed to have to pull himself back from some distant land. "Genevieve? Awake? I don't know..." his look became introspective. "Yes. Yes, she is. She's eating breakfast with... Marianna Loveress and Elaina Solway." He frowned. "Aren't any of your people up there, Alanna? The one isn't trained yet and the other isn't even on the try-outs list, last I knew."

Lady Alanna looked askance at his willingness to discuss this in even so public a venue as a hallway empty of any but the Secret Cadre... and Rosa. But she didn't see how not to answer a direct question from her king. "The Crown Prince asked Lady Aryllis to add Miss Solway to the try-outs last night. Lady Emily and Lord Aaron were supposed to be on duty with the Queen this morning. I would assume they are still up there unless she has dismissed them. Sir Otto and Sir Rodney were on door duty. Your Majesty," she said with some concern, "One of your knights should surely be at your side. I *cannot* understand how they would have..."

"Let me out by myself like this?" the king said dryly.

"*Damien...*" Rosa hissed. And pointed at the young lady trapped in her curtsy when he looked at her quizzically.

He flushed slightly. Damien was usually the most courteous and thoughtful of people. "Please rise, Lady Alanna. And please accept my apologies."

"You don't seem yourself, Your Majesty," the young woman said sympathetically, rising as gracefully as if she had not just held that position for far too long. Twenty-five-year-old muscles, the Duchess of Dalziallest thought mournfully... and a body that had never housed another living human being. Not that she regretted having her daughters... she simply missed having her body the way it used to be. Zachary kept telling her she was more beautiful now... which was nice to hear, but didn't bring back her muscle-tone.

"No, I suppose not." The king ran a hand through his already rumpled – slept-in, not combed – hair, doing it really no particular damage since it was already such a disaster, then scratched at his short beard. His slight, wry smile was more normal, however, as a pair of knights came dashing up towards them, apparently having given up and abandoned discretion for haste. "I see. Excellent tactic, milady. Delay me long enough to get a *proper* escort for your erring king." He nodded politely at the two knights. "Lev. Angelos."

"Damien, you need a change and a shave," Rosa instructed him firmly. "A wash if you can squeeze in the time before Council. You *look* like you could use three days' sleep, but–"

He gave her a poleaxed look. "Before *what?*"

She sighed. "You *do* remember telling everyone that we would resume Council meetings after the coronation."

"Well, yes, but I didn't mean the *day* after..."

"Then you should have specified. Besides which, some of the nobles with longer times to travel are planning to leave tomorrow at dawn." Which should have included herself and Zachary, actually, though they were delaying their own departure to try to spend some time with their old friends. They had seen Genevieve when she passed through in the early Fall with Jason, of course. Rosa had given the Queen back the Heir's Ring at the time and then felt guilty about it for the next several months after thinking on how dreadfully worn and ill Genevieve had seemed.

At the time, Rosa and Zachary had hoped that having the Ring back in her possession would tame Genevieve's inclinations to serve as a Warrior-Queen. They were well aware of how many babes she had lost, carrying out her duties to reclaim the Lost Provinces – and they knew both her and Damien well enough to know *he* would never risk his soul-bonded love that way. So, it had to be Genevieve's own idea, and that meant there was a hope that she could be reminded of the primacy of her *other* duty: bearing an Heir to the Throne.

She'd certainly seemed envious of their own two precious little girls... but when they'd seen that Jason had to practically lift her into the carriage that she was riding in – instead of the warhorse they'd only ever seen her on before – they had begun to rethink the move.

Neither of them had anticipated Damien Naming Jason to the position of Crown Prince and Heir in the absence of a child of his and Genevieve's own.

Rosa began to steer the distracted and dismayed king back towards his apartments again. "By my estimate you have just enough time to at least make yourself *look* like you're awake enough to lead a country..."

Damien groaned and rubbed at his hair and beard again, but resisted her pull to turn to the pair of knights trailing them. "Cousin, I have a different errand for you. Please let your lord father the Baron know that I'd like to talk to him after the Council meeting."

Sir Angelos Eldridge – Damien's cousin at a few removes on his mother's side – looked warily between Lady Alanna and his king. The Royal Guards had been read quite a lecture by their former-as-of-two-days-ago Captain not all that long ago. The Secret Cadre ranked them, it had been explained in no uncertain terms, because the ladies and gentlemen were able to follow the King and Queen in places that Royal Guards were not. Lady Alanna was standing with her arms crossed and looking disapproving. Sir Adam had *not* explained how to deal with conflicts between royal orders and chain-of-command. Or rather, when Sir Drake had asked about it, Captain Loveress had given him an extremely sardonic look and said "Pray." Which was not helpful at all.

Rosa nudged the king again, and Damien startled as if he had forgotten again that he was supposed to be going someplace. "Don't worry, Angelos. I'll have Lev here. I'm sure he and our lovely Lady Alanna can handle walking me back to my quarters." He looked at Rosa. "I'm sure you have things to take care of before the Council meeting, Your Grace." The king held out his arm to Alanna. "Milady?"

Rosa shook her head as Damien walked off with his official and unofficial Guards. This Council meeting certainly promised to be... less than productive.

Damien fiddled with his pen as one of his vassals droned on and on about... something. It was a baron, he thought, but at the moment he couldn't find the energy or attention to identify the man. Or, really, to care.

He knew his posture of almost aggressive disinterest bothered the members of his Council of Peers and Vassals. This wasn't what they'd seen out of their king these last five years. Damien had been careful to always show them attention, strength, and a cast of supporting characters who backed him up even when they disagreed with him.

Genevieve wasn't here now, and the Council couldn't be allowed to know why.

Jason and Adam were enjoying the morning after their wedding night, he assumed.

Aldred and Ciriis were up in Cloudcroft, her pregnancy proceeding well by the reports he was receiving, though their relationship had grown somewhat rocky.

Sir Tim was here, in his role as Captain of the Royal Guards, as well as a new, albeit extremely minor, Peer of the Realm. But Tim was a relative unknown to most of the nobles and a harmless-seeming fellow to the rest. Hardly a match for the architects of the king's reign or the Rebel Duke and Duchess. And the few who knew either Tim or Damien well enough to guess there must be more to this cheerful, mild-mannered fellow... were not likely to challenge the king in any regard.

Those included his Dukes and Duchess of Siovale and Dalzialest. Tomas Elsevier, Duke of Siovale, as the most senior, had begun directing the meeting when Damien left them all waiting for his permission to move on. That presumption had caused a few raised eyebrows, but the king hadn't cared. Perhaps it would even have some positive fallout, a distant part of him wondered, when he backed up the Duke of Siovale's actions. Perhaps *at last* they could be done with this air of suspicion.

The baron continued to drone on... or perhaps it was a different one.

Something was stealing *all* of Damien's attention.

Something to do with the Realm, thank the Gods, not Genevieve... though it seemed half his attention was always with her these days. More than half... she'd seemed to be *glowing* to his perceptions these last three days, and he hadn't dared ask if anyone else noticed. If it was real to others. By the lack of commentary during and after the wedding he'd guessed *not*.

He couldn't remember her *glowing* in the past.

The Realm.

He dragged his attention back.

The Realm, but not a part of it Bound to anyone in this room – and that covered most of the Realm. Jason's investiture as Heir had been a welcome break after the harvest was in and before the winter snows bound them all up in their own demesnes, so most of the country's nobility had shown up, though it had taken fast riders indeed to get the word out to the farther flung provinces in time for them to travel to Emeralsee. Who was missing?

Countess Solway of course, but Brindlewell was enfeoffed to Elaarwen again, and had been bound to Emeralsee while Aldred – and Genevieve – rebelled and Damien's grandfather ruled. Damien was nearly as Bound to Elaarwen as Genevieve, and his direct bonds to Emeralsee would never really fade as long as the Castle and Throne claimed him, despite both now being Bound to his Named and Confirmed Heir. It wasn't something in Brindlewell, though things were not *well* there exactly.

He ran through the list of all his vassals who hadn't made it, testing his connection to their lands absently, but sure in his heart that it wasn't any of them. They were all represented here today by their immediate liege-lords or -ladies anyways, who were magickally Bound to their lands as well, so it shouldn't matter that the lesser vassals weren't present.

It had to be one of the Lost Provinces, and since the Realm hadn't yet demanded he do anything about Farivera or Everfields, it had to be...

"Elendria!"

The baron looked offended and startled as the king's hands slammed down on the table, interrupting whatever it was he'd been saying. All eyes focused on Damien, but he barely noticed. The force of his movement had propelled him out of his chair – which had only not fallen with a great crash due to Sir Tim's quick reflexes at his side.

"Your Majesty?" Tomas Elsevier, Duke of Siovale ventured. His very slightly raised eyebrow suggested that the king had better have some explanation or it would be a political mess. "Baron Rivencour *was* just explaining how trade with Elendria will impact his people in Flowerdell."

Damien shook his head.

"There's an ice-storm out of Deltheren just starting to hit Elendria *now*. It will be *here* by evening. By morning there will be an inch to two inches of ice coating *everything* in its path." He frowned. "The winds are wrong..."

"Hail?" Tomas had started out of his chair.

Damien shook his head again, then hesitated. "I can't tell. Freezing rain, sleet... *An inch or more of ice coating everything.* We're going to lose a lot of trees to this." His heart grieved, but this was not the time. "If we're lucky, we won't lose *people*. Or animals."

The king looked around at his Bound and Sworn vassals. They knew the map of the Realm as well as he did, knew what fiefs lay between Elendria and the capitol. Damien named them off anyways, giving them estimated times before the storm hit. Their faces paled as he did so.

And then he gave them an instruction he had hoped he'd never have to. He knew Adam – and perhaps even Genevieve – would be wroth with him. But that would be later. And hopefully it was a *later* that would involve recriminations for giving away still more power, not for losing large numbers of his subjects and their livelihoods.

"You should all be able to feel your lands through the Bond that formed when you swore your Vassal's Oath. There's no way to get word to your people in time," he met their grim nods with his own. "Not the normal way anyhow," the king continued. "The Realm – your lands – won't let you do this for long, but if you work together, liege-lords and -ladies with your vassals, you *may* be able to give your people a sense that they need to get themselves and their livestock under cover."

"How?" Zachary demanded, his face white beneath that healthy tan he always sported. Rumor went that he worked the harvest and the planting as hard and as long as any of his people. And therefore likely knew a fair number of them personally.

"Join hands," Damien was making this up as he went along. He could feel Queen Marian hovering behind him, but she'd been no sorceress; this was far beyond her purview. The answers were coming from *somewhere*, though, and it didn't seem to entirely be the Realm. Where it *did* come from – he'd have to figure that out... later.

"Form circles around your liege-lady. She won't need to contact anyone herself, since you are each closer to your own people, but she can stabilize your connection." The king refrained from adding that the rulers of his duchies all had at least a trace of magick in their blood – and that there was likely more than a spark in scions of all the lesser families as well, given how they tended to intermarry. Damien had begun to suspect that there was a connection between the magick and why those particular families had risen... and it explained why the Alsterling line inevitably bred the strongest magick-wielders.

"Keep it simple," the king went on. "Don't try to talk to each individual. Don't think in *words* at all. You want to spread your awareness thinly over the area that is bound to you with the single thought '*get under cover and stay put.*' That way, even runaways and recluses should hear you." He also refrained from mentioning that what they would be doing was placing a powerful compulsion spell on every human – and perhaps even the animals – in their demesnes. They wouldn't – most of them – be able to sustain the connection – or the spell – for more than a few moments, but there were some of them...

Damien would be spending the next year – or lifetime – making sure that what he taught them in this moment of peril wasn't abused.

But surely the lives saved would be worth it?

"Go to your Duke or Duchess' rooms. Do this sitting down. On the floor, if need be, but somewhere that you won't be hurt if you fall down." He gave them a dry look. "Madame Elista's people are used to dealing with *me*. They'll have food and drink ready for after." He hesitated, then sighed. "Ladies, forgive my boldness, but loosen your corsets. If you faint before your people are warned, you will truly have a killer fashion." A variety of reactions from relief to embarrassment, but no outrage at least. A few of the men looked surprised, perhaps that he had even thought of it.

People began rising quickly.

There were no objections, surprisingly enough, and the speed with which they moved... Damien had a frightening suspicion that he was *glowing* as they said he had done in the battle with Lord Prydeen, five years ago. Which might be more than appropriate... this would surely tax his magickal strength and cleverness far more than that skirmish. With the Realm alive and awake and angry behind him, dealing with Prydeen had ended up taking little more effort than swatting a fly. This time it was Nature itself to face, and the Realm was more than half asleep with the onset of Winter.

"Your Majesty," Rosa's eyes were filled with determination. "Can't you turn this storm? Or blunt it?"

Dalzialest... Zialest itself – the county which she had inherited – lay straight in the storm's path. Damien had permitted her to merge it with her husband, Zachary's, county of Dalizell to create the duchy of Dalzialest when he had come to his throne.

He didn't have time to tell her that with *both* her and Zachary Bound, they might be able to do *more*. On the other hand, their lands *had* been counties until this generation and although both of them had magick, it was just a trickle. He suspected their tiny daughters had much greater potential, but they were too little now...

He gave her another grim nod. "I'll be doing what I can, but Elendria is being hit right *now*, and that's my first concern." He gave Duchess Laura Marseill of Alpinsward and Baron Densal Krakenroost of Minglemere a nod. "The Realm doesn't accept our human boundaries. I'm as Bound to Elendria as you are to your lands. They are just as much my responsibility."

Tomas Elsevier rose to face him with folded arms. "No. They're not."

The room fell silent of rustling skirts and papers as everyone froze.

"What do you mean, Your Grace?" Damien positively *itched* with the need to be away from the Council table and warning the people – the *animals* – of Elendria. He could *feel* the shock of the storm devastating the far western edge of the province; feel animals dying, tree branches beginning to bend past the point of recovery, and humans suffering the first symptoms of frostbite and hypothermia.

There wasn't *time* for discussion.

But he owed the Duke of Siovale his throne.

Despite being manipulated magickally for two years, Tomas could have looked to the main chance and thrown in with his brother Harald. Brother of the King surely sounded a lot better than the whispers of 'the Traitor Duke' that had followed him ever since, despite his sacrifices. Whispers that followed his family as well. Damien had never asked for Tomas' children to serve as pages in the Castle – it would have looked too much like he was taking hostages.

And... Tomas was a friend. And perhaps the only person in this room who was willing to call the king out on a poor decision. Perhaps the only person here who was thinking straight at *all*, with all but the northern edges of Siovale likely to be spared by this storm.

Damien owed the man a fair hearing for putting his personal and political capital on the line.

"Elendria is *not* a part of your Realm, Damien."

Tomas Elsevier did nothing that was not deliberate. Using the king's given name, for instance.

He unfolded his arms and leaned forward on the table, supporting himself with only his spread fingertips. "Countess Miraly – and her mother before her – *left* the protections of this Realm and has not chosen to accept them back. Let her – or Queen Estelle – protect their own. Your energies are vast, my king, but even you have limits. How vast or how limited, perhaps even you don't know, but your *duty* is to the people who are sworn to you through these, your Sworn and Bound Vassals." His nod encompassed the room. "Not to unrepentant rebels."

Damien stared at him. "Tomas... six years ago, that could have been *Siovale*."

"Yes," the older man agreed. "And *I* would have been responsible for what happened. Not King Reginald." His eyes flickered to Rosa and Zachary. "Or not King Reginald alone. Of course," he added with a small smile, "six years ago, our king wouldn't have even *tried* to protect the country from a natural disaster. Even if he *could*."

"How about an *unnatural* one?" someone muttered from near the door. "Isn't this happening because of what the king did to the weather yesterday?"

Damien looked for the speaker, but apparently the sentiment was sufficiently shared that no one gave her up. "No, it's not actually. There hasn't been time." He closed his eyes for a moment so as to *see* the weather patterns without the distraction of it all being superimposed over the people in his field of view. "*That* storm is brewing out in the ocean. It should bring us an out-of-season near-hurricane in three days to a week. The warm air I created is pushing against the colder currents normal to this time of year..."

He frowned without opening his eyes. "We shouldn't *have* winds *out* of Deltheren at this time of year."

"I should say not!" exclaimed the Baron of Flowerdell, who'd been speaking earlier, one of Rosa's vassals near the Elendrian border. His face was pale beneath his florid complexion.

"You *cannot* protect Elendria," Tomas recaptured the king's attention – and the rest of the room. He had straightened up again, and his posture was still hard and unrelenting, but his eyes were sympathetic.

"Tom," Zachary Miramar tried to intercede. "It's His Majesty's decision."

Tomas Elsevier looked at his brother-in-law. "No. It's not." His eyes went back to Damien. "How many of our people will die if you waste yourself defending Elendria, Damien?"

The king couldn't meet his duke's eyes. He could *feel* the glow around himself dimming.

He swallowed hard.

Tomas was right. There was only one way to make this come out right in any way at all.

"Duke Elsevier, since thy province is largely out of danger, I entrust the Realm to thy most capable hands as Regent until such time as I or the Queen or Prince Jason is capable of resuming rule." Damien pulled off his signet ring and held it out to the startled duke. "Take it, Tomas." he said, too quietly for almost anyone else to hear. "Shortly you – and Tariana – may be the only people of any authority with the ability to see straight." Embervest wasn't in the storm's path at all... but its cheerful young duchess had never fought a battle. That wouldn't be lost on Tomas Elsevier any more than the fact that his king had just demonstrated his utter trust in him.

Hopefully it wouldn't be lost on anyone else either. *Enough* with this 'Traitor Duke' nonsense.

"Captain Ancellius," Damien began turning away as Tomas took the ring – and the power to issue royal proclamations up to and including executions and war. "Summon the Queen to – ah."

He stopped because Genevieve was entering on Jason's arm, Adam a half-step behind. It didn't matter that it was a crisis of unspeakable proportions, Damien's heart lifted at sight of her, and everything began to seem more manageable. And he didn't have to wonder if she was glowing for anyone else *now*.

Based on the way people were staring, she most definitely was.

Suddenly Damien realized his vassals of Emeralsee had gathered around him as he had instructed. Except... this wasn't his place anymore, no more did he have time to spare just for Emeralsee just now.

He gave them a small smile. "Your Duke is here, good people. Jason," he said with relief, "Did Gen– did the Queen explain what you need to do, Your Highness?"

Jason looked harried as he made his way over. "I think so. Yes." He ran a hand through his golden hair as he looked around at the men and women who were Bound to the fiefs in the Duchy which he had accepted only yesterday. Counts and barons and... Adam's mother and the man Jason now knew as a cousin, Baron Eldridge, Sir Angelos' father. The former Champion and newly made Duke and Prince had met them all briefly yesterday after the wedding. Properly done, it *should* have been immediately after his investiture as Duke, but they had seemed to accept Damien's explanation that the Vassal's Oath had taken Jason hard. They had seen enough other oaths sworn to have some idea of what he'd meant by that.

None of them probably realized that Jason had been literally *blind* for several hours after his sunrise investiture. At least the title of Crown Prince didn't require a Binding to the entire Realm as did a Crowning, or more than Jason's meeting his new vassals might have needed to be delayed. Though Adam had sworn he could have gotten his love through the wedding ceremony without sight, they had deserved to be able to look into each other's eyes as they spoke their vows.

"Your sitting room should be sufficient to seat everyone, with a little rearrangement," Adam's mother put in. She and the rest of the Loveress family had been breakfasting in Jason and Adam's suite, but his brothers and nephews had been sleeping in that space. "I'll just have the boys rearrange the furniture..."

She caught Adam's eye, and he started to turn away, but Damien called him back.

"I'll need you in the Throneroom as soon as you are able, my Champion."

He tried to apologize with his eyes, but wasn't sure if he'd succeeded when Adam gave him a curt nod and stepped out of the Council chamber. To summon his brothers, Damien presumed.

The king had always hated to keep them apart for any reason, and Jason surely could use his husband's support in his first attempt at a spell... not to mention that the population of the city of Emeralsee was double that of some of the duchies, and the surrounding counties nearly doubled that again. Thank the Gods that the city itself had its own count – a rather terrified looking man running to elder years; Damien knew him well as a solid administrator though the king felt his no-corruption policy needed rather better enforcement than Count Antonin had been giving it, no doubt to a certain lining of the man's own pockets. But the king had no doubt that the Count of Emeralsee would hold steady today, and be an anchor for his new-made Duke; Antonin had more than a drop of magick in his own blood, after all, likely due to the occasional royal scion trickling down to his family's lineage.

In the brief span while the door closed after his Champion, Damien's eyes had gravitated to Genevieve – as they always did when nothing else claimed them.

She smiled faintly. "It's a good thing Elaarwen isn't in danger," she said wryly, and he nodded.

Indeed. Doubly-Bound as Damien was to Elaarwen – both as King and as Duke, for being Genevieve's husband – it would have been incredibly distracting to have his focus pulled away to deal with the mountain province... though less so, admittedly, than Emeralsee would have been.

It also meant Genevieve could devote all of her energies to helping *him*. Her eyes went to the small number of her own vassals, awaiting instructions, and she directed them to put themselves at Duke Elsevier's disposal. There would doubtless be a number of administrative tasks that needed doing in the absence of the usual chains-of-command.

Damien wanted badly to reach out and touch her hand... but that would have to wait.

"Captain Ancellius. Would you kindly escort the Queen to the Throneroom and see that she has whatever she requests? I'll be there shortly, my love," he added to Genevieve, not even noticing the endearment until it slipped out. Normally they were more careful in public.

"I'll await you there. Your Majesty." Genevieve never curtsied to him. They had established that early on. She might be Queen-Consort, legally, rather than holding the Throne in her own name, but that was not the way they ruled, and not only because she very well *could* be ruling in her own name.

She held out a hand to Sir Tim, and he came over and offered his arm to her properly, but his eyes gave sharp orders to the Royal Guards scattered around the room, and they edged closer to their king. As long as Sir Tim had been by his side, he had been the king's personal guard. As he departed, Sir Leverett and Sir Marcus took his place. Damien almost cracked a smile, wondering if any of his vassals noticed that it took two men to replace his new Captain... just as it had his old one.

Too much else to do. "Baron Eldridge," he caught the man's attention as he followed Jason out of the Council chamber. "Our meeting will have to be delayed, my lord. I shall send word to re-schedule as soon as I am able."

The baron inclined his head politely. "Of course, Your Majesty." He paused and stepped closer. The room was almost emptied now. "Is this about our... mutual relatives, Your Majesty?"

Damien gave the man credit for being observant. "It is."

The baron smiled. "It was good to see my younger brother's reputation restored. Not that Alexa Solway made her slander so public as to tarnish the rest of the family, but that she used it to punish my nephew... and that she wouldn't let any of us *see* him, any more than His Majesty allowed us to see *you...*" He shook his head. "We'll have much to discuss, I'm sure. *After* this crisis is over. If I may borrow my son as a guide, Your Majesty?"

The king nodded and the baron turned to the young knight hovering nearby.

"Angelos, please show me to your cousin's rooms." He grinned at the king. "Your *other* cousin."

Damien began to think that he'd made a mistake in not getting to know this side of his family again once he'd been free to do so. He remembered – vaguely – how his mother had always tempered his father's tendency to seriousness with gentle humor... Genevieve would say 'I told you so'.

But for now, there was a storm to thwart.

Mangala McNamara

Chapter TWO

Preparation

THE ROOM HAD CLEARED COMPLETELY while he spoke to Baron Eldridge, leaving only the king and his handful of Royal Guards. Damien strode out, leaving the Guards to their tasks of surrounding him in a shell of safety while his thoughts surged ahead to his own tasks. For once, that shell would be useful: he didn't think he dared leave any energy powering his personal, physical protections while fighting the storm.

Genevieve had caused the Throneroom to be setup as the work-space they needed it to be. Huge fires blazed in the three hearths, taking the edge off the chill air, and a half-dozen braziers glowed with heat nearer the Throne itself. She had cushions stacked near the Throne to the right, and there would be broths and teas in the insulated hamper on the other side. They'd discussed plans for this sort of crisis shortly after she was crowned.

Damien gave her a nod and tried for a moment to put aside what they were about to do.

Adam strode in as he did that, looking sour. "What do you need *me* here for, Damien?" he demanded as soon as he was within speaking distance.

The king shook his head. "Not yet." He looked at Tim, standing near the dais, waiting for more instructions. "Thank you, Captain. You and your men are to stand guard at the entrances to this hall. On the *outside*. Do not enter until Sir Loveress lets you in. If that takes longer than a full day and night…" he met Genevieve's eyes, but avoided Adam's, "you are to inform Duke Elsevier that he is to support the new king in all ways."

Sir Tim's face was shocked, and he looked from King to Queen to Champion. "Damien… you can't be serious…"

The king drew breath to answer, but Adam spoke first. "You have your orders, Captain Ancellius," he ground out. "I believe time is of the essence."

Tim responded automatically, years of drilling under Adam's steely gaze and caustic tongue triggering old reflexes, though Captain and Champion were technically two separate chains-of-command.

"Yes, sir!"

A few flicks of Tim's hand sent the other Guards to secure the various entrances, while Tim himself took the main door. They had too few Royal Guards for these sorts of duties… but Damien knew there would soon be ladies-in-waiting and gentlemen-of-the-chamber keeping the good knights company at each door, and Castle Guards supplementing them as well.

As the echo of the doors closing faded away, Adam turned to Damien with a look of resignation. "So, you think *none* of us are going to make it out of here alive?"

"No," Genevieve said firmly, "exactly the opposite. But after this, no one will underestimate the seriousness of the situation… or interrupt us."

"So, what am *I* here for then?" Adam demanded again.

Damien cringed slightly, only halfway at Adam's tone. "In the *best* case – neither of us is going to be in fit shape to move. In the *worst…*" He looked up at Genevieve standing next to the Throne with apology. "In the *worst* case, my dear friend, one – or both – of us won't have a mind or a soul left."

The king reached into his doublet and pulled out a gem on a slender chain.

"This…" he held it out to Adam, "will end what life is left in my body that remains."

Adam, in the act of reaching for the proffered jewel, froze. "*What?*"

Damien swallowed. "The Throne is a concentrator of Power, Adam. But more than that, of the Realm itself. I need to access it at a deeper level than I have since the very first time it Bound me. And it nearly consumed me then. Our people don't need a breathing body of a king withering away without a soul. The jewel will stop my heart without leaving any external marks. No one will know what you did."

He dropped the gem into the hand that Adam hadn't, quite, begun to withdraw, and marched up the steps towards the Throne. He probably should have made one to use for Genevieve as well, just in case – but he couldn't bear to truly imagine his soul-bonded beloved in that state. And... if Damien died, the soul-bond would likely take Genevieve along after him in short order.

"And you just carry this thing around all the time just in case?" Adam muttered, staring at the now-ominous-looking faceted red stone with a dark center.

Damien glanced back at him. "No. I altered that pendant on the way here from the Council chamber. I *do* carry a few gems and threads and things around just in case."

He put his arms around his silent wife. "I'm sorry," he whispered to her, then turned back to Adam. "This is why *you* have to be in here, Adam. There's no one else I trust for this. But the part about you not coming out – that was just to scare Tim into moving. Nothing should happen to *you.*"

Damien tried a grin. It didn't work very well. "*You* can't even access that spark of magick you have, so it's not likely I could draw you in to try to do anything with it anyways. Accidentally or on purpose."

"You have a morbid sense of humor, Damien. How in hell am I supposed to know when to use this thing? And what about Genevieve?" Adam glowered at the Queen. "I can't see as how *you'd* be all right with this."

She shrugged. "I'm not. But he goes down this rabbit-hole often enough that I'm done arguing about it. He's going to do what he has to do, I'll keep the Realm from eating him alive, and you'll make sure we get moved back to our rooms if it takes too much out of us."

She freed a hand from the arms she'd slipped around Damien's neck to gesture at the cloth wrapped basket. "Mostly rich broths and honeyed teas to give us a quick boost of strength when I can get him back out of his spell, but some heartier food for you as well. Feel free to send for more." Genevieve smiled slightly. "I had a couch brought in for you – and a stack of reports on winter wheat production in Elaarwen. Since we had so much fun with potato production in eastern Siovale a few months ago."

Damien wasn't looking at his old friend anymore, but he could almost *hear* Adam roll his eyes. "*Thank* you, Your Majesty."

Genevieve's lips were moving again... more instructions to Adam. "You *may* need to get Damien off the Throne. If... if he and I lose physical contact for any reason... then pull him off the Throne as fast as possible – no matter what you have to do."

So... she wasn't as blasé about this as she pretended. He wanted to kiss away the fear in her eyes... but it wasn't possible.

And *he* had some last instructions for Adam as well.

"You... three... can still try for an Heir once I'm... gone. Provided you do it quickly. If I've gone into the fabric of the Realm there should still be... *enough* of me to keep Genevieve alive. For long enough to bear a child, anyways." His heart ached for the child he would never get to see, to hold. "Now that the Sword has spoken for Jason, it's even possible it would speak for his daughter. I still don't know exactly how it works..."

"Damien..." they both objected at the same time. One of them he could ignore. The other he could prevent any further objections from. So he did.

There wasn't any reason not to touch Genevieve now, and this was probably his last chance. He kissed her, believing it was the last time he'd ever do so.

You idiot, came clearly down the bond. *We won before. And I'll do what I had to do last time if that's the only way to bring you back to me.*

You will not, he ordered her. They both knew she couldn't carry a child of his to term – and just how likely it would be that this time losing the babe would kill her as well. The plan to have Jason sire their child was the only way, but the soul-bond wouldn't care if she took these extreme measures to save Damien; it would ensure she conceived immediately. *All these months... only to have another miscarriage that might kill you? No.*

She smirked at him. *Then you better not let that be necessary. Because it's all I can manage not to rip your clothes off of you right now. Crisis or no crisis. **You've** gotten to have your fun, while I have had to just be **patient.***

He chuckled. She was right after all, and was there any point in wasting their last moments with blushes and embarrassment? *And Adam or no Adam? That's the other reason I insisted he be here. I know how well patience sits with you, my brilliant beauty.*

Genevieve's blue-green eyes blazed. *Adam or no Adam.* And Damien's breath caught.

Aloud, she said, "We should get on with this. The storm won't wait."

Without thinking, he answered, "The storm would wait just fine. It's the wizards driving it who won't." He realized what he'd said when the silence of two held breaths assaulted his ears. "A suspicion, nothing more," Damien tried to pass it off.

"Then you'd *better* come out of this spell-weaving safe and sound," Adam said dryly. "Without you, we won't have *any* defense against another attack if that's what this is."

Damien reluctantly let his warm, wonderful wife go and undid his sword-belt. He unsheathed the Monarch's Blade and dropped belt and scabbard to one side.

"That's the beauty of it, Adam," he said absently, regarding the Throne with trepidation. "I've used the Vassal's Oath to wake the magick in the blood of every landed noble in the Realm. And most of them are having their first lesson in magick right now. The *Realm* will defend itself, using the web of magick-users I've been Binding to it for the last five years. And a weather-wizardry of this magnitude is unlikely to be seen again. *I* could probably do it, but I have some idea of the cost to someone *without* the resources of an entire Realm behind them."

He ignored Adam's reaction and quit temporizing.

The Throne enveloped him as soon as he sat down. Genevieve's hand was a link, a golden gateway to a world he could no longer directly observe. The Sword was useless for this task, he realized. There was nothing he could point it at – the disturbance was too far away.

Distantly, he heard the clatter as the Sword fell out his hand. Doubtless his beloved and his Champion found that alarming, but it no longer mattered to Damien.

He was in contact with the deeper fabric of the Realm as he had not dared to be since that first time. Since he'd completed his own Binding to the Realm by sitting on the Throne after having been first claimed by the Sword. It had yearned for this deeper contact every time he had sat upon the Throne since. Its yearning for him had only grown stronger when he kept the contact light and brief – and redoubled during the long intervals when he avoided it entirely, not needing to use either the magickal or secular Power of the Throne, and lacking Genevieve's presence as his anchor.

Damien tried to convey his purpose to the Realm and received a wholehearted approval. A warning to all the wild creatures first – even in Elendria. Preserve Life… that was the Realm's purpose in many ways. He barely needed to touch the fabric of the Realm to do it. He had needed only to give it the Intention.

His next task was more difficult.

While the Realm was delighted to have him, it was like Genevieve's delight when he came to bed long after she did; muzzy-headed and tired, and mostly asleep. No more than she would enjoy leaping out of bed to spar beside him did the Realm want to fight off the oncoming storm. Ice and cold *belonged* to Winter, after all.

Damien tried to prod it out of somnolence by pointing out the breaking branches of trees at the edges of Elendria, the unprepared animals dying and suffering.

Some died every year, however. It was part of the cycle of Life. More dying earlier in the Winter might mean more food left for those that survived to make it through to Spring. Not a tragedy in the ages-long view of whatever entity the Realm itself was.

So, the king turned instead to exploring the storm. It was far too late to simply stop it. His only hope was to divert it, or to blunt its force somehow. But there was nowhere to divert it *to,* save elsewhere in his own Realm – unless he could somehow double it back on itself and send it into Deltheren. Which could easily be seen as an act of war... unless he could find some proof that the storm had been sent by wizards on Queen Estelle's behalf in the first place.

In which case it was *still* an act of war, but *he* was not the provocateur.

His people were weary of war after so many years of Rebellion.

How then to blunt it?

Damien felt for the edges of the storm, climbed around the gusting winds, and searched for what was driving it.

Clever... clever... they had started this long ago, and far, far away to leave few fingerprints of who they might be. He could see, touch, taste, *feel* the remnants of the spells that had started this mass of air moving, seen to it that it picked up moisture and kept it, that it stayed just warm enough to carry vast quantities of water... and then that it would hit his own poor country just when the local temperatures dipped below freezing enough to turn it into an ice monster.

Was it chance – or vile purpose – that had the thing hitting the day after Jason's coronation and wedding, with most all the nobility of Ilseador stuck here in Emeralsee? Or... was it a boon in disguise, since he had all of this help here to teach and tap? Did the wizards who had sent the storm even know?

It was moving past Elendria now, and his heart ached to feel his people – who did not acknowledge him their sovereign, but were *his* for all of that – dying as overburdened roofs collapsed, as temperatures plummeted and poorly constructed chimneys permitted fires to be smothered, as branches collapsed and crushed brave souls who ventured out to see to their livestock. It wasn't *their* fault that their countesses had sought safer vassalage with Deltheren when his grandfather was terrorizing their own Realm...

But past Elendria meant into Ilseador proper, beginning with Flowerdell, whose pompous baron had been expostulating in the Council so recently. Their major industry was supplying the florists of both Realms – their fields were Winter-barren now, but the rosebushes and the flowering trees and vines were delicate. It would have taken *days* to prepare for a storm like this... not the bare hour they'd had. And the greenhouses, their roofs made of glass – on supports that might not bear extra weight, or where the torsion caused by interior heat against exterior ice might cause the glass to shatter with no other cause. Flowerdell was known for its mild climates...

Damien could not understand how Queen Estelle could possibly be involved. This *must* be rogue wizards, not ones in her pay. Elendria was hers for now, and it had been devastated, as had the provinces within Deltheren just past it. Even if she were not Bound to her land, as Damien was, it would do her no good to destroy the county and her own unquestioned territory just behind it.

How to blunt ice? And wind?

Warm, still air...

... such as still hovered around Emeralsee, though its gradual dispersal out to sea was building the almost-hurricane that he knew would hit his capitol in less than a week.

But he needed the warm air in Flowerdell *now*.

Could he create a similar bank of warm air over Flowerdell? Warm air rose... that air had to come from somewhere. It might simply suck the icy winds in even faster. And even if it melted the deadly ice... he risked creating tornadoes. That part of the country was prone to them anyways... those broad flat plains so suited to the agriculture that fed the rest of the Realm...

So... warm air. But not too warm.

Damien's magickal attention was distracted again to the near-hurricane brewing out in the sea in answer to his magick of yesterday. It was farther away from the Realm than he could normally hope to affect, but it was attracted to his magick. It was chilly, but well above freezing temperatures – part of the Trade-Winds that kept his city of Emeralsee temperate all year long... along with Dalzialest in the central plains. Elaarwen and Siovale were nearly the only duchies that were to be spared, though Duchess Tariana's Embervest in the far north might also be and Duchess Laura's Alpinsward would only be struck a glancing blow...

This was definitely going to overreach him: as King of Ilseador, Damien had no reasonable jurisdiction for his magick beyond the continental shelf, and the tropical storm was far beyond that demarcation.

But he could *feel* the alien, tropical plants in Flowerdell's greenhouses dying... Perhaps they *didn't* belong there, as the Realm tried to tell him was the case, but it wasn't *their* fault that they had come. Any more than it had been his grandmother, Queen Rena's, fault that her ambitious father had sent the young princess here from faraway Dawil to be his grandfather's sixth wife. She had never thrived here, never put down real roots, but the seeds she had sown had given rise to Damien...

The Realm relented.

With a prayer to the Gods of Wind and Sea, and a breath of apology to his poor people of Emeralsee caught in the middle, Damien began to call the storm.

Chapter THREE

Battle

THE OCEAN PROTO-STORM RESPONDED WITH an almost unholy glee, following him back to where he had birthed what called it: the warm bubble of air still slowly dispersing from Emeralsee.

It might have paused there, to see what damage it could do to these mortals who dared trifle with that which belonged to the Gods, but Damien had counted on the momentum of those winds to keep the storm going. And he was right: it rushed through the city rattling doors and shutters, but barely slowing.

Then out to the open plains where it picked up speed again, still feeding on the warmth of the Autumn just past and the plentiful islands of human-generated heat surrounding the city.

The storm didn't want to be guided, so Damien had to chivvy it along. Not *this* way. Not *that* way. Around *this* side.

Not straight into the ice-storm, but curling around to knock into it from the side.

And... Damien had realized that Tomas' point that he should not protect Elendria – though he had not said so openly – was also that if he *could* protect Ilseador then it would make the case for Elendria to rejoin its mother-Realm all the stronger. Elendria had already been iced over... there was only so much the king could do anyways...

Flowerdell had never seen such a strange, soaking rain so close to Midwinter.

And it was a rain that stopped exactly on the border with Elendria.

Exactly. The downpour followed every twist and turn of the river-branch that demarcated the two fiefs without once splashing onto Elendrian soil.

Damien was not done, however. The ice-wind had been diverted, some of its force blunted... but it now had all the moisture of the sea-storm that Damien had co-opted from its vengeance on his temerity. The warmth of the sea-air was sucked up into the stratosphere almost as if with a siphon, and the king searched for signs that the instigators were still at work.

He hardly had time to look, however, since the enemy storm was still seething forward over Dalzialest.

It was the heavy coating of ice that had to be avoided. These provinces were used to high winds, thin coatings of ice, and even occasional hail.

Small hail was acceptable, he reminded himself. Even pea-sized hail could cause damage; but cherry-sized hail shattered the glazing on windows struck head-on and left substantial bruising – though hopefully all animals and humans were under shelter by now – and anything larger could be deadly.

The glassmaker's guild was likely to see its fortunes increase despite his care, it seemed.

Grimly, Damien surveyed his options.

The storm was coming up on the orchards and vine-crops that the region was famous for. The people might survive, but it would take decades to rebuild their livelihood if the ice broke or shredded these plants.

And farther along – he didn't need to magickally survey the route. He'd memorized the maps of Ilseador long before he'd been Bound.

The storm could not be swayed from pouring across the very center of his lands and funneling down into Emeralsee. Nothing he'd done had altered its trajectory by even a few degrees – his suspicion that it had been somehow Bound onto its course was confirmed by the fact the enemy storm *itself* had suppressed any nascent tornadoes when he had smashed the sea-storm into it. He'd watched vigilantly, knowing the risks, but *not one* twister had emerged... though he'd seen several swirling masses that had looked all-too-ready to spawn.

This storm wanted to devastate his entire Realm – but *particularly* to hit his capitol.

Thank all the Gods that Damien was no longer quite so tightly Bound to Emeralsee himself... and that Jason wasn't an Earth-mage by nature. The tall, blonde knight-and-duke would *feel* the effects, but it should be more at a remove than Damien would have done. The blow wasn't likely to cripple Jason, as it most certainly would have done to his king.

How could one Bind such a thing as a storm? Damien had no idea. And perhaps the enemy *was* merely using the shape of the land to do their dirty work...

The longer the storm stayed in one place, the more ice it could deposit.

High winds... or crushing ice...

Damien gritted his teeth... and put all his own strength to driving the enemy storm faster and faster. It was inclined to pick up speed across the plains anyways. He felt its malice like a wicked grin – thinking he was helping it do its work. It was being *summoned* to Emeralsee, it *couldn't wait* to get there...

The ice layer over Dalzialest was thin enough for most of the trees to survive.

Across the plains it spread out, and Damien thought, briefly, that he could persuade it to spread itself out into nothingness...

But the storm laughed at him, its front turning into a line hundreds of miles long, and he began to realize he might have made a mistake. The passage between Alpinsward's mountains and Elaarwen's – where Flowerdell and Elendria lay – was relatively narrow and he hadn't seen how *large* the storm really was.

The *entire* central plains of Ilseador now lay bare and vulnerable to its attack. And Damien, fool that he was, *he* had given it more strength, more speed...

Yet if it hoped to provoke him to helpless rage, the storm – or its progenitors – did not know Damien.

The king prodded his sleeping Realm for more Power, dug himself deeper into the fabric of the Realm. If brute force in the form of the sea-storm had failed, and pushing it along had only given it more scope... there must be *some* other way he could affect it.

He came back to himself, momentarily.

He was in the Throneroom, sitting on the Throne...

Genevieve was in his arms, wrapped around him...

Her hand had found a way inside his clothes... his pants...

She was using the soul-bond to fight the Realm's claim on him, as she had promised she would...

Though not yet by risking all they had planned for before the storm.

"Now, Adam," she said, and withdrew her fingers, sliding off his lap as Adam yanked his arm half out of its socket to pull him up and away from the Throne.

"What...? Why did you...?" Damien couldn't collect his frozen thoughts to form a coherent query.

"You went icy cold, love," Genevieve told him. "And it's been hours. You need to eat and rest a bit."

Damien shook his head, trying to speak calmly rather than with the panic that was threatening to overwhelm his ability to plan. His mind seemed filled with slush. "There isn't *time*. I melted it in Flowerdell before it could do harm, got it past Dalzialest, but now it's over the central plains. *Reyensweir*. I thought I could get rid of it by making it move faster, but I just made it *stronger...*"

He wasn't standing, the king realized, he was sagging bonelessly in Adam's sturdy arms.

"Grab his legs, Genevieve," the Champion told her. "No, we won't try to carry him anywhere, just set him down away from that... Thing." Adam's tone held revulsion. What had he seen in the Throne? What *could* he have seen, with his own magick still tied up and sealed away?

Damien could feel the Throne reaching for him.

He wanted to go back to it.

He wanted to go back to his *work*...

Rich, salty broth assaulted his tastebuds. Damien spluttered, then took a deep drink. It was *warm,* thank the Gods. And warm all the way down through the icy core of him. No, not thank the *Gods* – thank his *wife,* who had prepared so well, and his *Champion,* who had waited so patiently and made sure the broth was still warm when Damien needed it.

The king realized he was leaning back against Adam's warm chest, and his friend had wrapped his own body around Damien while helping him to drink the broth. The king was still too chilled even to shiver. Genevieve was a few feet away, drinking carefully from her own cup.

"Thank you," Damien managed between sips.

Adam simply nodded. "He's still like ice, Genevieve. We don't need him losing fingers and toes to frostbite, or sick with hypothermia."

She looked pensive. "What do you suggest?"

Adam snorted. "You're mountain-bred, Genevieve. You know as well as I do."

His beautiful Queen sighed.

"All right. You look so comfy there," she said dryly, her ironic tone acknowledging that *she* dared not be the one to warm Damien by holding him close. Not with the soul-bond ready to pressure them into another ill-fated conception given half a chance.

"I'll have Tim send for trays of hot rocks," Genevieve said. "Or potatoes. Or whatever Elista can come up with. Then, while we're waiting, we'll get his boots off and I'll warm up his feet. That should be safe enough. Do what you can with his hands – maybe he can hold a mug on his own now, and warm up his hands that way?"

She paused. "Ears... that would be the other part to watch out for... maybe you can put your hands over them?"

Genevieve shook her head and went to the main doors of the hall.

Adam poured some more broth into the mug, and wrapped Damien's icy, nerveless fingers around it. The king tried, but could not make his hands grip the vessel. "Sorry," he gasped, feeling like even the – he knew objectively – cool air of the room was a furnace in his lungs.

"Hunh." Adam wrapped his own hands around, sandwiching Damien's between the warm mug and his own still-warmer hands. "Now where is *she* going?"

Genevieve had slipped out of the Throneroom entirely, closing the door behind her.

Damien had finally warmed up enough to begin shivering... and shivering violently enough to spill the broth even with Adam's stabilizing hands. The tall knight swore softly, and peeled the mug back out of the king's hands and set it down to the side.

"Sorry, sorry, sorry..." Damien's teeth chattered, and he wasn't sure if he was apologizing for making a mess... or for not being able to save his country... or for keeping Adam apart from Jason... or what.

"Stop that." Adam slipped out from behind him, settling him on a large cushion that had absorbed the knight's own body heat and helped Damien for about two seconds before his chill body had sucked all the residual warmth out of it. Adam pulled off his boots and stockings, exclaiming with shock at the bluish-white color of the skin of the king's feet. Damien couldn't feel his ankles, let alone his toes.

Adam shook his head and propped Damien's feet on a cushion, then layered them with a blanket that Genevieve must have requested as well. Then he came back up the steps and stripped both the king's and his own tunic and shirt off and put himself back in his original position, now able to transfer his own heat better with the skin-to-skin contact.

"Brrrr. Even your core is cold," Adam complained as he tucked the soft fabric of the shirts around Damien as best he could. "Here, give me your hands again." He shook his head. "Not much I can do about your ears this way though."

The Champion paused. "Well. There's this." Adam blew softly on Damien's left ear, his breath hot and moist and...

"Maybe... maybe you *shouldn't*..." Damien managed to say, his entire body tensing.

"You *would* like that." Adam blew again. "You *did* say it wasn't only about Jason."

"I'm... I'm sorry about that, too..."

Adam chuckled. "You're not shivering so badly anymore, though. And I'll bet your core is warming up." He freed a hand and ran it down the king's abdomen. "Yes, indeed."

"Adam..." Damien had no idea what he wanted to say. *Stop, please...* didn't quite seem to cover it. He retreated into something that made sense... because *this* very much did not. It just barely made sense that *Jason* had been willing to... to *help* them fight the demands of the soul-bond. That was all it had been. Really. *Really.*

"I need to get back to work. That storm..." the king's voice trailed off as he realized that he was out of ideas. "I don't know what to *do,*" he said helplessly. "It's hitting Reyenweir and the northern edges of Siovale *right now.* I got it past Dalzialest without too much damage...there *has* to be away I can protect those provinces..."

"And Emeralsee?" Adam's family's holding was a solid day's ride to the north, but still beholden to the province.

Damien shook his head. "It's *aimed* at Emeralsee. At *me* is my guess. Someone is testing me. To see if I can thwart their plans and protect my people."

He didn't need to add that it was a test he was *failing.*

"To soften us up for an invasion," Adam said softly. "I wondered why no one tried when King Reginald died."

Damien shrugged, then caught his breath. Adam's hand was still very low on his abdomen and his own movement had jogged the position... "Grandfather died rather suddenly. After all those years, he could have been on the throne for another twenty as far as anyone knew."

Or... forever, given that King Reginald had had no particular qualms about using his Power to accomplish just that. Granting himself eternal life and youth along with invulnerability to most normal risks was more or less *de rigeur* for an Evil Wizard, from what Damien had read.

"Surely it takes more than a few months to muster an army," the king finished. "And in those few months we'd proven that I was an unknown quantity. Perhaps it was worth waiting to see what other surprises we would come up with?"

Adam, Jason, and Genevieve, along with Ciriis and Lord Aldred had been that 'we' that had likely flummoxed potential invaders. Lord Aldred's and Genevieve's proven savvy as leaders of the Rebellion might have done it alone, but Jason's famous prowess with a sword, Adam's cleverness with developing the doubled Royal Guards to protect Damien and Genevieve against assassinations, and Ciriis' less visible role as Royal Spymistress had also been essential to underpin the rumors that had spread quickly of Damien's magickal defeat of Lord Prydeen.

Adam sighed, and Damien tensed again. This sigh had been much, ah, *deeper* than those light, ear-warming breaths. This time the other man's breath flowed down his neck and chest as well.

"Well, at least if we have to have most of the nobility exhausted from using magick for the first time," Adam noted, "that won't include Tomas Elsevier and, apparently, Genevieve. For all that you tried to scare *me* half to death. Between the two of them, and your commissioned generals and admirals we should be set to defend against non-magickal forces."

"Even with half the Realm and Emeralsee iced over?" Damien tried to relax, but the topic was chilling in and of itself. "And surely *you* belong on that list as well."

Adam huffed a laugh into his ear. "I've *fought* in battles, my king. Tomas *commanded* them. And Genevieve *planned* them."

Damien wriggled uncomfortably. "Adam, I don't think you're doing this intentionally, but–"

His Champion slid his hand farther down. *Much* farther. "What makes you *not think* that, my king?"

"Because this isn't *like* you, Adam!" Damien yelped.

He tried to move away, but it wasn't very successful, given the way Adam was holding him.

And the fact that Adam was taller, heavier, and *stronger.*

And that he was himself of two minds about this.

And that he couldn't feel his feet. "Who are you, and what have you done with my best friend?"

Adam shrugged... another movement which was altogether too *interesting* in and of itself. "Maybe I just want to see what kept Jason coming back to you. Or maybe I've just come to terms with the idea that this is what you'll *need* from me when Jason and Genevieve..." He stopped abruptly. Clearly, he wanted to think about *that* as little as Damien did. No matter *what* he was doing right now.

Damien sighed. "I *do* have other ways of coping, Adam. And I wish I hadn't had to ask Jason for... any of it."

There had to be *some* way of coping anyways. He'd figure it out.

Those fingers wriggled a little lower. "Or maybe I'm just finding you incredibly attractive right now."

"Adam... you got *married* yesterday."

This was impossible... completely impossible. The storm... the Throne... it must have done something to Damien's brain and he was hallucinating... fantasizing... How messed up was he, if his maundering mind went to this sort of forbidden fruits instead of to his beautiful and beloved wife? He wasn't seventeen anymore... or *four*teen...

"Damien. Jason's been my love and my life for fifteen years. Well over *twenty,* if I get to count the years I spent waiting for him. Yesterday was... freeing." Indeed, Adam sounded more relaxed than Damien could recall. "He's mine now – *forever* – and I don't have to fear anything coming between us anymore. There's nothing that *can.* Didn't you and Genevieve feel the spell that the wedding ceremony casts? Though I've heard it said that a wedding between a soul-bonded couple is just a formality..."

The king smiled, distracted from his previous self-recriminations and feeling warmed in an entirely different way. "It didn't feel like a formality to *me.* It felt like the first sunrise on the first day that ever was." He paused, slightly embarrassed by his effusive description. "I suppose there might have been a spell involved. But I've felt like that every time I've looked at her, so it's hard to tell."

There was a moment of silence.

"Well." Adam moved aside, reclaiming his fingers. The king... wasn't sure how he felt about that. 'Relieved' probably *should* be his answer...

"I suppose we should check on your feet. I wonder what's holding up your Queen of the Dawn," Adam added sardonically.

Damien frowned. "Something's wrong... but she's not letting me see what."

The Champion frowned, distracted in his own turn from... whatever. "That doesn't sound good."

He uncovered Damien's feet and shook his head.

"It's worse than 'not good'," Damien disagreed. "That storm is still out there." He looked at the Throne and bit his lip. "The Realm is mostly asleep. I can probably do this alone."

Not a good idea, grandson, Queen Marian appeared before him.

"I wondered where you'd gotten to," Damien replied. Adam looked up in confusion, saw his king focused on empty air, sighed gustily, shook his head, and went back to trying to warm Damien's feet out of numbness.

Well, I certainly can't warm you up. And your good Captain seemed to be having such a good time with it.

"He's my Champion now," Damien muttered, feeling himself flush.

Yes, I know. Heaven help the next poor boy to fill that post.

"Do you actually have anything *helpful* to say, Grandmother? I more or less have my hands full here. In case you didn't notice." He didn't have *time* for this right now. And blushes stole blood that his feet needed. So did other things, for that matter.

More like you **were** *a handful. I'm not criticizing you, grandson. You have excellent taste in lovers. And putting them in the position of Champion is quite clever. I did the same thing, after all.*

Damien buried his face in his hands. "I could have gone a whole lifetime without knowing that."

Pffmf. You can't really be such a prude while going on the way you have been. Abruptly she became serious. *You can NOT go back on the Throne without Genevieve either. The Realm will sense that and … that will be that.*

"Then what am I supposed to do about that storm?" he demanded.

Nothing.

"Nothing? What do you mean, *nothing?*"

Adam looked up at that. "Queen Marian says to let it go? I agree." He nodded in what he apparently guessed was the direction of the ghostly Queen, getting it vaguely right. He and Jason had had practice with these weird, half-audible conversations over the last five years after all.

Damien transferred his outraged glare to the tall, blonde knight. "I can't *do* that."

"The Realm has survived storms before, Damien. We only have one of *you.*"

He's right. And **handsome.**

"So you've said before," the king replied to Adam and pointedly ignoring his ancestress.

"You can't do everything. Stand up, Damien." Adam stood up and stepped back, standing at parade-rest with folded arms. "I dare you."

"Adam, it's going to look like favoritism. I saved Dalzialest and then let Reyensweir suffer. Elaarwen isn't in the path and Siovale is barely going to be touched. You *know* how Duke Quillian will see this. *And* his vassals."

"And Emeralsee is going to get smashed. So much for favoritism. Stand up."

"Adam," he pleaded, tears in his eyes, "Whoever is out there is *testing* me. We don't dare let them think I'm too weak to protect my Realm."

"Or they're trying to wear you down so you can't deal with whatever they throw at us *next*. Stand up, and I won't argue about whether you're fit to sit in that fancy chair again and do whatever it is you do." Adam gave him a look that brooked no argument.

Damien glared at him. "Fine."

He still couldn't feel his feet, but as soon as he tried to put weight on them, *that* was solved.

Numb was infinitely preferable to excruciating pain, Damien decided instantly. He cried out and would have fallen, if Adam hadn't been ready and caught him. The Champion's powerful muscles were entirely too warm beneath his smooth skin.

*Clever **and** sexy. Keep this one, definitely.*

Damien tried to keep from flushing by focusing on the pain in his feet.

"Just as stubborn as when you were seventeen. Do I want to know what the old biddy is saying?" Adam asked with sardonic amusement as he lowered his king back down onto a cushion.

"Not half what she's going to say after she gets over her shock about what you just called her," Damien replied. Clearly, he hadn't avoided the blush as much as he'd hoped.

"Hunh. Well, from what you said before, she and I agree on at least some things." Adam sat down and began rubbing Damien's feet again. Now that sensation had returned, it hurt to blazes, and Damien yelped and tried to pull away. Adam simply held on tighter and kept at it. "The sooner you get your circulation back, the sooner it'll stop hurting. Quit being such a baby. Your Majesty."

"I just – ow!– choose to – mmpf – risk myself in other ways." Damien glanced as pointedly at the Throne as he could manage under the onslaught as a reminder of *what* other ways. And ignoring the fact that the pain was entirely due to having risked himself that way already.

Adam sighed, and grabbed for the other foot before Damien had the presence of mind to snatch it away. That one had managed to go numb again, but the Champion's determined massage soon fixed that, to Damien's dismay. "It says all kinds of good things about you that you're willing to sacrifice yourself for others, Damien. But somehow, you've gone rather too far in that direction. I'm beginning to think you have no sense of self-preservation at *all.*"

"Of course I do." That was ridiculous.

Not that I've seen.

Oh, you're still here? He forced himself not to look for the ethereal shape of the woman.

Oh, so you've decided not to share your half of the conversation with your new lover?

Adam is **not** *my lover.*

He could hear the smirk. *Not* **yet.**

"Not that I've seen," Adam told him.

Damien blinked. "What?"

Adam gave him an odd look. "You claimed to have a sense of self-preservation."

"Oh. Hmm. Queen Marian had just said the same thing."

In the *exact same words...*

"I knew she was an intelligent woman." Adam smirked.

I take it back. He's far too full of himself. Find someone more biddable.

Damien covered his ears, as if it would do the slightest bit of good, then glared at Adam. "You win this round. But only because I have no ideas left to try on that thrice-damned storm. I've pushed it, I've pulled it... I pulled in the storm that was brewing out to sea and would have hit us here in about a week and used it to keep Flowerdell alive. And *not* Elendria."

He bowed his head in shame.

"Good." Adam said firmly. "From what Jason's been telling me, Cousin Miraly needed a good kick in the backside."

Damien's head popped up.

"If you weren't so damned determined to put the whole Realm back together just as it was in Queen Marian's day," Adam went on, "We'd all have told you. Miraly didn't leave the Realm because of some terrible thing your grandfather did to her people. She – or rather her mother – took Elendria over to Deltheren because Queen Estelle offered them lower taxes."

Damien frowned. "Elendria *already* had lower taxes than the rest of the Realm." He paused. "Though I never understood why."

"Father is Elendrian, Damien. He's been going on about this since I was a child. He was shocked when he realized how Elendria had manipulated the rest of the Realm. Ilseador. And now Deletheren as well. The people are actually paying *higher* taxes, but Countess Miraly gets payments from the Crown simply for keeping the county as part of Deltheren."

"'Payments from the Crown'..." Damien echoed. Something was trying to come together... and abruptly it did. "Those payments are a percentage of the taxes and fees paid by her people, aren't they. So, she's essentially taxing them twice, once as their liege-lady, and once by accepting a share of Queen Estelle's taxes on them. So, the taxes have to go up, just for Estelle to afford to pay Miraly and still make it worth keeping Elendria."

His expression cleared. "*Now* it makes sense. I couldn't understand, if the weather wizards who created this storm are in Queen Estelle's pay, why she'd be willing to let them trash Elendria, and some of her native territory beyond it. But if Elendria is beggared, she won't have to pay Miraly a penny. There's probably even some clause in their treaty about this sort of 'natural disaster.' And the countess – or her mother before her – would have discounted that clause... because they *never* get ice-storms in Elendria."

Adam stared at him. "That's... almost word for word. Father saw the original. He said it was the final straw for him, and that his sister's greed would destroy Elendria."

"A prescient man, your father." Damien shook his head. "That makes it more likely to be true that it's Estelle who's our enemy. The storm was definitely *sent* from that direction. But it felt like it was being *summoned* this way."

A strange howling started up, seeming to come from above them.

"It's here," Damien said with trepidation as they both stared at the clerestory windows high above. He shuddered convulsively. "It's *looking* for me."

Chapter FOUR

Guilt

THE STORM HIT EMERALSEE HARD and fast.

The winds howled along the Castle's stone walls like a pack of giant wolves out for blood, and the tightly shuttered windows all over the structure shuddered.

Adam insisted on hustling his king out from under those all-too-fragile-looking clerestory windows in the Throneroom despite Damien's insistence that the spell protecting the windows was part of the deeply-laid foundations of the Castle itself. He barely acquiesced to Damien's dry suggestion that they should put shirts and tunics back on first.

And Damien flatly refused to allow Adam to carry him out.

"If I'm unconscious, Adam. Nothing less," the king insisted.

"I can knock you over the head," the Champion offered, not entirely sarcastically.

"Thank you, no." Damien rolled his eyes. "I will hobble out on my own two feet. With your help, Sir Loveress." He bit off the 'if you please' he would normally have added. Adam clearly did *not* please. "Um... I think I may need some help getting the Sword."

Adam growled and retrieved blade, scabbard, and sword-belt. Damien put on his stockings, then strapped the sword back around his waist. "Help me up?" He held up his left hand.

"This is a bad idea," Adam said again, but he took Damien's hand in his right and slid his left arm around the king's back.

Damien planned to make a joke about it, but the words died on his lips as he felt himself going white with pain as he put weight on his feet.

"Still determined to walk?" Adam asked, watching his face with a certain grim satisfaction.

"Yes," Damien gasped. He tried not to look at how far it was to the main entrance of the hall. A hundred feet. He'd measured it once.

The Champion sighed. "Healer, Heal thyself."

Damien didn't bother trying to answer. He was too busy trying to *breathe*. Healing other people rarely took any more from him than the Intention to do so, though he hadn't tried to deal with anything particularly complex as of yet. Healing *himself*... tended to be *long* and *protracted* and required his *full attention*. It was rarely worth it, Damien had discovered, when he'd tried ridding himself of a simple cold – that he'd cured everyone else of by pretty much just walking past them. He had managed to cure his own cold, but had been left with a splitting headache for two days. What's more, Adam knew all that, having had the delight of dealing with him for those two days.

Adam stooped down, and Damien's stomach turned over. The pain was making him nauseous and light-headed. Oh. Adam had grabbed the king's boots.

One step. Two.

Three.

Four.

It was *thirty-eight* steps at the usual length of his stride.

Five.

Six.

Fifty maybe, with the length of the 'steps' he was taking now?

Seven...

Damien started to crumple, and Adam caught him before he could, sweeping his feet off the ground so there was no more pressure. The sudden cessation of pain was almost painful in itself.

"Enough of being the idiot?" Adam asked.

Damien nodded, his eyes tightly shut. His feet were *pulsing* with pain now, and Adam's arms were as warm and safe and reassuring as they had been when Damien was... well, sixteen and had finally dared to accept such comfort.

Of course... that safe comfort had also engendered the *fantasies* that had inspired Damien's insistence on walking his own way out of the Throneroom. Well, half of his insistence. He hadn't a great deal more desire to appear weak and vulnerable before the vultures of his own Court than to any watching sorcerers that he might have to battle later.

Adam's quick, long stride covered the remaining distance to the doors in half a moment. He kicked at those doors until Tim threw them open. The Champion carried his king out and settled him on a bench at the side of the Great Hall, then sat down beside him, breathing heavily. Damien wasn't some light maiden after all, but a muscled fighter.

"What happened?" Tim asked quietly, the look in his eyes was alarmed, but his demeanor was as calm and full of confidence as the Captain of the Guard should always display. Adam had sometimes covered anxiety in that role with an excess of his usual acerbity, but that wasn't Tim's style.

"Frostbite in his feet," Adam dropped the boots he was still somehow carrying. "Don't ask me how or why. This magick stuff is all mumbo-jumbo to me." His ironic glance met Damien's. Adam was the next best-educated person on the topic in the Realm as far as either of them knew, for all that he had no practical use of the knowledge. "Idiot tried to walk on them first."

Sir Tim gave his king a sympathetic glance, some of the concern fading from his gaze. "Be fair, Adam, you would've tried walking, too."

"Oh, *he* would've *crawled* before he let someone else help him," Jason's lighter voice came from somewhere nearby. Adam's eyes lit up even as his husband added. "As I recall we had to bring you along to deal with Harald's Usurpation, even though you were nearly as broken as poor Tim here."

Sir Tim winced in memory, his fingers creeping unconsciously to where his ribs had been broken.

Damien winced – hopefully internally – for a different reason. This was *not* the time to remind everyone in hearing distance that Harold of Siovale had briefly usurped the Throne. Not when Damien had left Harald's rehabilitated brother, Duke Tomas of Siovale, in charge of the Realm a few hours ago.

And not when Damien himself somehow needed to project an impression of strength.

When he couldn't even stand on his own feet.

Ah, well, Jason had been Crown Prince for all of a day and night. As Champion – until two days ago – he had kept quietly in the background and rarely needed to speak publicly. Keeping all these finer details in mind… would surely come with time. If they had time.

Jason came closer. "It's good to see *you* have more of a sense of self-preservation, Damien."

No one but Adam – and Queen Marian, though only Damien could see her disgruntled expression – understood why the king burst into uncontrollable laughter. Adam simply glowered at him.

Hysterics, they probably assumed; that he'd broken under the stress.

It was a little too close to the truth.

"Thank you, my Duke of Emeralsee," Damien said as he regained control of himself, wiping tears from his eyes. "It's been a difficult time, and more to come, I fear. That was... helpful."

"A pleasure to serve Your Majesty," Jason said automatically, though his face was baffled. "I came to report that the duchy is as secured against the weather as it may be." He tilted his head. "Though an incredibly strong wind swept through some hours after the Council ended. Coming from the *sea*."

Damien nodded, slumping down. "I brought in the storm that was brewing at sea to fight the ice-storm. The *good* news is that we won't have a near-hurricane hitting us in a week. And that Barony Flowerdell was spared because the sea-storm was warm enough to melt the ice before it coated anything."

He looked around the Great Hall.

His Peer Council was mostly there. And many of their spouses and children, nieces, nephews, cousins... abruptly Damien realized that they would *all* have to bed down in the Castle somehow. It wouldn't be safe to go out into the city until the wind and ice died down... and possibly not for days after. Madame Elista and her staff were going to deserve medals after this. No, bonus pay and vacations... and maybe *also* medals.

Damien's eyes sought out Rosa and Zachary. "The sea-storm kept Dalzialest relatively ice-free as well... but then it ran out. I... tried to hurry it along so that it wouldn't leave as *much* ice in any one place, but then it spread out across the plains of Reyensweir and up into the edges of Siovale... and even Embervest." He met Duke Quillian's and Duchess Tariana's eyes in turn. Then Jason's. "And it's still heading straight into Emeralsee..."

The king looked down at his stockinged feet. "I'm sorry."

Baron Rivencour of Flowerdell pressed forward and threw himself at the king's feet. "I am Your Majesty's most devoted servant." He would have actually tried to kiss Damien's feet if Sir Tim hadn't snatched him back muttering "*Frostbite.*"

Rosa was embracing Duchess Tariana, and Zachary had an arm around Duke Quillian. It was clear they were promising what aid they could. Which words they might yet have to eat – Dalzialest *had* been treated lightly but it had not been *spared,* except by comparison to Reyensweir.

"You did more than anyone could have expected, Your Majesty," Duchess Tariana said to him, her chin lifted in determination. "Embervest is used to Winter storms coming down the mountains at us."

The auburn-haired beauty didn't look towards Duchess Laura of Alpinsward, whose mountain province funneled the winds into her own hilly demesne. Duchess Laura had the grace to look slightly embarrassed, not that *she* had any control over the weather.

Not like her king.

"Not like this one," Damien muttered guiltily, tearing his eyes away from his northern vassals and returning them to a contemplation of his stockinged feet.

Duke Quillian broke away from Zachary Miramar's attempt to settle him, and stalked forward.

Quillian had been a thorn in Damien's side since the beginning of his reign. The younger man hadn't appreciated that his mother's loyalty to the Crown, as Duchess of Reyensweir, had not been more rewarded than the rebellious duchies… nor that Rosa and Zachary had even been elevated in station by combining their counties, not least because Dalizell had been enfeoffed to Reyensweir, though Quillian himself had once been fast friends with the easygoing Zachary and the hotheaded Gavin Teraseel, Rosa's younger brother. Quillian also hadn't appreciated that he'd inherited his title because his mother had *collapsed* when she'd tried to take the Vassal's Oath. As had his elder sister and brother, who had tried next. Damien had explained to him later, privately, what that meant, and expressed his appreciation of Duke Quillian himself. Being told that his mother was more of a traitor – to the Realm itself, if not the king – than Duke Tomas of Siovale, who had 'helped' his own brother usurp the throne had been… difficult. Duke Quillian had helped spread rumors that the story of Tomas Elsevier's ensorcellment was just that: a fairytale.

"Quill–" Zachary stepped after him, but Rosa held him firmly back.

Damien looked up guiltily and wearily at the man whose lands he had failed today.

"You did more than any other man could have *done*," the young Duke of Reyensweir told him gruffly. "You're not a *God*, Your Majesty. We don't expect you to change the *weather*."

The king inclined his head in exhausted appreciation of the concession.

"Put your king to bed, Champion," Duke Quillian growled at Adam. "He looks like he's about to collapse anyways."

He stalked off again.

"That sounds like a good plan," Jason said mildly. "Though I think technically that's the Captain's job."

Sir Tim grinned. "Already on it. Madame Elista said there was a sedan chair in storage. She's sending it up. She thought His Majesty might appreciate it a bit more than a stretcher."

Jason frowned. "A what?"

Tim started to shrug, but Adam explained.

"It's a chair with handles for carrying. They used to be popular a hundred years or so ago." He gave Damien a sardonic grin. "Among nobleladies."

Damien resisted the urge to make a rude gesture. Normally it wouldn't even occur to him, but he was so very tired that anything more clever was simply beyond him. The exhaustion hadn't really hit until he was out of the Throneroom. Say what you might like about his hungry Throne, it did its best to take care of him... and probably had no idea how dangerous it was itself to his continued existence.

"Where's Genevieve?" he asked instead, hoping his voice didn't sound as plaintive as he suspected it did.

It was never a good sign when Jason and Tim exchanged a look before answering. It probably also wasn't a good sign, he realized, that his good friends, Rosa and Zachary, hadn't come up to check on him yet. Rather, the pair of them were continuing to circulate among the gathered nobles – settling ruffled feathers and smoothing riled fur, he supposed. And Tomas Elsevier hadn't yet appeared to return his signet ring.

Genevieve was still blocking her end of the soul-bond. And he was beginning to wonder if it was intentional. When she was very, very focused on something, that had occasionally worked to block him as well. And she had to be nearly as tired as he was – he was all too aware that serving to anchor him back to the world siphoned her own energy.

And she was so recently well enough to even consider another pregnancy. Even one that met the demands of Lord Prydeen's prophecy, so that they dared hope she might not lose it.

There was no normal thing in the world that he didn't think she could handle. Or that Tomas could. Probably better than himself. But it was still *his* Realm and his responsibility.

He had to *know,* and help her if he could. Damien stretched out his awareness to *feel* for whatever was wrong. It couldn't be *very* far away if they had gotten word of it just before the storm hit Emeralsee...

He heard Adam mutter, "Damnfool *idiot!*" as he pitched forwards off the bench and the blackness closed in.

Chapter FIVE

Trapped

DAMIEN AWOKE IN A SPACE that was both familiar and unfamiliar.

It took him a moment to realize that it was the bedroom of the suite below his own. The proportions of the room were similar, but it lacked the clerestory windows – any windows at all, actually. Damien had never been sure if he thought it was cozy or claustrophobic.

It was also the suite that the Castle staff had arranged for Adam and Jason to share, in acknowledgment that a proper honeymoon was next to impossible at this time of year. And that, with the Queen's health so chancy, it wasn't really possible for both Heir and Champion to be absent for any length of time.

And, of course, now they were all trapped inside the Castle for the foreseeable future anyways.

"So, you're back in the land of the living." Adam noted from a chair that must have been dragged in from the sitting room. He was half-dressed, in pants and a shirt, but swordless and tunic-less, and with his boots stacked neatly by the door alongside the king's own pair. Damien realized that he was similarly clad; someone had removed his tunic before laying him down to sleep off his faint.

"Why am I... *here?*" Damien asked, still feeling disoriented.

Adam raised an eyebrow. "You didn't think we were going to let you and Genevieve sleep upstairs under all that glass, did you?"

The king *was* awake enough to roll his eyes. "That's all spelled, too, Adam."

He looked around. "Where is she, anyways? What time is it?"

"In your office. With Tomas Elsevier. And Jason." Adam narrowed his eyes. "And it's much too late."

Damien scrubbed his hand through his hair. "Is it just me, or is none of this making sense?"

He started to slip out of the bed, but Adam was at his side and preventing him before he could do so.

"Do you not remember what happened when you tried to stand on your feet last time?"

The king gave him a mildly irritated look. "I need to use the washroom. Adam! *What* do you think you're *doing?*"

The Champion had scooped him up and was carrying him to the washroom. As Damien spluttered in outrage, Adam seated him on the raised edge of the bathtub.

"Don't faint trying to stand up," the golden-haired knight advised dryly as he strode out. "Or we'll be stuck with me having to be in here with you. Call out when you're ready to go back to bed."

Adam closed the door all but a hair. "This is your wife's orders, by the way. I think she may be getting back at you for all these months stuck in this tower. And apparently at me as well."

Damien contemplated the tasks he needed to accomplish and the way to put as little pressure on his feet as possible. His Healer's sense told him that his feet hadn't improved very much.

Adam continued to talk from just outside the door. Damien imagined him propping the wall up and listening for any sounds of pain that the king might admit. He resolved to bite through his own tongue before that happened.

"There's a fleet sitting just outside the bay. The word arrived just before the storm hit, so we haven't been able to get more details. Genevieve says they have some preliminary numbers on the size and makeup of the fleet. No word on what flag they're flying, though." A deep sigh. "The ice storm may be all that's protecting us. It's blowing in from Reyensweir and out into the bay. The enemy fleet is probably sheltering behind the Cape – our fleet is iced in, we suspect, but that should be keeping the enemy out as well. They're doing a lot of guessing, since the storm is still howling and it doesn't show any signs of stopping soon. We can't really even get word in and out of the castle, let alone the city."

"Damn..." Damien gasped in pain as he came to the door.

"Idiot." Adam scooped him up again. "I *told* you not to walk."

"You're my *Champion*, not my *bodyservant*, Adam," Damien said uncomfortably. "This ... isn't appropriate."

The tall knight snorted. "That didn't seem to bother you when it was a matter of me looking after *Genevieve*, and arguably that was *far* more inappropriate. I can tell you just exactly *how much more*, because I got to hear about it from Aryllis, Ciriis, *and* Lord Aldred. Shall I call in some of your gentlemen-of-the-chamber then?"

"I suppose so..." That *was* what they were ostensibly there for, after all. No reason *not* to ask one of those young men to serve the place of valet or... whatever. Except that Damien had never really grown accustomed to relying upon servants for anything he could do for himself, and the fact that all of his gentlemen-of-the-chamber were noblemen of greater or lesser degree made the whole thing even more awkward. Some of those young men could grow up to be Bound and sworn as his vassals... he'd as soon they not see him naked.

If he said any of that aloud, Adam would likely remind him that that had never bothered him with their first set of ladies-in-waiting. But *those* twelve young women who had been selected by Adam to be trained to protect their prince had been the founders and core of the Secret Cadre of Royal Guards. They had *also* been selected by *Ciriis* to fill Damien's bed, both to protect him at night and to ensure there was no chance for unscrupulous members of his grandfather's Court to lure him into any unwise or compromising situations.

And Ciriis had chosen carefully – all twelve young ladies had personal and powerful reasons to protect the naïve young Heir to the Throne and to help preserve his innocence and faith in humanity. All of them had dark and horrible histories at the hands of his grandfather, Lord Prydeen, or his youngest uncle, Prince Oskar. All of them had been both terribly fierce and terribly vulnerable... giving *Damien* all the reasons in the world to develop feelings that were rather similar for each of *them*.

It would have been ridiculous to worry about any of *them* seeing him undressed after all of that.

No, the problematic part had been when Genevieve entered his life and those twelve women became *her* first ladies-in-waiting. Luckily, his Rebel Duchess had a broad streak of ruthless practicality; she had accepted that

Damien hadn't come to her bed an untried virgin and that there was a deep and genuine affection between him and 'His Majesty's Ladies,' as even the servants and Castle Guard described them. And that there was nothing that could possibly disrupt his utter adoration for her – soul-bond inspired or otherwise.

Well, she'd accepted those things after they sorted out the first few rocky weeks. She'd even managed to befriend his Ladies, and they had quickly become as devoted to their new Queen and her safety as they were to Damien.

These newer members of the Secret Cadre didn't have that complex shared history with their king – thank the Gods. But Damien didn't feel anywhere near as comfortable with them, male *or* female.

Adam sat down on the bed, still holding his king in his arms, and thence in his lap. It was... wholly undignified, but... While it had been patient Jason who had lured the timid young Prince Damien out of the Royal Library, where he had hidden since his parents' murder... it had been acerbic Adam who had always made him feel safest. There had never seemed to be a question that Adam would sugarcoat a hard truth – he'd tell Damien whatever was going on straightforwardly, if with whatever gentleness was possible.

Jason – especially after what had happened when Damien was seventeen – had always himself seemed to need to be protected to some degree, despite being the most formidable knight alive. He'd sacrificed so much for Damien – that sacrifice had to be lived up to. Damien couldn't admit to Jason how woefully inadequate he felt at trying to do so.

With Adam – Damien had felt safe enough to fall apart.

Before he was Crowned, anyways.

He owed the both of them so much... then *and* now. It was a continuing and growing debt of monumental proportions.

But it was damned undignified to be carried in Adam's arms like a little boy, and now to be held in his lap. Even if no one else was watching.

The king's mind had focused on the conundrum of trying to reclaim some personal space without seeming ungrateful. Likely, utilizing the services of one of his gentlemen-of-the-chamber *would* make this less awkward...

So, Damien was startled by Adam's reply.

"How is it *their* privilege to serve you and not *mine*, when *I'm* the one who found you in that damned Library in the first place and took care of you for all those years?"

Was it Damien's imagination that he almost sounded... hurt? The king looked up into his newly-named-Champion and former-Captain's golden-hazel eyes and was reminded of how much *Adam* had given up all these years to care for the younger man. Months-long separations from Jason and the loss of his honeymoon being just the first things to mind.

"It'd take two of *them* to lift you," Adam added, slightly defiantly, his arms tightening a little around Damien in ways that were rather too reminiscent of what he'd been doing in the Throneroom. "*They* have no idea how much muscle you have under all these fine clothes."

Damien sighed. He *was* secretly rather pleased that he'd been able to put on enough muscle, despite his late start, to please his demanding arms-instructors. "That's your doing. Yours and Jason's. And Genevieve's. And you know why... For the Gods' sakes, set me *down*, Adam."

The king wriggled out of his Champion's arms, despite his intent not to seem ungrateful, and scooted into a tailor position on the mattress, taking care not to use his feet. He really needed to spend some time getting the Healing started. He might not be able to fix his own feet as fast as he could someone else's, but he could speed the process along a bit.

For now, however... "I should go down and help. Late or not. Even with the storm, I should be able to get some sense of the enemy fleet's position, and maybe who they are, if they aren't too far off our coast. And I can see how much storm we have left coming at us, see how far the ice extends."

He didn't turn back to look at Adam when he said it. He didn't quite dare.

His Champion's voice went back to its normal acerbic neutrality. "And just *how* do you intend to get down there? I have strict orders from Genevieve that you're to rest, and *I'm* certainly not disobeying my Queen when she speaks in that tone."

"I *do* outrank her if it comes to that," Damien said mildly, glancing back now that the moment seemed past. Adam had folded his arms as if to close up the space where Damien had been and looked more like his usual self.

Adam snorted. "I've seen you pull rank on her once? twice? In all these years. Besides, she's right."

The king shook his head. "I wasn't going to put you to the test. I'll just vanish myself over to the office."

Adam snorted again. "Try."

Damien frowned, but summoned his Power and... nothing. He tried again, and the same result. In a slight panic, he tried to *feel* beyond the suite and – *nothing*. Nothing besides the vague, closed off sense of Genevieve anyways, and the similarly ever-present sense of the Realm. Yet he could still gather his Power.

To test it, he snuffed every fire in the suite, from the hearths to the lanterns beside the bed... then re-lit them almost instantly. Even the brief cessation brought a measurable chill to the room.

"Testing yourself, my king?"

Damien turned to look at Adam. "What have you done?"

The golden-hazel eyes gleamed with their usual sardonic humor. "Locking you in your room was about the only way to make you rest when you were seventeen, too."

"Nineteen," Damien corrected absently, his mind still probing at the boundaries of his confinement, rather like the way one prods at the place where a recently lost tooth should be. "You couldn't have locked me in the Royal Library. Lady Theresa would have had a fit."

"Not to mention that you wouldn't have rested worth a damn with all the books in there."

The king looked at his friend seriously. "You used the cord I gave you. But why? I can just vanish myself onto the couch in the office and keep resting my feet. No walking, I promise. Right now, Jason and Genevieve can't get back in here if they ever decide they can take a break from planning. Speaking of which, I'm the only one with the rank to make all of *them* stop to actually *get* that break."

He paused, and added hesitantly, "And do you really think it's going to work to have all four of us in here? I'm having enough trouble not touching her right now... and she's in the same state, so even if *I* can't walk..."

Adam gave him a direct look. "She says it's more than your feet that need to rest, especially if we're facing an enemy who potentially has magick. You'll just have to trust that the three of them possess that sense of self-preservation *you* so clearly lack – Jason's comments notwithstanding," he glowered at Damien's remembered mirth, "and that *they* will take a break before they run themselves into the ground. Since *they* are the ones you left in charge of the Realm, it seems you *do* trust them, so quit worrying.

"But as to your other points, no. They can't get back in here. And, no. We don't think it's a good idea to have *all four* of us in here tonight."

Damien frowned. "You're still not making sense..." something down the bond from Genevieve caught his attention. The *soul-bond* couldn't be blocked by his wards, at least.

"Tomas just left the office. Why is she re-setting the wards? What... Oh!" Damien shivered and tried to pull his awareness back from the sensation of Jason kissing him... no, kissing *Genevieve*. He knew the feel of those skilled hands along his own skin already and this was... different and the same in an exceedingly uncomfortable mix.

Damien tried to blink himself back into his sense of his own body, and turned to look at Adam. "Jason and Genevieve are..."

His voice trailed away as he realized that Adam was looking anything but surprised.

"You planned this." It wasn't accusatory... exactly.

Adam didn't look away. "We'd *all four* agreed that they'd do this – after the wedding and coronation. Which is where we are now. This way is actually a bit easier. Jason and I were assuming that he'd take the secret passageway up to your suite and send you down here."

"Easier..." Damien looked away, trying to block off the bond more thoroughly. "I suppose." His heart and soul were elsewhere... and none of this was *easy*.

"Hey..." Adam's large hand on his shoulder was gentle. "We're in the same boat, in this, you and I."

Damien hunched in on himself. "Not exactly." No. Adam wasn't soul-bonded to Jason – he couldn't feel Genevieve touching his new husband in ways that should only have been his. And none of this was *Adam's* fault. It was *all* Damien's.

"You have that look of taking all the world's trouble's on your shoulders again." Adam's tone was calm.

"*You're* the one who taught me they were mine to take." The younger man blew out a breath. "I'm sorry. That wasn't fair."

Adam snorted. "It was entirely fair. We took you from your nice, safe library and turned you into a king. No," he corrected himself. "Jason and Ciriis and I helped you to your *throne*. It was you who turned yourself into a *king*."

"And Genevieve," Damien hunched a little further, trying not to think of her, because that only brought her closer through the soul-bond. But how *could* he 'not think' about her? Genevieve was always in his thoughts.

Well, except for when he and Jason... which was not *helping* right now, not at *all*...

"From what *she* tells me, *her* only role was to convince you that you *are* one." Adam's hand that had rested on Damien's shoulder now trailed down his back, and the king shivered in reaction. His *body* apparently remembered what Adam had been doing in the Throneroom.

He shook his head, trying to clear it of... *things*... that shouldn't be in it. "Adam, please. It's hard enough to keep the other end of the bond blocked..." Impossible, rather. "Don't... don't *touch* me."

Unexpectedly, Adam chuckled. "Or you'll do... *what?*"

He ran his hand *up* Damien's back this time, and the resulting shiver was more of a shudder as the younger man tried to overcontrol it away and failed... dramatically.

Damien swallowed hard. "Adam, *please*. I've done too much to you already. To you *both*. I... don't want to take any more advantage of your kindness. Of *you*. You've trapped me in here. You don't have to do anything *else*."

A quiet sigh, and then an answer that had not the slightest bit of sarcasm in its tone. "You've given me – us – more than you seem to understand, Damien. A country where we can be free together – even *married,* as I had never dared hope and Jason never even tried to imagine. A country where my brothers and sisters – my nephews – can grow up without fear. Positions of honor and responsibility – and the ability to fulfill them honorably without risk of execution for doing our duty."

Adam took another deep breath.

"And personally, you have been the very dearest of friends, you and Genevieve both. Even if you were not my king and needing an Heir, I would have wanted to do this – to save your lives, yes, but also because I want you to be happy and I can see that you need to have a child to fill your heart as much as *I* do... and now you're giving *me* a child as well. A child of my own true love's blood and bone."

Adam hesitated a moment. "I've been trying to talk Jason into adopting for years now. He's been too scared, and after what his mother and sister did to his self-image, I can't blame him... and yet somehow, my Healer-King, you've even managed to set him on a road to recovering from *that*."

Adam chuffed a laugh. "You rehabilitated the image of the father he never knew, freed him from his mother – and... didn't you see how he picked Megan up and swung her around? Did you see her give him a hug back? Did you see how her children came up to him? She and Alexa made them terrified of him before they were *toddlers*." Adam shook his head, distractedly. "Megan tried to say something to me about being sorry and her husband, David, told me it hadn't been her fault. After seeing her and Jase together, I could almost believe it."

He refocused and gripped his king's chin with a gentle thumb and fingers, making Damien look deeply into Adam's golden-hazel eyes.

"And *somehow* you loving him has made my Jason start to truly move past those dark days with Prince Oskar. That was always between us before – I couldn't accept that he had really been in love with Oskar. When I saw him falling in love with *you*–"

Damien made a strangled sound of denial, but Adam smiled. "Oh, but he has. Jason doesn't love *easily* – Alexa and Megan wounded him too badly for that. But he loves *fiercely* and he does not let go. He loves you. He loves Genevieve... but it's *me* he married and *me* he has come home to for fifteen years. I can share his heart with you... and with the child – the *children* – who are to come... Even with his memories of Oskar, now.

"You haven't somehow *broken* things between me and Jason, Damien... You've helped fix things I hadn't even realized *were* broken."

Damien could read the unshielded sincerity in Adam's golden-hazel eyes.

And he liked the title his friend had come up with: 'Healer-King.' He liked it much better than 'Sorcerer-King,' as his people had become wont to call him.

But this seemed too pat, too much like the perfect fairy-stories he had read in his years hiding in the library.

Normal people didn't accept such *abnormal* arrangements with equanimity.

Damien must have said some of that thought aloud, though he hadn't been aware of it. Adam smiled again.

"And when did any of *us* have a chance to be 'normal?' Your youth may have been the most unusual, but Jason and I were living here in the castle in your grandfather's Court since we were eleven. And I, at least, knew my preferences early on. Early enough to learn how to hide who I was, and who I loved, until I was strong enough to defend myself. It's an incredible gift," Adam's eyes shone with sudden extra moisture, "it is such an incredible *gift*, Damien, simply to not have to hide that part of me anymore. And you've given that gift to how many thousands more like me?"

Damien twisted his head away. Adam was applauding him for things that he didn't have any right to take credit for. And there were still so *many* problems he hadn't fixed. Might never be *able* to fix. "Legally, maybe, though there was never any *law* forbidding same-sex couples to wed. But you *do* know why we were so careful of the two of you throughout yesterday's ceremonies? Tim and Aryllis must have shared those threats with you."

"I was reading those reports for myself less than a week ago," the former Captain of the Royal Guard said dryly. "I'd already spoken to the

City Guard about stepping up vigilance regarding people being persecuted because they are following our example and Duchess Laura's. Whether it follows in the provinces... will depend on the various liege-lords and -ladies."

Damien wouldn't meet his eyes. "If I had Bound them to *me* instead of just the land, I could *make* them all enforce the change."

That earned him another snort of sardonic mirth.

"My king, *you* could probably go into your connection to the Realm and make all the individual *people* change their minds to accept same-sex couples."

Adam's face was still more gentle than Damien had ever seen it. "But that wouldn't be right. I don't always challenge your decisions to disperse power because I disagree with them, Damien. I do it to make you think things through and not just imagine the best-case scenario."

Damien cringed slightly. "No worries of that."

Adam's gaze on him was knowing... and understanding. Just as it always had been since Damien had been fourteen. Sympathy cloaked in insulating sarcasm. He had been girding a prince to become a king, after all.

"But you also can't spend every moment anticipating the *worst*-case scenario. Think about it, plan, then set it aside and move on. You're an optimist by nature, my friend," Adam said kindly, "and there's no shame in that. You're a pragmatist by training – mine, mostly, I'll admit."

Damien had to stop and think about that, and while he was distracted, Adam had slid a leg around to sit close behind him, pulled his own shirt off, and was working on Damien's.

"Now, where were we earlier?" the tall knight asked rhetorically as he tugged the satin-woven cotton fabric over the king's head and pulled Damien skin-to-skin against his too warm chest.

Too warm, too well-muscled, too... much everything. Damien could feel the *too* rapid heartbeat and breathing – or was that his own?

"Oh, yes," Adam chuckled wickedly into Damien's ear, sliding one hand lower and lower across the younger man's abdomen. Under and past the waistband of his pants. "And *you* suggested this might not be intentional. I may not have had as many lovers as you – or Jason – but I think I know how to make love to someone when I want to."

Damien couldn't find the breath to reply.

Chapter SIX

Realizations

"**I** DEFY YOU TO TELL me that that didn't distract you from what was going on in your office tonight," Adam murmured sleepily rather later.

"*Is* going on," Damien corrected absently. "They're on round two. Or possibly three. But, yes. Mostly. Neither of us had the concentration left to block the bond, so... there was some... erm... leakage." He twisted around for another kiss. "*This* was... *wonderful.*"

It was impossible to believe the king didn't mean every word. Those beautiful, clear, grey eyes of his shimmered with almost as much silver *intent* as when Adam had seen him focus them with coldly suppressed fury on Countess Alexa during what had turned out to be her trial two days ago... or when he was performing some feat of magick.

At least Damien wasn't *glowing* anymore. It had been... *disconcerting* for Adam, to say the least, to realize that their fun really *did* light up the room.

The king had also glowed with that cool, silvery effulgence all the way from the Council chamber to the Throneroom earlier, and Genevieve had been glowing a brighter golden light. It had been almost blinding when those two had kissed, though the glow had gradually dimmed as Damien worked his magick, almost as if he was using it up.

The king and queen had been...moonlight and sunlight, to put it poetically. Perfectly matched and complementary, as if they completed something within each other – which was the usual description of a soul-bond, after all.

To realize Damien had reacted the same way to *Adam* – if not so brightly – had been... unexpected.

Adam kissed him back with interest, adding rather distractedly, "Round *three*? Where the hell is Jason getting the stamina? Even at nineteen, that's the kind of thing it takes a soul-bond to..."

Between what had been some rather delightful follow-up kisses, Adam noticed Damien's guilty expression, and tried to ignore the sinking feeling in the pit of his stomach. He tried to put a stern and acerbic tone – a *swordmaster's* tone from the training ring – into his voice and keep any tinge of panic out. "What have you not been telling me?'

"I mentioned it to Jason. And Genevieve. It was just a suspicion. They both thought it was silly." Damien's eyes were just plain, clear grey now as he tried to avoid Adam's sharp gaze. He started to squirm away.

Adam rolled over on top of his king, pinning him down... and resisting the urge to kiss him again. He could feel his own body responding, and where the hell was *that* coming from? *He* hadn't been up for a 'round two,' as Damien had so discreetly put it, this quickly since he was nineteen himself.

"What did you not tell *me?*" Adam demanded.

Those clear, grey eyes met his reluctantly. "I thought that Jason might have ended up soul-bonded to Genevieve if I hadn't run into her first that day."

Adam's core went icy. He sat up, moved a little away, trying to fold his arms and not wrap them around himself. "What does that mean *now?*"

It was only with effort that he managed not to scream out, *And how is it that none of you three ever mentioned this to* me?

Damien scrambled to a sitting position, wincing as he clearly barked his feet against the mattress. It... probably said something that Adam had to stop himself from moving to ease that pain – or kiss it away. He tightened the grip of his hands on his elbows – he'd seen the king take far worse. Had inflicted it on the younger man himself in the course of serving as his swordmaster.

"I wasn't sure if I was overworrying things – as you all tell me I tend to do – or if they just really needed to believe it wasn't possible." Damien's wry expression didn't completely cover his anxiety. "I know that's true for Genevieve. She's constructed this whole Grand Destiny story that we were *meant to be together* and that with each failed opportunity – like my parents not managing to flee with me to Elaarwen when I was a child – it meant that Fate had to twist itself into more exotic contortions to *bring* us together."

The younger man winced slightly. "It's *pretty,* but it sometimes feels like it's all just a story she made up simply because she had to justify to herself how she could have fallen out of love with Rosa so rapidly. Genevieve resented the soul-bond originally, you know. She didn't like it making her choices for her."

Adam had known that the Rebel Duchess had been lovers with the Rebel Countess. He hadn't realized it had been as deep as being *in love* – somehow dismissing it as two lonely and injured women helping each other. To his eyes, Rosa Teraseel had always seemed so deeply in love with Zachary Miramar – and she had, after all, been about to marry him when everything fell apart with Prince Oskar.

But it hadn't been Zachary and his county of Dalizell to whom Rosa had turned for help and protection against King Reginald's retribution... Or for the Healing of heart and body that she'd sorely needed.

And she'd stayed in Elaarwen for two years, long past the time when Genevieve's rebels had made Zialest safe for her return. Nor had she married Zachary until *after* the Rebellion was done and a new king was on the throne. After the soul-bond had Bound king and queen beyond all hope of undoing... *after* Genevieve had wed Damien.

Adam had been naïve, or even condescending, to dismiss their relationship, he realized belatedly. And if anyone should have known better...

But...

"What about *now?*"

Damien shook his head apologetically. "My bond with her doesn't *feel* any different. I can't sense Jason..."

The king looked wry again. "All right, that's not quite true. I can sense Jason quite clearly, but it's through her physical sensations, not as if he was entangled in her soul."

He came close and put an arm around Adam's shoulders, the comforter instead of the comforted, for once. "I can't answer what you want to know. You said yourself that Jason loves fiercely and doesn't let go. The four of us are tangled up together anyways – forever. We'll have a child together – and others who'll be yours as much as they are mine, just like the first."

They were words that should have warmed Adam's child-hungry soul, but that somehow felt... pale and unsatisfying right now. Truth... didn't always help.

The king paused. "They've always had something special between them that pre-dates either one of us, Adam. This is going to make that... tighter. But I don't think they'll leave us out."

"Not *you*, certainly." Adam felt sick.

It was one thing to give Jason up for a night – or even a month of nights as they'd... not joked – *feared?* He'd even enjoyed making love with Damien this evening, once he'd come to terms with it in his own way. But if he lost Jason *forever...*

Likely Damien had felt this same way many a time over the years. It was Adam's own approach of absolute truth in all cases – if gentled and tuned to his own nature – that he was serving back.

It was the right thing to do, Adam had always felt. Don't lie, don't soften more than is true. A harsh truth isn't eased by hiding or pretending it away... it's merely deferred to cut sharper and deeper later.

As, indeed, this one was doing now.

"Not you, either." Damien put his other hand on Adam's face and made the Champion look into his eyes. He was *smiling*.

"You told me that the wedding ceremony cast a spell on both of you. Can't you still feel it? I could – I *can* – now that I know to look for it. It *feels* a lot like the outside of a soul-bond. I've had occasion to meet a few other soul-bonded people, and this feels very similar." Damien tilted his head. "I haven't thought of looking for it before, but it wouldn't surprise me to find that *this* is what distinguishes a real love-marriage... I'll bet if we asked Mother Alayana, she'd say the same thing. The thing with the fire – I think it must *create* a soul-bond. Just... one that you got to *choose.*"

Adam tried to summon a glare. "You aren't just making all this stuff up to try to make me feel better, I hope."

It was working, if he was. Adam did feel less icy inside... and that together with his attendant hyperawareness of Damien's nearness...

"Lie to you to get you to go to bed with me?" Damien raised his eyebrows, that small, sweet smile still blessing his lips. "Seems a little late for that. Try to see if you can feel Jason right now."

"Of *course* I can feel him," Adam retorted, trying to focus on some other part of his king than those lips. "I've been trying *not* to for all the same reasons *you* have." His eyes widened as it came to him what it was that Damien meant. "Oh."

And... damn, but he'd let something more slip himself than he'd intended...

Damien chuckled, then gave him a wide-eyed look as *he* realized what Adam had implied. "This isn't new, is it? When did you realize that you knew what Jason was feeling?"

Adam put on a baffled expression. No way out but through sometimes... Perhaps Damien could be led to believe *Adam* didn't know what he'd been doing... It wasn't his secret alone to be kept, after all.

"What do you mean *when?*"

"I mean, when did you..." the king stopped and looked thoughtful. "Is that how you knew Jason was the one you were waiting for? From the very beginning? But you *couldn't* have known when he was with Prince Oskar or... oh." Damien stopped, his eyes going *silver* again, this time with compassion. "This is why you nearly went crazy with missing him. Both times. You *did* know."

"I knew the first time I saw him," Adam admitted. He'd never told anyone – never told *Jason* – any of this. But his young king was just too damned *clever* to be put off the mark for long or far. "When Mama brought me up to the city to become a page."

Which had been Adam's idea more than Mama's. He hadn't *needed* to come study for his knighthood after all, he'd been – he still *was* – Mama's designated Heir to the baronetcy of Lynnscrag. Learning to manage their lands should have been all he had time and energy to *do*. But Adam had been adamant and obsessed as only an eleven-year-old *can* be...

Papa had supported him, and Mama had brought him to Emeralsee and Court at last. They had both understood after all, though they'd warned him that it might be years before he found The One that he knew would be there... eventually.

He'd known it was Jason as soon as he'd laid eyes on him, and that had led to years of hiding that knowledge from his loving, supportive parents who were expecting him to bring them home a *daughter*-in-law-to-be...

And then when he'd started to wrap his mind around *that* mess... then had come Lady Miria and Prince Eric's assassination in the middle of public audiences and his first real glimpse of a certain terrified young prince... and that *feeling* of *Destiny* knocking on his door had nearly overwhelmed what he'd been exposed to that horrifying day...

"I had a feeling there was something else drawing me here," Adam went on, hoping only now to keep the king on *this* topic. Damien was an incredible romantic, especially when it came to his no-longer-so-vicarious interest in and always-unflagging support of Jason and Adam's relationship. "So, I kept looking around... and *there* was Jason. I swear I could hear something go 'click' in my head like one of those mechanical puzzles Ciriis loves... and from then on, I've always known what he was feeling."

Adam looked down, the one fragment that had always disappointed him escaping at last from the cage of silence he had built for it. "I don't think it goes both ways."

It went both ways for Mama and Papa. And for his sister, Desirée, and *her* husband, from what he'd learned in getting to know them all again these last few days after Adam's long estrangement from his family. He had been able to guess that it *hadn't* gone both ways for his brother Lorry in either of Lorry's two failed marriages.

Which had become more than a niggling worry for himself and Jason...

Damien gave him that *intent* look again. "Maybe not *before*, but I'll bet it does *now*."

The king grinned wryly, his eyes growing distant enough as he seemed to look through the walls of the castle to where their wedded loves were that perhaps he didn't see the look of hope and relief that Adam gave him. "I'll bet Jason could give you a play-by-play description of what *we* did tonight... if he was willing. Which he probably wouldn't be, gentleman that he is. Even distracted as he surely has been with his own activities."

Adam was startled and slightly... disturbed by the idea. Yes. Disturbed. Not aroused. Because that would be... entirely too strange.

A snort at Damien's usual effusive praise and idolizing of Jason might be better...

But before Adam could compose himself to scoff properly, his king was gazing deeply into his eyes. Damien's own had gone that shining *silver* again, and Adam had the oddest sensation in his head, nor could he seem to look away. That family secret surely wasn't going to be one for much longer, the Champion thought resignedly. But perhaps he could still limit the damage.

Damien broke off that oddly intent gaze, looking away with a satisfied smile. "It's your own gift, my friend. It's... not *quite* magick. You *do* have a gift for that as well, and if you stay on as your mother's Heir and end up becoming Baronet Loveress and are Bound to the land, that gift will be accessible to you. I could wake it now if you wanted..." Adam shook his head quickly with some alarm. "No? Well, there's no rush. And it's a doorway you can only cross once; I don't think I could lock it down again. But what you have right now... what led you to Jason in the first place... that's different."

"You're being mysterious again, Damien," Adam complained, trying to play the part of the innocent who was stubbornly refusing to be enlightened. "I've probably read enough of your books to know what you're talking about – *if* you'll give me some specifics."

60

Yes, that was it. Force Damien to reason everything out for himself. Though it was still pretty likely that he'd manage it, given how very good the king was at assembling disparate clues. Not a thing Adam had ever taught him – it was his own *gift*.

Ridiculous, all of it. He trusted his king in every way imaginable. But he'd promised Mama when he was eleven never to volunteer the information to anyone, but *especially* not to anyone of Alsterling descent. Why, Adam still didn't know, but he'd never seen his mother look as grim and determined before or after. And his Papa had refused to discuss it, looking sadder than Adam had ever seen him and quite nearly as grim as Mama…

Normally, Adam didn't do *anything* that he didn't have good reasons for. Especially in cases that involved him walking the boundaries of truth with his liege-lord and -lady – since Genevieve was also 'of Alsterling descent.' And now his husband… he'd planned to tell Jason everything… *some*day… but now *he* was an Alsterling as well… As was Adam himself. Though by marriage, not descent, so maybe that didn't matter.

But he'd hinted around it to Mama the last few days and she had managed to avoid his every attempt at discussing the problem.

Damien tilted his head. "You and Ciriis found me in the library when I was fourteen. How?"

"Damien, if you're changing the topic…" Which was surely too much to hope for.

"I swear I'm not," the king's smile was slightly apologetic for his usual, roundabout approach. "I always thought it must have been Ciriis – and how did you ever become friends with *her* anyways? – because she would have had more unstructured time than a squire. Or so I thought. As lady-in-waiting for both my grandmother and Queen Eliza she may have been busier than I realized."

Damien's eyes were curious. But these little tangents of his were usually quite effective at gathering more of the clues that he then assembled so adroitly.

"I… nudged Ciriis," Adam admitted without addressing the question of how he had met Ciriis at all. "Though it *was* her idea to search for an uncorrupted Alsterling scion." Her idea with a little help, anyways. "She was scouring the archives – coming and going regularly in the Royal Library. She saw you, skulking around, but she didn't figure out who you were. Just thought it was odd to see you there that often. She brought me in to show me something in the Library, and as soon as I saw you, *I* knew who you were. I… told her it was because I recognized you from… That Day. Jason and I had been on Guard duty. We saw it all."

Saw it. Had nightmares over it. Spent years feeling like he'd failed in some obscure way by standing there and watching Prince Eric and Lady Miria killed – though he'd been all of fourteen himself. "Ciriis hadn't come to Court till the next year. She'd never seen you, so she accepted my explanation."

With luck, so would Damien. He typically shied away from anything that edged the memories of his parents' death.

"But that wasn't it at all," Damien said softly. Typically... but not today, it appeared.

Adam shook his head.

He'd never promised Mama that he would *lie* about this. She'd known better than to ask that – because at the time she'd made him swear, *lying* to someone of Alsterling descent had most likely meant lying to King Reginald or one of his scions, like Prince Oskar. Or Damien's father, but it hadn't been until a year or two later that Prince Eric had been summoned back to Court with his wife and younger child. *Lying* to most anyone in the Alsterling clan might have proven a death sentence, even for a child.

Not to mention that Adam found *lying* to be morally abhorrent and always had. Likely he'd have refused to make Mama the promise if she'd suggested that. At eleven... everything had seemed much more black-and-white. He'd learned... later on... that obfuscation and even outright prevarication had their place – at least if one hoped to survive in King Reginald's Court.

Those hard lessons had served Damien well in the end. There was nothing Adam wouldn't have done for his prince – who was now his king in no small part because of that.

So... he'd tell Damien. Or rather, confirm his king's suspicions when they came too close to deny.

Adam took a deep breath in preparation, and...

"My dear friend," the king asked with gentle concern and... amazement? "*How* have you managed to stay here in Emeralsee – in the *Castle* – around so many people at all?"

Adam frowned. That hadn't been what he was expecting to hear.

"Jason was here." What other reason could he need?

Damien gave him another silvery *intent* look. "You have some very tight natural – or rather instinctive – shields. You're a natural empath, Adam. Possibly with a touch of telepathy as well."

The king tilted his head again as his knight – and swordmaster and friend and Champion and advisor... and lover – tried to look surprised, rather than laugh at the way Damien seemed to think he had to explain this fact of life as if Adam wouldn't actually know it. It seemed he'd already made up his mind and Adam wouldn't have to confirm or deny anything...

"I wouldn't be surprised to find that it's a Loveress family trait," Damien noted. "Though whether it came from your mother or your father – what you told me about him earlier makes me wonder."

And since that was fully *half* of what Mama hadn't wanted the Alsterlings to know... It felt almost like a blinding strike of lightning for Damien to just state it outright like that, even if merely as a speculation.

"Or both?" Adam felt an obscure need to defend his parents. "Papa had to come halfway across the Realm to find Mama after all."

Dammit, that was practically the confirmation Damien needed. And he hadn't even asked for it; Adam seemed to have somehow volunteered... He was as susceptible to Damien's gentle interest and leading questions as any of the Peers or Councilors or subjects he'd watched his king carefully quiz – and after observing Damien at work so many times, surely *Adam*, of all people, should have been wise to the tricks.

Well, the 'trick,' of course was that they weren't tricks. Damien was genuinely interested in what everyone else thought or had to say. Of course, it 'worked.'

"That would explain why your empathy is so strong, then." The king smiled with the mischievous expression he sometimes wore after solving a particularly challenging intellectual puzzle. Adam had always found it endearing. *Before.*

"It's been staring me in the face for so long," Damien went on. "It's how you knew that Jason and I could help *each other* Heal. It must have driven you crazy..."

He let his words trail off, but Adam could practically hear what he had planned to say – by telepathy? He knew nearly as much about these things as the king, after all. His own reading had been nearly as much to understand the Loveress family gifts as to help Damien understand *his* gifts.

Damien had been *going* to say that it must have driven Adam crazy to not be everything Jason needed then. To know that his best chance of helping his love recover from having heart and soul broken by another man was... to connect him to *Damien.* Granted that Damien had been a half-feral child, if immensely self-educated.

"It did," Adam answered the thought. "And it didn't. You were a scrawny, unkempt little thing then. Not *competition*... though I always knew that Jason wouldn't leave me forever in any case. He's the other half of my soul, so how could he? I had no idea," he said dryly, trying to go back to the safe, sardonic tone that had served him so well in the past. "That you were going to grow up into such a handsome, sexy man."

True... but a red herring to some extent. Bait and offering to divert Damien's attention in... well, *one* direction or another, but away from the secrets that weren't all Adam's to share.

Damien went rather appealingly red at that, but gave Adam his usual half-smile. "'The other half of your soul'? You 'always knew'? That sounds like a soul-bond, just not the flashy kind."

Adam was startled for real, though the suggestion dovetailed on Damien's earlier assertion that the marriage ceremony *created* something like a soul-bond. Just one that was *chosen* by the participants. "There's more than one kind?"

Damien shrugged. "I'll have to do some research. Empirical research, not literature," he clarified.

His arms around Adam didn't *shift,* but somehow they went from comforting to... something *more.* And Adam was unavoidably reminded that his king had far more experience in the bedroom than he did.

"For now, though," Damien said softly, "it certainly sounds like we have *two separate* soul-bonds spilling over to us.... Shall we enjoy it?"

"Mmmmn," Damien murmured peacefully into the firm, warm muscle of Adam's broad chest. "I should just 'vanish' Jason and Genevieve up here. It will be less peculiar than if they come out of the office in the morning together."

Adam pried an eye open. "What about your poor Royal Guards doing duty on an empty room all night."

"The night's mostly gone, love. I can't do much to fix that."

"They finally fell asleep and you want to wake them up..." Adam sighed. "I don't know if I could *handle* any more." But he dropped a kiss on Damien's mop of messy black hair, possibly in a silent answer to what the younger man had inadvertently called him.

Inadvertent... but heartfelt, as such things tended to be. It had always been a truth of Damien's life, at least from the age of fourteen, but he'd never before dared say the word even inside his own head.

He tilted his head up to meet Adam's eyes. Those lovely golden-hazel eyes – always so warm and kind, even when he was playing his role as Professional Cynic to the King. Mentor, best friend, safe harbor, swordmaster... lover. Love. It was too complicated and yet entirely simple. Right at this moment, anyways.

Damien's mouth curved into a smile and his heart raced a little as he replied, "It might be fun to find out. But I didn't plan to wake them."

Adam glared at him... then softened. "Another time, please. I'll be close to worthless tomorrow as it is."

Damien felt more than his heart racing.

"You mean it?" he breathed, sitting up to see Adam better.

"What?"

"Another time?"

Adam shook his head with what appeared to be fond disbelief. "How do you get anything done if this is all you can think about? You're as bad as a teenager. No wonder all those knights and lordlings keep propositioning you."

Damien's jaw dropped. "What – what are you talking about?" he stammered not very convincingly. He thought he'd managed to be discreet in discouraging such interest.

Adam gave him a lazy, knowing look. "You're the handsomest man at Court – barring only Jason, who is most definitely *taken*. And I saw the look you gave Genevieve when she said the men of the Court don't throw themselves at you like the young women do."

"I'm *taken*," Damien objected. And rather carefully ignoring the physical – and emotional – context of this discussion.

"Your grandfather set a precedent about that not making a difference," Adam's lazy look became wicked. "So how many have you had to fend off, and how has she missed noticing?"

"Perhaps the bigger question is why only the *women* accosting me bother her," Damien muttered. Though he had the same reaction to men admiring her... and he hadn't particularly noticed any women doing the same. An... oddly disturbing thought, now that he'd had it.

"So. How many?"

"Eight different knights," Damien relented, and blushing furiously. Not that any of it had been his fault. "I haven't kept track of the 'lordlings,' as you put it. A couple of the Royal Guards – they were polite, they didn't make it awkward," he added hastily as Adam frowned over that lack of professionalism in the ranks of the people *he* had commanded. "You were with me almost every waking moment. How is it *you* never noticed enough to have a tally?"

Adam chuckled. "Oh, we noticed." He watched with amusement as Damien mouthed the word 'we' with some dismay. "A number of them couldn't figure out how to get to you directly. I doubt there's a single member of your Royal Guards who hasn't been asked to be a go-between by both men *and* women." He grinned. "Your fault for being so devastatingly handsome."

Damien snorted. "My fault for being *king* and people thinking the way to get things out of me is to fill my bed. I won't even mention all the mothers and fathers, aunts and uncles and cousins who have offered their own younger kin." He shuddered. "What part of 'soul-bonded and happily married' do they not get?"

Adam gave him a deeply ironic look. "You *do* hear yourself right now, don't you?"

Damien blushed again, but said firmly, "You're different, you and Jason. And this is nobody else's business. Actually, it had *better* not be. Could you please remove the magickal barrier so I can vanish them up here?"

The tall knight groaned. "I should have known this all came down to me getting out of bed and into the cold air."

Damien grinned. "Oh, I'd never ask that of you. I promise you won't be cold. Especially certain parts of you."

"Like my *feet,* I hope. I haven't yet tried to find if Elista's people brought my slippers up here."

Several minutes later, Jason and Genevieve were also asleep on the bed. Damien, true to his word, had managed not to wake them in transport. He'd remembered to snatch their scattered clothing off the floor as well. Cleaning staff didn't enter his office, but since it was apparently serving as a war-room, doubtless others would be in and out.

Damien dimmed the lanterns as Adam adjusted sheets and blankets over them all. With a practiced Healer's eye, he surveyed Genevieve's beautiful sleeping body, looking for the signs of a new conception that he knew so heartbreakingly well. To his surprise, he couldn't be sure he'd found them. A part of him had been utterly positive that she would 'catch' instantly.

Well, he had survived this so far. And he'd discovered how much he loved his two friends. A little longer before he could make love to his beloved wife.... he could survive that, too.

Chapter SEVEN

Attack!

THE STORM WAS STILL HOWLING by the time any of them woke up.

For once, that first person was Damien, and he lay very still, not wanting to disturb any of… his loves. He was still tired, but not sleepy. He'd exhausted the Realm's excess resources the day before, but had also fed it well on his own joy. And so had Genevieve. He wondered idly if his reactions to Adam's lascivious explorations in the Throneroom itself had been more effective at, ah, *getting his attention* because of the special nature of that room; likely the Realm could absorb magick from Damien there better, just as It could provide him magick better when he sat on the Throne.

It hardly mattered. The Throneroom was an entirely awkward place for such things and he didn't intend to test it further.

He closed his eyes again and kept his breath even and slow. Adam didn't seem to have noticed last night, but he hadn't reset the barrier-spell that kept Damien and his magick confined to this room after he'd opened it up to allow the others to be transported in. The Champion had probably assumed that his king was too sleepy to attempt anything he 'shouldn't' in their overprotective opinions… and after all the effort Adam had expended in making certain of that sleepiness, he'd been right. Then.

But now Damien was fully awake and rested. It was an excellent time to send his awareness out to check on the progress of the storm – and that mysterious fleet.

His plan came crashing in on him. "Adam!" he sat bolt upright. "Put the magical barrier back up. Now!"

Despite having seen Adam crawl up out of sleep as if he had to claw his way to alertness just a few weeks earlier, the Champion was wide awake and halfway across the sitting room before Damien could *feel* more than the first edges of the enemy storm stealing around the castle, orienting on the tower. He felt the wards activate, one level at a time, as Adam wrapped the long thread in its loops, tracing the infinity symbol over and over... When the highest level – the one that trapped Damien himself in these rooms – dropped into place, he relaxed. Somewhat.

Adam trudged back into the room with a heavyfootedness that belied his previous instant response and gave his king a wary glance. "Done, but I suppose you know that. Care to explain?"

"Yes, please do," Genevieve hadn't bothered to sit up. "*And* perhaps how we got up here? I recall falling asleep in your office..." She blushed. Jason lay still beyond her, his blue eyes open and curious, one arm out from under the bed-coverings and resting lightly across her abdomen. *Possessively.*

Damien gave her a tight smile, then nodded to Adam, entirely ignoring Jason for the time being. He'd never imagined he'd have to *see* the two of them together – knowing he'd have to *feel* what they were doing to conceive that baby had been bad enough. As he'd admitted to all three of them not so very long ago, he'd effectively banished a couple of knights to far corners of the Realm for being too bold in pursuing their queen's 'favor.' Or rather '*favors.*' Distant, miserable postings... that really *did* need a knight to fill them...

Not that that could work with his newly named Heir. For *Jason*, whom he loved so dearly himself...

He *could* handle this... but maybe not right now.

"I was awake, so I decided to see how the storm was progressing. It sensed me and decided to come looking for me." Damien fixed his gaze on Adam and wrapped his arms tightly around himself. Even that slight contact with the storm had chilled him to the core. "It was a foolish error. I knew the thing had been targeted to me. Adam got the magickal barrier up before it figured out exactly where I am..." He nodded at his Champion. "I *think* it didn't get into the Castle, but with the wards up... I can't *look* to check."

"'Targeted' to you..." Genevieve murmured. "I *thought* I felt it seeking you when we were in the Throneroom. But everything I sense *through* you is so heavily filtered that I can never be sure." She sat up, the blankets – and Jason's arm – falling away from her lovely curves and the light, golden tan that never seemed to end, and reached out to him, pulling back in surprise. "You're icy again!"

He nodded. "Not as bad as yesterday. This was only a brief touch. I... wish I could ask *you* to warm me up, sweetheart, but..." He finally glanced at Jason, trying to keep it as brief and neutral a look as he could manage. Trying not to show *disappointment*. Or *disapproval*. Or... *hurt*. Or *anger*. He'd asked Jason to do this after all. And Genevieve had resisted as long as she'd been physically able. "You're not pregnant yet, as far as my Healing sense can tell."

She sighed, but it didn't seem an *unhappy* sigh, to his overly-sensitive ears.

Jason looked at Adam and shrugged, also not seeming particularly put out.

Adam came back to the bed and laid a warm arm around Damien's shoulders. It helped... more than he should want it to. But not nearly enough. *His soul-bonded wife in another man's arms...*

Guilt – and justifiable indignation – trickled across that very bond.

The king looked up at the ceiling and around at the walls of the windowless suite, doing his best to barricade her out of his end of the soul-bond. "No insult intended, sweetheart, but honestly right now I'm more concerned with the storm. We don't dare take that barrier down, but I can't *see* past it. I have no idea what it's doing to my Realm... my province... my *city*... I can still *feel* the Realm, but it's mostly sleeping and I can't get any *details...*"

And details were how he held his entire reign together. Details that other people didn't notice or couldn't correlate as well or as quickly or as broadly. There might be other ways to rule, but Damien had begun this way and what he had learned from Duk– *Lord* Aldred and Genevieve – and to a lesser extent from Tomas Elsevier and Rosa and Zachary and even Count Antonin of Emeralsee – had been things he simply piled on top of the house of cards he was already juggling.

What he'd gotten from them had been things he hadn't known about how the *people* would respond to his changes in policy, and how to *persuade* his vassals and subjects better to his own viewpoint. As Adam had pointed out last night, he probably *could* have forced a change in every individual person's views through their innate connection with the Realm – or even just ruled by fiat without regards to their preferences. He had sufficient Power to do that. But it wouldn't have been *right,* even when the changes he was making were to the ultimate benefit of the people who were objecting.

Damien needed those details to keep the whole damn thing from collapsing.

It was beyond frustrating that he was trapped safely in this room and couldn't get them.

Jason sat up at his statement however, shedding the remaining blankets to his waist and looking like a golden god, matching the golden goddess beside him far better than the small, dark-haired husband who didn't even dare touch her right now. "No. *My* province. And *my* city... and you didn't set up that barrier to stop *me,* did you?"

Damien eyed him warily. This was *another* unintended and unexpected sore spot between them.

He'd removed as many of his own threads of connection to Emeralsee as he'd been able to identify during Jason's Investiture as Duke... but the province and city had been *his* more intimately than even Elaarwen for so long... from even before he'd been Bound by the Realm, Damien had discovered in trying to extract himself. Emeralsee seemed to recognize its proper Land-lord or -lady by the fact that they wore the Heir's Ring.

It had seemed... very *happy* to have a properly Invested Duke and Heir at last... passing the Ring between Genevieve, who had been so often gone, and Rosa, in faraway Dalzialest, these past five years had been nearly as stressful for Emeralsee as when King Reginald had not allowed the Ring to sit on anyone's finger for more than a brief time.

Anyone besides Damien, because he'd run out of other potential heirs... and Damien's father, Prince Eric, some ten years earlier, who had worn the Ring for nearly two years himself for reasons the old king hadn't even written down in his coded journals. It might have been a concession to King Eldrig in Dawil, far across the sea – Prince Eric had been Eldrig's nephew, after all. Dawil was still more powerful than even its king seemed to realize, with Wave – the former capitol of the Turquoise Empire – right there on it's southernmost coast.

But Reginald's notes made no such suggestion.

Well, now Damien could appreciate a bit better why his grandfather had seemed so loathe to give up Emeralsee to any Heir. Even his own Investiture as Crown Prince had been... as lacking in the proper transfer of magickal Power and connection as it had been lacking in pomp and ceremony or any real secular power.

Since his grandfather had never been entirely Bound to the Realm, his connection with Emeralsee – which served as a concentrator of Power and power nearly as effectively as an actual Binding – must have been truly painful to divest for even brief periods. Damien had done a proper job of it and it was still... sore.

And now... He could *feel* there was something *wrong* in city and province, but not *what*.

"The barrier should stop *all* magick from going in or out," Damien told his... friend. And former-Champion. And love. Not his *rival*. "It's the other one that stops magickal spying... but the Seeing Eye hasn't been one of my stronger gifts. I... don't what you might be able to do with it."

Seeing magick and using magick to See had turned out to be very different things, to his dismay.

"It probably *is* one of yours," he admitted a little reluctant, "given that you told me you were *seeing* stuff with it before you were even Bound, and how strongly the magick affected your sight when you took the Oath."

Jason had settled himself cross-legged and his eyes were closed. "There's an inch of ice on everything..." he said after a moment. "Doors are sealed shut, windows... most of the chimneys still seem to be smoking at least. Less ice outside the city, but it's still pretty severe. The river is frozen as far back as I can tell... The bay is iced over... that seems to be several inches... several *feet?*... thick. The cape seems to be sheltering the enemy fleet from the ice... but they won't be able to make it into the bay for some time. Even after the storm is over, there's going to be chunks of ice floating out towards the barrier islands. *Big* chunks of ice. Of course, *our* fleet is mired in the ice as well..."

The new-made Duke blinked, coming back to himself. He glanced at Damien, but he focused on Genevieve, as if aware that there was too much tension between himself and his king just now. Or simply because he preferred to look at her. "That was... strange. Very strange. I could actually *see* all of that, but not as if I was flying from place to place. Just as if I happened to be right there. Though the perspective was... unexpected."

Damien frowned as he watched Jason watching Genevieve. "Could you see the storm itself? How much of it is still left to hit the city? Did it make it into the Castle?"

Jason closed his eyes again. "The storm – it doesn't seem to be adding more ice, but it's still howling." They could hear *that* much even within the solid stone walls of the windowless tower room. Damien tapped his fingers on his tightly folded arms impatiently. It would do no good to rush him. "I can't find the trailing edge of it."

Which probably meant it was still beating on Reyensweir.

"And... the castle..." The blonde knight's usually serene face took on a look of strain. "I... can't..."

Abruptly he slumped over, his head drooping over his lap. Damien saw Adam make a movement towards him... and then halt himself as Genevieve laid a hand on Jason's shoulder.

She *was* right beside him after all. Adam's expression went completely shuttered.

"He's exhausted, love," she told Damien a little sternly. "Don't push him."

Damien glared back at her. "I did no such thing."

Jason laid a hand over Genevieve's, and lifted his head slowly. "It's all right, Genny. It's my duty and my privilege." He gave her a tired smile, then looked at Damien. "I couldn't see inside the Castle, Damien." It was the first time Jason had capitalized the noun to the king's knowledge. It was... interesting to hear the difference so easily. "It was like trying to look inside someone's beating heart. *Your* heart, actually."

The tall knight's lips curved up wryly... but somehow with a tenderness that reminded Damien that it hadn't been so very long since *he* had been in Jason's arms himself... Better not to think of that right now. Adam had withdrawn to sit alone again on the wide bed...

But Jason's statement made Damien's eyebrows fly up. The Castle felt like Damien's heart to Jason's Seeing Eye? He didn't know what to make of that. He was Bound to the Realm... and the Castle was a *part* of that...

But this seemed a more... *intimate* connection somehow. Thinking about that was easier than meeting Jason's blue eyes just now. For too many reasons.

Jason gave him a dry look as he added, "I think if the storm had gotten in, you'd know about it."

His eyes went, at last, to Adam, who was seated beside, but no longer so close to, the king. And then back to Genevieve. Damien could feel Adam trembling despite the small distance between them.

"Damn," Damien muttered, trying to stay focused on the bigger problem that... he *also* had no real ability to affect. "That means there's no way to find out what's going on outside these rooms without dropping that ward. And..."

He shivered again, turning to lean momentarily into Adam's shoulder for comfort as he had done when he was a *boy*... and to give Adam an excuse to not look at Jason looking at Genevieve.

Adam's arms that had come around him, seemingly automatically, did make him feel a little bit less lost and hopeless at least. As they always had.

He straightened up before that comfort could be flavored with any acerbic commentary, however. It had felt as if Adam appreciated – perhaps even *needed* – the gesture of trust as much as Damien... but that didn't mean he wouldn't say something to prod his king and former-protegée to buck up and remember who he was. Though the normalcy of that might have been welcome...

"It doesn't have to be anytime soon," Jason suggested. "It's just past dawn now, and with nowhere to go, even the early-risers are likely to sleep in. You can wait until you feel it safe to try opening up the ward."

The dark-haired man snorted. "Until *Adam* decides it's safe to try, you mean."

Jason shrugged. "I suppose it won't be you taking it down with your feet injured. But whichever of us." He seemed ready to lay back down and go back to sleep, tugging Genevieve with him... Granted, she'd been up as late as he...

But Genevieve had narrowed her eyes at her husband, and resisted lying back down. "You did something extravagant again, didn't you, love? Why does it have to be *Adam* who undoes the ward?"

"Because he's the one who set it. If you'd set it, you could undo it."

She gave Damien an exasperated look. "I thought that when you gave him the extension to add the last level – like you did me," she lifted her wrist with its own single line of red cord, "that it was because you'd decided it wasn't a good idea for you to be trapped in a room. I wondered at the time why you couldn't just go over and *undo* the ward *yourself,*" the king blushed, and she raised an eyebrow. He'd had to sketch in for her what had happened with Jason a few days ago and just why he was changing the ward-system when he'd given her the extension cord.

For his own part, Jason just chuckled as Genevieve finished, "Or even just use your magick to *unwind* it at the first opportunity. But *you* decided to be *clever* again, *didn't* you?"

That wasn't a *mildly* accusatory tone she was using.

"I had my reasons." Damien shrugged uncomfortably and tried to lean into Adam again – for more warmth, *not* protection from his beautiful and fearsome wife. He'd largely recovered from his magickal brush with the storm, but the air of the room was still chilly on his bare skin and the blankets were all either underneath them or wrapped around... *Jason* and Genevieve.

But Adam wasn't having any of it, either.

He grabbed the king's bearded chin and forced Damien to look into his eyes, though he did slide his other arm around the younger man's waist. "You young idiot. Suppose I *died* after setting that ward?"

Jason made a sound of muffled protest, and Adam flickered a *very* brief glance at him. "It may not be likely, but it could happen. Are you telling me you'd doom Jason and Genevieve to starve to death in here with you? It was bad enough to think that if you weren't *willing* to get past someone, you were trapped," he glanced at Jason again, who had the grace to blush this time, "but I figured that would only last until you got *bored.* You made the thing to keep yourself *out,* not *in,* you said."

An ironic glance exchanged all around suggested that everyone else was aware how quickly Damien became *bored.* And clearly placed most of the blame for the previous episode on *him.*

"I made it to do both..." Damien dropped his eyes as best he could. "You need a solution, all of you, against the day that I turn into the monster my grandfather was."

If Adam's golden-hazel eyes were... pitying, his voice was anything but. "So your *solution,* my fine young prince, is for one of *us* to trap ourselves in here *with* you?" he demanded harshly, though he did release Damien's chin.

"I thought it would mean you had taken the problem seriously," Damien tried to explain. He rubbed at the hair of his beard, wondering if there was any point in trimming it even shorter. Adam seemed to find that the extra friction of the hair made it easier to grab his chin, but he'd had no trouble with doing much the same thing *before* the beard either.

"And if you'd turned into such a monster as all that, you don't think you could simply *torture* any one of us into undoing the ward?"

Damien gasped. He *loved* them – *all* of them, How could Adam even *suggest..?*

"I... *never...* I *could* never..."

Genevieve reached a hand out to him, her smile gentle if also rather... pitying. "And *that* is why you never will turn into that kind of a monster, my love."

Adam shook his head. "That's not it, Genevieve. He was *hoping* he'd be trapped with one of us if it came to that..." He glanced at the other two sardonically. "With me or Genevieve, rather. Since *we* would force him to re-think his behavior in such dire straits. I notice you didn't saddle *Jason* with one of these things," he said rather pointedly to Damien, though he didn't withdraw the warmth and support of his encircling arm.

"Um." Damien didn't have a lot to say. That *was* more or less what he'd been thinking.

And, actually, he'd considered giving cords to Jason, Tim, and Aryllis. Except that Tim and Aryllis both had vital roles that would be even more crucial in such a situation. And so did Jason, as Crown Prince... not that that had been his major reason for not giving Jason one.

"Adam," the tall, blonde interlop– um, sexy– hmmn... *Heir* to the *Throne* interjected gently, "give him credit. He was trying to do what he thought was right."

Adam rolled his eyes. "And *now* I see why you didn't give one of these shackles to Jason."

Well, yes.

And the fact that evidence suggested that Jason might find the notion rather too entertaining.

On the other hand, it was vindicating that at least *one* of his dearest friends and advisors took his fears seriously. Although Jason had said *'trying.'* And if he took Damien more seriously than the others about his potential of becoming and Evil Wizard... hmmn, indeed.

"I don't know if you can understand," Damien tried to explain, moving his eyes between Adam and Genevieve. "I've never been able to determine *why* Grandfather became the monster he did. How can I be sure I *won't*? He was the most Powerful sorcerer in the family that I've identified to-date. Other than *me*. They say that power corrupts... How can I *not* leave you with some way to defeat me when it happens?"

Genevieve sighed deeply, and then, unexpectedly, she chuckled.

"You see what I mean," she said to Adam. "He keeps going down *this* rabbit-hole, too."

Adam grunted and fixed his king with a steely eye. "You are going to *fix these things*. Or make new ones, or whatever. You are going to start by talking to me – or Genevieve – about all the details of what they do *before* you do that. And you are going to talk to *one* of us before you create any *more* of these crazy spells." He paused. "No. More. Death. Gems."

Damien dropped his eyes, while Jason sat up more alertly and said *"What?"* and then Adam had to get up and show him the one that Damien had made yesterday.

Jason's face went pale. "Damien, what were you *thinking?*"

Genevieve sighed. "Give it to me when we get out of here, Adam, and I'll put it with the rest of them."

Jason went, if possible, even paler. "The *'rest of them'*? How many of these dreadful things has he *made*?"

She shrugged. "Five? Ten? Not all the curse stones are for instant death or entrapment. There's *one* that was rather entertaining..."

"*Genevieve...*" Damien tried to give her a warning look, which was not easy to do while blushing furiously. He wished he dared come close enough to use a more effective method to keep her from explaining.

But she decided to be merciful. Mostly. "Oh, very well."

Unfortunately, Adam wouldn't let this one drop. "Entertaining? This I have to hear."

He slipped his other arm around Damien as well, pulling the king into his chest. Which *was* nicely warm, but Damien hadn't missed that at least some of the point was to keep him from noticing the broad smirk on his Champion's face.

Adam had handed the ruby 'death gem' on its chain to Jason, who was now cringing and holding it as if it were a live spider on a leash.

"Let's just say that it was one of his other attempts to help us solve the miscarriage problem." Genevieve grinned, taking entirely too much enjoyment from her husband's discomfiture in *his* opinion. "It was the first one, I think. It didn't work... rather dramatically. So, I haven't worried too much about the rest."

She leaned back against... *Jason,* who... slipped an arm around her. Automatically, it seemed.

Damien glared at his hands rather than look at the pair of them. A man wasn't meant to be able to look at his *soul-bonded wife* in another man's hands and think straight. And nevermind that he was snuggling up to Adam – Genevieve had never even seemed to notice his 'knights and lordlings' propositioning him, after all.

Let them think he was upset for looking like an incompetent sorcerer. He could vanish himself away – to the sitting room anyways – but there was no need to act the part of a sulky child any further than he already was.

He was aware that Adam was watching him carefully. And, Damien suspected for much the same reason he was staring at his hands. "That... may have been a mistake, Genevieve. Damien, is this thing keyed to *only* work on *you*?"

The king pulled himself out of his thoughts and looked at the red jewel dangling from Jason's hand. "It should be." He met Adam's eyes. "I wouldn't make something that could hurt one of you accidentally. Or anyone else."

"And Genevieve has five or ten *more*?"

"Some are to bind his magick instead," she put in. "Though I haven't kept them sorted." She snorted. "Just locked up. And sealed with the locking spell he taught me, Adam. No one else should be able to open the box."

"Hunh." Adam looked at the jewel. "How do we destroy these things, Damien? Will fire do it? Or do you have to take the spell apart bit by bit?"

"Probably the latter," Damien muttered, looking down again.

Sitting here and listening to them telling him he'd been an idiot – and marshalling all their arguments so logically that they wouldn't even listen to his – was frustrating. And embarrassing, because they weren't entirely wrong.

And Damien couldn't even buy himself some emotional space by getting up and walking a little ways off with these damned feet.

He *did* turn and sit facing away from everyone, his feet dangling off the bed, but safely away from the floor.

"I didn't really make them to be *un*-made," he added, aware that he probably sounded like a child. "*I* don't know what fire would do to them."

"Damien..."

"Don't bother, Jason. I saw your face. *All* of your faces. And Adam and Genevieve are doing a fine job at making it clear I'm an idiot."

He knew he sounded sulky. What was he supposed to do? Leave them with no protections at all? Or with a slowly starving husk of a king after the Throne had sucked out his soul? Or... worse yet, what if they managed to feed the husk and it just went on, and on and on...?

Was it his fault if his worries seemed exotic and unreal to them? Two days ago, the idea that the Realm would be under attack by a killer ice storm sent here by magick and with an unknown fleet hiding just outside of Emeralsee Bay would have seemed just as ridiculous.

"His early writings suggest that he *loved* Princess Lindrea and his oldest children," Damien heard himself saying. "Not that he was ever particularly scrupulous, though I've yet to see any corroboration with what Queen Marian told us about him being a regicide. He resented her for passing over his father, Prince Anthony, and for blatantly having an 'Autumn child' in an attempt to produce an Heir acceptable to the Sword. He claimed Princess Alexandria was spoiled and hotheaded... he wanted his own eldest son, Robert – *your* grandfather, Jason – to have a chance with the Sword, but he claimed Queen Marian wouldn't allow it. It's all so *reasonable*. From what I've heard about Uncle Robert, he *might* well have been an excellent candidate for the Sword."

"What does Queen Marian say?" Genevieve asked quietly.

Damien tried not to imagine his beloved wife snuggled into Jason's chest as he answered. "I haven't asked her. She's... not entirely reasonable herself on the topic of her 'miscreant grandson.' All she'll do is assure me that *I* won't turn out like him, and then lately she–" He broke off, flushing again.

Adam came over and sat closely next to him on the edge of the bed – though *his* feet rested comfortably on the floor. "Do I want to know what the old biddy's been telling you?" the Champion asked, a smile in his voice as an arm went around the king's waist.

Damien shook his head as Genevieve gasped "Adam!" in a shocked voice.

"I'm sure she's been called worse than a gossipy hen, Genny," Jason's tone was also amused. "That *is* all you called her, love?" he asked.

"Out loud anyways," Adam retorted, and Jason chuckled again. Then yawned.

"I need more sleep," Jason murmured, and there were rustling sounds as he laid down.

Then more such sounds as Jason doubtless pulled Genevieve back into *his* arms... Damien dropped his head into his hands, elbows digging holes into the muscles of his thighs, but the discomfort should help distract him from thinking about...

"Damien? Join me?" If her tone hadn't gone from light to sultry in the space of three words...

"I love you, Genevieve," he muttered, and vanished himself to the sitting room before he could do as she asked and risk her life on yet another miscarriage.

The sitting room of the suite... where he discovered that brocaded upholstery on bare skin *really* wasn't all that comfortable.

"So, this is where you went." Adam strode in, closing the door firmly behind him.

"Not a lot of choices right now," Damien replied tightly. "*You* can stay in there and sleep in a proper bed. Beside *your* spouse."

Adam sat down on the sofa and winced. "This is going to cause all kinds of friction-burns in all kinds of places. I don't want to stay in there anymore than you do, my sweet prince." He put an arm back around the younger man. "We'll get through this, somehow."

Damien sighed, and leaned his head on Adam's shoulder. "The impending invasion or our weird relationship?"

"I was thinking of the latter just now. But both."

"Not without blankets..." And sheets and blankets there were. Magick could do a *few* useful things, after all.

Adam chuckled and got up to lay a sheet over the sofa, making Damien scoot over so he could cover the other half, and then sat back down to lean against the armrest, commenting that for once he was grateful for the little, decorative pillows people always seemed to leave on these things. He invited Damien to lean against him again, and tucked a blanket around them both.

"You realize that by stealing half their blankets we're making it more likely that they'll have to share body-heat."

Damien snorted. "Like they wouldn't anyways."

He tried to prevent the tears he felt filling up his eyes from falling. He was just exhausted, that was all. Too many emotions, too much magick... too many enemies on the horizon.

"I'm sorry," he apologized again.

"I've yet to see anything you could have done much differently, Damien," Adam said with sleepy gentleness. "I *suppose* you could've adopted one of your grandfather's acknowledged bastards... or one of their offspring, but I've been with you when no one else has. I know you've found an excuse to get that bloody Sword into the hands of every one of them that you could. No point in going through all the trouble to legitimize one of them if the Sword won't speak for them. You'd be better off naming one of Tomas Elsevier's children." He yawned and fell silent.

Damien closed his eyes, but couldn't sleep. Did Adam remember that he'd suggested Jason name one of Desirée's boys his Heir if it came to that?

There were just too many things to *plan* for – to *worry* over. And he was too tired for any of it. He gave up and let himself fall asleep, comforted by the warmth of Adam's body... and what he was beginning to suspect was an overflow of *emotional* warmth meant to soothe him... if an empath could even do such things.

Everything was just *too hard.*

MANGALA MCNAMARA

Chapter EIGHT

Sleepless

GENEVIEVE HAD HER OWN TROUBLE falling asleep.

This was all just *too easy*.

Damien should be *raging* to see her in Jason's arms. So should Adam. *She* should have felt something closer to jealousy at seeing Adam follow *her* own true love into the other room. After all she'd sensed from Damien across the bond, her relationship with both of the tall blonde knights should have been *strained*, to say the least.

She knew her husband was struggling, knew that was why he'd turned away. She hadn't meant to hurt him when she'd leaned back into Jason's embrace. Wouldn't have done it if she'd realized beforehand.

Probably.

It was *too easy*, Genevieve reflected, to lie here in the circle of her old friend's arms, his chest so warm against the bare skin of her back. She felt herself warming in other ways, *again*, and strove to keep her breathing slow and even, though she could do nothing about her heartbeat. But Jason was sleeping, and she'd let him...

"I imagined holding you like this, that Summer," he said unexpectedly. So. Not sleeping. He'd learned to lie still and pretend to sleep as effectively as she had then... and possibly for much the same reason, though that reason would have been named *Oskar*, rather than *Harald*.

"Holding you... and *kissing* you," he added.

Jason's hand slid down her arm, gently, delicately.

Genevieve chuckled and kept her voice light. "I didn't think you were interested. I was flat as a boy after all."

"That... might have helped," he admitted. "Then."

Her breasts clearly didn't bother Jason *now* as his hand was making exceedingly clear. After last night, she was no longer entirely convinced that his preferences for male lovers were as set as she had thought.

"Why didn't you?" she asked. "It's not as if you didn't have the opportunity, since we spent most of that Summer together."

"I wasn't sure how you felt..."

She snorted. "I did everything but pounce on you and kiss you myself, Jason. I insisted on swimming and climbing trees *naked*. I suppose I could have played dumb about swordfighting..."

"You mean somehow *after* that first day?" he said dryly. "When you knocked me on my rear-end because you told me you wanted me to teach you? *Without* mentioning you'd been using a sword for longer than I had?"

Genevieve chuckled wickedly. "You deserved it for not noticing that the sword I brought along was perfectly fit to me and well-used. I *did* feel bad about it, though. You had such a cute rear-end. I didn't want it to have any bruises."

She reached around and squeezed said body-part and felt him twitch in surprise. She'd been... almost docile last night, giving herself up wholly to the demands of the magick... and her own touch-starved body. She was ready to admit, now, that Damien might have been right. It wasn't just about tricking their soul-bond to accept Jason in his place; there was something nearly as strong between herself and her old friend.

Jason bent his head to kiss her shoulder where it met her neck and she shivered in response.

"Not sneaky enough apparently," she sighed. And not *girly* enough at the time to know how to flirt so he'd notice. Though her ploys to get the attention of the kind, handsome boy *had* worked... just not as much as she'd wistfully hoped. Genevieve wasn't sure how it was that she'd found it less embarrassing to taunt him into climbing trees and swimming naked than simply trying to kiss him.

"I... didn't trust myself then," Jason said quietly. "I was afraid I'd do what my father... what I *thought* my father had done."

Damn Countess Alexa and her self-serving slanders.

Genevieve snorted again. "You weren't all that much taller or stronger than me at that point, Jason. And my father had made sure I was trained to defend myself beyond using a sword. Which you *knew,* since you kept objecting to my use of 'dirty tricks'."

Her father… and the secret tutors he'd agreed to have give her *extra* training. Genevieve had a suspicion of just *where* those secret tutors had come from and who they were. Why they thought of *her* as valuable enough to be given such education she wasn't sure; surely it couldn't be because of her *other* great-grandmother, although Duchess Shalla *had* been a daughter of Lady Giovalla Elemandros of Wave…

Nevertheless, Genevieve had excelled at the training they had offered – and the extra protection that had been implicit in that offer. Because the point of teaching a target to defend herself was to buy the handful of minutes needed for the *real* protectors to arrive.

And it was that training – and those trainers – that had made it possible to consider forgiving Megan Solway for how she had treated her younger brother. And consider accepting Elaina Solway as one of her ladies-in-waiting. Genevieve knew that her *special trainers* had been provided through the auspices of a certain Captain Daffyd Metreedi… better known in Ilseador as Lord David Solway, husband to Lady Megan and father of Lady Elaina.

David had given up a great deal to funnel arms and finances to the Rebels in Elaarwen – including romancing Countess Alexa's daughter and Heir to prevent Brindlewell from being a bottleneck for those resources. Genevieve didn't think that was why he'd gone so far as to *marry* Megan – and after twenty-five years he seemed to be deeply in love with the brittle, unhappy woman as well as to adore his children.

If a man of David's character could feel that way about Megan Solway, there had to be some hope for her. *And* the obnoxious Elaina.

She'd never told even Damien – or anyone, actually – about any of this. The Metreedis' role in supporting the Rebellion was over and becoming less relevant with every passing day; there was no need to disrupt trade by riling up the old dispute between Rebels and Loyalists. And her trainers had given her too many gifts to betray their trust in her discretion – gifts she planned to pass on to her *own* children and which she had shared to some extent with the Secret Cadre already.

But when she was twelve, it had all seemed like a wonderful game of *Spy.*

"Hmmn. I was also *older*," Jason was pointing out, "and if they ever caught us, *I* would be the one expected to have acted responsibly."

"Jason, they were talking about *betrothing* us. How could a few kisses or caresses – or even more – have mattered? If anything, *your* mother would have been pleased if it sealed the deal."

He stiffened. "What do you mean?"

Genevieve sighed. Surely, he wasn't going to go all withdrawn on her *now*. Even if that *was* his usual reaction to unexpected new information. "When I thought Father was dead, I ended up going through rather a lot of his papers. Old correspondence. You did know that Alexa and my father had been childhood sweethearts?"

Jason relaxed slightly. "She... mentioned it."

"He'd saved all of her letters," Genevieve went on. "They clearly were important to him."

She hesitated. It was one thing to have read through those papers after her papa's presumed demise. It... was another to share what she'd learned from them after he'd been found alive. On the other hand, this would be important to Jaso. And it, too, was less relevant to anyone *else* with every passing day.

"There was some suggestion that your mother married *Megan's* father almost by accident, trying to make him jealous after he'd met *my* mother."

Jason shifted uncomfortably, but he didn't try to move away from her. "Mother never did have a good word to say about the late duchess. In our home, anyways. But... that wasn't exactly unusual for her. With regards to *anyone*."

"There was *another* series of letters, after Mama died," Genevieve went on. "I think she was hoping to go back to the way things had been between them. It all apparently came to a head the Spring before that Summer. She was suggesting that even if Papa wasn't ready to marry again, you and I were of an age for a betrothal... and that, with Megan old enough to manage Brindlewell on her own, it would be a perfect excuse for you and she to move up to Elaarwen."

Jason was silent. Genevieve wasn't bothered, though. She knew that he always closed himself down when he received startling new information and he wasn't trying to move away from her, so that was positive in and of itself.

Hearing that his mother had tried to volunteer herself into the ducal bed – and *without* a plan for a marriage and *with* the intent of using him as bait – surely had to qualify as 'startling and new.'

"I didn't know any of that then, of course," Genevieve added. "But Papa seemed interested enough in a betrothal that it seemed worth finding out about you."

He relaxed again, slightly.

"And what did you find out?" Jason asked, a hint of teasing back in his voice.

"That you were intelligent, kind, brave, curious, sensible, and could be lured into adventures if I could get you past your o'erweening sense of responsibility. And good with a sword. And not bad to look at. Although," she added candidly, "not moreso than a half-dozen boys I knew back in Elaarwen."

She laughed as he stiffened slightly at her last comment after having grown progressively more relaxed and even a little *smug* – though she wasn't sure how she knew that, since he was still stretched out along her back and she couldn't see his face at all – as she had recited her litany of his virtues. Jason wasn't *terribly* vain about his looks, but he'd been told so often that he was the handsomest man at Court that it had become a part of who he was.

"You grew into being handsome," she assured him. "But at the time you were already all the things I could think to want in a husband – or the future Duke-Consort of Elaarwen."

She could feel Jason shaking his head, his beard stubble catching in her hair. "You were thinking all of that at *twelve years old?*"

Now Genevieve really chuckled. "My mountain-folk start early, Jason. There were girls and boys I grew up with who were married and with babes of their own by fourteen. And I was my father's only Heir. Of course it was on my mind."

He sighed, and traced a pattern on her abdomen. "If... that had worked out... there would have been no Harald for you."

Genevieve hesitated. Not even to Damien had she admitted this. "I... waited, you know. Even after you quit answering my letters. I wouldn't have married Harald – treaty with Siovale or not – if you had come for me."

He went very still and quiet again.

"Mother said it was unwise to correspond with a known rebel if I wanted to earn my shield," he said at last.

"I thought as much. But I knew you'd earned your shield when you were nineteen." She sighed. "I'd wanted to earn mine as well, though I knew it wasn't possible under King Reginald. I made our spies keep me up-to-date on your progress for the vicarious thrill... and because it was *you*."

Jason was quiet. "I was assigned to Prince Oskar the day I was knighted. And... I didn't know you were waiting, Genny."

He left it unsaid that Adam had also been *waiting*... and *he* had been right here.

Genevieve nestled her head into his shoulder. "I know. I'd more or less given up at that point anyways – a childish dream. When I met Harald... he made a poor comparison to you. Which wasn't really fair to him, but I couldn't stop myself."

"I met Harald," Jason reminded her dryly. "He would have made a poor comparison to almost anyone."

Now she was glad he was wrapped around her back, as tears pricked her eyes. "He called me 'Genny,' the first time I met him. I was torn between his temerity at using a nickname for me when we'd barely met... and thinking it might be a... a *sign*, since that's what *you've* always called me." She paused. "If we'd been betrothed, you'd never have won your shield, and there would have been no Oskar for you."

"No..." He sounded wistful, but not in the way that she regretted her marriage to Harald. Though, as she'd said before, she'd do it all over again to make sure Siovale joined the Rebellion. But marrying Jason would have brought Brindlewell into the Rebellion, and possibly Cedarwen before Lady Theresa had time to betray her husband and Princess Kandra.

The princess might have had time to bring her parents – and Damien, who'd been but a child – to Elaarwen for safety... and because Prince Eric had been the Named and Confirmed Heir and wore the Heir's Ring. While Genevieve's father, Duke Aldred – and she herself – had a solid claim to the Throne via his mother and grandmother's line, the Heir's Ring and Prince Eric would have given the Rebellion a sheen of legitimacy that the scions of Queen Marian's reckless youngest daughter had never quite mustered up. King Reginald, after all, had been the eldest child of Queen Marian's eldest child – and Eric had been *his* eldest surviving child at the time.

Having Eric *might* have made it easier for Zialest and Dalizell to join up... And Tomas had once said *he'd* merely been looking for an excuse to join the Rebellion, so perhaps even Siovale...

Damien might have grown up with his parents still alive and his beloved elder sister... which seemed worthwhile all on its own. And she'd have known him as a child... Though she would have been married to Jason...

"No Damien for you," Jason added quietly. And *that* didn't bear thinking of.

"And no Adam," she agreed, setting aside the useless *might-have-beens* as the pointless fantasies that they were. "For all that we went through to get here, I'm glad we're here."

"*Right* here?" his voice was warm, and she felt his body responding with interest.

Right here? In bed with him? Genevieve had had months in this blasted tower to examine her thoughts and feelings on the matter... and she still was torn. It would have been so much easier if she'd simply been able to bear her beloved husband an Heir. She could have lived a lifetime with this mysterious bond to Jason unexplored.

Not-so-mysterious, she realized as familiar white flames started to dance around the bed, beginning the process of enclosing them.

Genevieve reached for Damien through the bond, panicking. But *that* bond was still there, still *firm* and *warm* and filled with the love and adoration that she never could bring herself to feel she completely deserved. Steady. Patient. Accepting...

"Please tell me that's not what I think it is," Jason had rolled back slightly to observe the white flames that didn't burn. She rolled onto her stomach to look at him.

"I can still feel Damien," Genevieve said. "Down *our* soul-bond, I mean." Her emphasis more or less answered the question he hadn't quite asked.

"*I* can feel *Adam*." He'd told her his sense of his love was new, only since the wedding ceremony. Still a source of wonder... he hadn't even mentioned it to Adam yet, not having noticed it until they were all caught up in dealing with the ice-storm and the potential invasion.

Jason shook his head. "This wasn't supposed to be *permanent*, Genny. It was supposed to be... to be our *gift* to you and Damien. A *one-time* gift." His voice was... a curious mix of frustration, resentment, and... something else that seemed more tender and accepting.

She sighed, guessing her own voice would have its own awkward combination of unresolved feelings. "I know. I have no answers here, though. I didn't particularly want to be soul-bonded to *Damien* either – I was completely in love with Rosa, even though I knew it couldn't last. We both needed to produce Heirs... and she was always deeply in love with Zachary. Even if she couldn't bear to be around men for... a long while." She bowed her head. "We helped each other out of similar places, but *she* always had Zachary waiting."

"You had Damien waiting," Jason reminded her.

Genevieve laughed a little bitterly. "Not as far as I knew about. And meeting him in the context of the soul-bond..." She shook her head. "I resented it. I tell myself *now* that it was this marvelous, magickal moment. I have to."

Jason looked thoughtfully up at the wreathing white flames. "Perhaps this is just to ensure you *do* conceive? Not... anything more."

She shrugged. "I wasn't able to resist it the first time. And Damien's attempt to resist it nearly killed us both. I've never heard of a second soul-bond happening to someone... but it's my *husband* who's memorized the Royal Library, not me." Her voice broke on the word. Somehow *this* seemed more of a betrayal than anything they had already done.

Reassurance and love came down the bond from Damien.

And humor: *I told you so...*

Genevieve couldn't respond in words without quiet and meditation to clear her mind – or physical contact and preferably *eye*-contact. Damien claimed it was because she didn't really want to hear him in her head all the time, not through any lack of natural ability.

But she found herself laughing now, through her tears of frustration. Damien had, indeed, warned her that her reactions to Jason were the stuff of which soul-bonds were made.

"I felt that!" Jason exclaimed. "That was Damien, wasn't it?"

She looked at him askance. "Yes."

Jason frowned. "It felt like he was laughing at you – or... at *me?*"

His brow smoothed suddenly, and Genevieve felt a soft, enveloping warmth that seemed to emanate from Jason. It brushed the edges of her sense of herself but didn't extend to her directly.

"And that was Adam?" she asked.

Jason nodded, looking relieved. "He knew about *our* bond already. He... doesn't seem to mind... this. Whatever it is." He clearly didn't want to name it.

Genevieve smiled a little grimly. "Good, because I'm not sure that any of us get a vote... my loving husband's tendencies towards democracy notwithstanding."

Jason tilted his head as he looked at her. "Do *you* mind, Genny?"

At last, the question that had occupied her on and off for five years. It had occupied her almost *entirely* for the last six months, ever since she'd last conceived and she and Damien had agreed that it would be the last time – that they didn't dare let her go through another round of this without trying the answer that Lord Prydeen had offered them with his dying breath.

Or cursed them with.

The question that she had been asking every time *Damien* and Jason had made love – and she had felt it through the bond. That she had asked herself every time she looked in her mirror... and that she had thrown to the winds last night when opportunity presented itself and her body was finally healthy enough to take it.

"No," she said at last, compelled to honesty with him, even if she hadn't found it possible with just herself. "It's not what I would have chosen... but I spent fourteen years regretting that I *didn't* pounce on you and kiss you that Summer. And the last five telling myself not to. What about you?"

His eyes were an incredible shade of blue. "No, Genny, I don't mind at all."

"Well, then..." She gave herself up to the urgings of the magick... and her own desires... and pounced.

"Mmmn, nice of them to share..." Adam murmured.

Damien chuckled. It would be a mess again come morning, but for right now... everything felt *right*. "Only fair, since we're sharing *them*."

"I love you, too, you know."

"I've never doubted that. I hope you know that I love you."

"If I didn't *before*..."

Mangala McNamara

Chapter NINE

Released

"**Y**OU'RE PREGNANT, LOVE!" DAMIEN EXCLAIMED with a mix of happiness, relief... and renewed anxiety after sending his Healer's sense through her the next morning. He wrapped his arms around her and hugged her close... and without fear for the first time in longer than he could remember.

Genevieve relaxed into his arms, and suddenly all was right with the world.

The king turned shining eyes on his oldest friends, not releasing his embrace of his wife by one iota. If he had his choice, he would never let her go again. "Thank you," he whispered, almost afraid to speak louder for fear he might shout. "I know it's just the first hurdle..."

"Just the first hurdle *today* even," Genevieve pointed out. "We have the aftermath of the storm and an invasion off our coast."

"Not to mention that we either reveal your ability to move yourself and others around magickally *or* you return Jason and Genevieve to your office to have spent the storm isolated for no particular reason," Adam said dryly.

Damien shrugged. "It was bound to happen sooner or later, Adam. If it shields my lady – and our child – from scandal, it's no great loss."

"And why none of the four of us stepped out of these rooms for close to two days."

Damien refused to let Adam's cynical practicality lower his spirits. "Genevieve and I weren't *here* for two days, of course. We were in our own suite, sealed in when the storm went after me. And you two were simply continuing your interrupted honeymoon."

"Some of this is going to depend on what's been going on out there without us, love," Genevieve pointed out. "It's going to seem extremely strange if people were pounding on the doors and we never noticed. Especially after the storm ended."

"In the middle of the night?" Jason asked. "It's just dawn now... so I think we have that one covered. You weren't taking down your wards after Damien was attacked, and with Genevieve's new pregnancy. And no one knocked here – I'm right that we would have heard it, Damien, even with the wards up?"

"So long as no one actually tried to *enter* your rooms during the storm," Adam said sardonically. "Since the wards up there weren't *actually* up."

"We'll cross that bridge when we come to it," Damien said firmly. "I'm going to make a big show of vanishing from place to place... to spare my feet and Genevieve. Get yourselves put together and we'll meet you in the Great Hall in an hour." To prevent any further argument, he simply vanished himself and Genevieve directly upstairs to their *own* bed.

"An hour?" she asked, amused.

He kissed her properly. "Should I have said two hours? You are mine again, at *last*. And I am all *yours*."

Genevieve's eyes softened. "We can make an hour work..."

It took longer than Damien had anticipated to wash and dress properly. He had managed to start the Healing on his feet a day earlier, and he was fairly sure he'd managed to save most of the skin and toenails... but they still hurt like blazes every time he tried to put any weight on them. And footwear was simply not to be thought of.

With Genevieve's help, he was able to vanish himself into the bath, and similarly manage other washroom activities, but none of it was easy... and the fact that they both remained extremely distracted by each other didn't help.

"This *is* what your gentlemen-of-the-chamber are supposed to help with," Genevieve commented dryly, as she helped him manage his pants.

"Shall we summon your ladies-in-waiting to help with your laces?" Damien inquired archly, pulling her close and kissing the back of her neck. "I'm sure that won't mess with our fun at *all.*"

Genevieve laughed, and kissed him back. "I see your point."

When it was time to go down, they faced a new dilemma.

"It will have to be your old favorite chair," Genevieve said from the sitting room. "The other one isn't in any better shape, and there's no real reason to move the couch. Vanish yourself in here, love."

"The reason could be that I don't want *you* standing," Damien pointed out, but he gamely vanished himself onto the old leather-upholstered chair that he had favored before Genevieve had become part of his life.

"Do I look regal?" he grinned. The chair was nothing fancy, the leather worn soft in some places and the stuffing lumped up in others.

Genevieve laughed and brought a footstool close enough that he could prop his feet up at the ankles. "You goose."

"I believe, my lady, that *you* are the goose and *I'm* the gander." Damien opened his arms. "Come here, beloved. Let's not give away more than we have to and make it obvious that I don't need to be touching things – or people – to move them."

Presumably he would have 'vanished' himself down to the office to collect Jason and Genevieve the first night, and then left Jason with Adam in their own rooms...

She raised her fine, golden brows. "Good idea. Make sure I'm not putting any pressure on your feet." She settled onto his lap, and into his arms. "Maybe the couch *would* be a good idea..."

"Too late," he whispered into her ear.

They were in the Great Hall.

The Great Hall at the main entrance to his Castle had been transformed in the two days. Pallets had been setup along the walls, mostly for his Castle Guards, he noticed, and some of the visiting men-at-arms. Damien wondered if the Guards had given up their barracks to the stranded nobility by choice or been evicted... and if so by whom. The main center of the room was still filled with noblemen and -women and entire herds of their cooped-up, energetic children.

Genevieve unfolded herself agilely from his lap, and stood up, as the anxious nobles of the Realm converged on them. Luckily, Jason and Adam were a step ahead of everyone else and had rounded up a handful of Royal Guards as well. Fear of an external invader didn't mean *someone* wouldn't see this as an opportunity for 'advancement' – and it was entirely possible there were secret colluders somewhere in the great mass of people. Those whom he had Bound and Sworn, he trusted, but that was a fraction of the total number of people here.

Damien snagged his Queen's hand and tugged her to perch on the arm of his chair, not coincidentally giving him an excuse to continue touching her. He *could* move anyone or anything without touching it, but his reaction times would be faster this way if he did have to yank either of them to safety.

Out of the confused babble, Duke Quillian of Reyensweir and Duchess Tariana of Embervest somehow caught Damien's eye. They were merely standing together, not even particularly closely, and merely talking... but suddenly the king noticed that they were almost *always* standing together like that. With a flash of insight, he realized that there might be a very *personal* reason indeed why the young duke had been so displeased to take his ancestral seat.

Damien was still considering that idea when Tomas Elsevier, Duke of Siovale, strode out of the welter of confused babble, lesser nobility scattering from his path like geese before a hunting hound. Rosa and Zachary Miramar trailed in his wake, and Duchess Laura of Alpinsward came up from the other side. Duke Quillian and Duchess Tariana made their way forwards as well. All the dukes and duchesses of the Realm, counting Jason and Genevieve.

Tomas stood for a moment, looking at Damien ensconced in his old leather chair, with Genevieve perched casually on one arm. Jason, as the Heir, and Adam, as Champion, had arrayed themselves behind the king and queen, and Sir Tim had their handful of Royal Guards arrayed behind *them*. Members of the Secret Cadre were scattered amongst the crowd, but there was no reasonable excuse for any of them to insert themselves between the king and queen and the highest nobles of their Realm.

For an instant, the room held its collective breath.

Damien looked back at his most senior vassal, his usual mild expression entirely unruffled. He saw the amused glint in Tomas' eyes and felt he had no reason to be ruffled. The older man was simply playing the moment for all it was worth.

Tomas knelt on one knee.

"My lord Duke of Siovale," Damien acknowledged him, and a ripple of bows and curtsies moved outwards from the still center.

"It's good to see Your Majesties out and about again. I believe it's high time I returned this to you." Tomas pulled the signet ring off his hand and held it out.

"Thank you, Your Grace," Damien replied. Genevieve stepped forward to take the ring and return it to the king's hand. "We thank you for your timely care of Our Realm." He dropped the formal mode. "We need to discuss what our next moves are."

"The city is too dangerous to go out and about, Your Majesty," Tomas informed him. "Even the Castle's battlements and the main bailey are iced over such that it's impossible for a man to walk across it and a horse would break a leg in a single stride. The storm may be over, but we're very nearly as trapped as we were while it still raged." The duke hesitated. "There *are* some urgent items that Your Majesty will need to be apprised of."

Clearly the word of the fleet was not yet common knowledge.

Damien nodded. "Her Majesty has given me some understanding of the situation. Perhaps we can repair to my office to discuss the matter in more detail."

He looked past Tomas to his other vassals. "We shall have a meeting of the Dukes and Duchesses in the small Council chamber after lunch. And a full Peer Council meeting in the hour before dinner. Prince Jason will see to your individual concerns following *his* meeting with the Royal Council."

He gave the room a nod of dismissal. Tomas stood up and stepped closer as did Adam, Jason, Tim, and Aryllis. Damien hadn't been aware of when his Spymistress had arrived, but he was glad to see her. Little Rico clung to Aryllis' skirts, looking with wide eyes at all the adults.

"So, *I'm* running a Royal Council meeting?" Jason asked with some trepidation.

"You'll be focusing on the logistics of getting help to the damaged parts of the Realm," Damien told him. "I want a plan of action to present to the Dukes and Duchesses after lunch." He nodded at Tim, and the Captain called one of his Royal Guards over to round up the Royal Councilors.

"That would be Alpinsward sending aid to Dalzialest," Genevieve clarified for Jason's benefit. "Siovale and Elaarwen to Reyensweir and Embervest sending assistance to Emeralsee."

"Wouldn't Embervest helping Reyensweir and Siovale sending aid here be the more obvious way to do it?" Jason asked, frowning. "Embervest doesn't even contact Emeralsee directly except to the far north where the storm didn't even hit."

Tomas and Adam both started to explain at the same moment, stopped and looked at each other.

"Go ahead, Sir Loveress," the duke told him.

Adam inclined his head politely. "Embervest and Reyensweir are already tied tightly, Jase. We'd like to see more bonds between Reyensweir and Siovale... or Reyensweir and Elaarwen. I think you can see why." He paused, then rolled his eyes as Jason still seemed somewhat baffled. "Your Majesty, you don't need me for your strategy session, right?"

The king shook his head. "You, Tim, and Aryllis will all be at the Royal Council to back Jason up."

Jason looked somewhat relieved.

Adam nodded. "Then I'll explain on the way. With your permission, Your Majesties?"

Damien nodded again, and Adam and Aryllis – and even Tim – began explaining certain political realities to the newly-made Prince.

"This is going to break his heart, Damien," Genevieve said sadly, watching them go. "Jason wasn't made for politicking."

"No, but Adam was," he answered her. "Unfortunately justifying giving *him* the coronet of the Heir would have been much, much harder. Tomas, you have a devious look on your face."

"Just thinking about building those connections between Siovale and Reyensweir, Your Majesty," the older man said innocently.

Damien winced. "Do *not* offer Arabella to Quillian. She's barely of an age to wed, and... let's just say I have a feeling it wouldn't go well." He saw Genevieve giving him a curious look, and touched her hand to share his insight about the Duke of Reyensweir and the Duchess of Embervest.

Tomas' eyes twinkled. "I suppose sending Mark to Embervest would not 'meet with royal approval' either, then." He chuckled at the king's expression. "I've been watching those two for ten years, Damien. Istvan married my cousin, so Tariana is my niece, as *you* should remember. You threw a wrench in their plans when you made Quillian duke over Reyensweir, and unlike Rosa and Zachary, there's no simple answer. Dalizell and Zialest had been asking the Throne for a merger for three generations, and those were counties. You can't exactly combine two duchies into anything less than a new kingdom."

The king gave his duke a rueful look. "I should just ask your advice before I do *anything*, Tomas."

The Duke of Siovale gave him a sly look. "You said it, not I." His expression grew serious. "But we need to discuss this *other* situation. I assume that your... rather dramatic appearance here was at least in part because your feet are still injured. Can you get yourself to your office the same way? Unless the Prince and the Queen put things away, the maps should still be out."

"Everything is just as it was when you went to bed, Tomas," Genevieve assured him.

"Then shall I meet you there?"

"Unless you're willing to go the faster way?" Damien suggested.

The duke looked torn between curiosity and trepidation. He hovered on the brink for just a moment of indecision, then shrugged. "Why not."

Damien turned to his Royal Guards. "I know Captain Ancellius left you strict orders to leave neither me nor the Queen unattended. I can take you with me by magick or you can simply use your own feet to go guard my office." The three knights exchanged a dubious glance.

Adam's sister, Marianna, suddenly stepped out of the swirl of colorful nobility just behind them, dragging – of all people – *Jason's* niece, Elaina, with her. She dropped into a deep curtsy, and Elaina followed suit slightly more slowly. "Do forgive me, Your Majesties, but Lady Alanna had sent us to attend the Queen when Lady Aryllis was called away, and we overheard Your Majesty's offer. With the Queen's permission, we'd like to come with you – by magick."

Sir Marcus and Sir Rodney were giving the two young women a skeptical look, but Sir Angelos wore the wry expression of someone who had found himself unexpectedly on the floor of a practice-ring. "If the ladies will be attending Their Majesties, I think we'd be redundant, Marcus," he commented dryly. Marianna gave him an impish grin, and even Elaina Solway had a small smile. "By your leave, Majesty, I'll meet you there." Sir Angelos bowed.

Still looking like they had misgivings, the other two followed his lead.

Tomas Elsevier regarded the young ladies with a speculative look, and Damien decided to head it off by vanishing them to his office.

The ladies were suitably impressed and thanked Damien profusely for the experience. Genevieve thanked the young women and let them out of the office, leaving them to stand unofficial guard until Sirs Angelos, Marcus, and Rodney appeared. They were instructed to have breakfast sent to the office as soon as possible. Damien reflected that the pair must have proven themselves more capable than he would have expected, and much more quickly than he would have expected for Alanna to have assigned them to Genevieve and for his knights to even momentarily leave them as the sole Royal Guards.

With the extra chair, the office was overly crowded. He quickly moved himself over to a perch on the edge of the sturdy map-table, much to Genevieve's amusement. The old leather chair was vanished back to their own sitting room.

"Those young women..." Tomas began, staring after them.

"My new ladies-in-waiting," Genevieve agreed. "Marianna Loveress and Elaina Solway."

Tomas looked back at her. "I believe I should like to apply for my Arabella to join their ranks. I think there are things she could learn from them, and from you, Genevieve. And... I believe her skills at riding and self-defense will give her a start at the other things *you* need from your ladies."

Genevieve raised her fine, golden eyebrows at her former brother-in-law. "Why, Tomas, surely you meant her skills at embroidery and flower arranging. What else would a lady-in-waiting possibly do for her queen?"

The duke snorted. "Your sworn knights backed down from their place to guard you and Damien on Miss Marianna's word alone. And neither of *you* objected. My children all learned to defend themselves early... for reasons *you* should understand only too well." Harald's name lay like lead weights between them. "It was Sildra's doing, of course," he admitted, somewhat hollowly. "*Her* eyes were open from the start."

Genevieve nodded slowly. "'Bella's sixteen now, isn't she?"

"Seventeen. Eighteen before Midsummer."

"Then she's most welcome. Provided it's something *she* wants as well."

Tomas and Damien both gave her dry looks.

"I've been putting off having Tomas' children here in case it looked like we were trying to keep them as hostages to his good behavior, Genevieve," Damien reminded her.

The duke nodded. "Mark was too old to go for his shield when you came to the throne, but 'Bella and Cindy were furious that I wouldn't let *them* try." He looked at the king. "But if things are changing... Denis is twelve – will your armsmaster still accept him for a page?"

Damien smiled. "We're taking Roger Solway at thirteen. I can't see why not." He paused. "Lucinda is fourteen, isn't she?"

Tomas nodded. "Definitely too old, I know."

"Maybe. At fourteen it was too late for *me,*" Damien said, "but *I'd* had no arms training at all."

Nor would he likely have lived to see his fifteenth birthday if he'd come to Prince Oskar's attention by enrolling as a page and moving into the training barracks.

The king made a face to cover up all those ancient fears and memories. "Actually, Jason and Adam couldn't convince me to actually even *pick up* a sword until I was *seven*teen. I was convinced that any skill at arms at all would bring me to my grandfather's attention in an entirely lethal way.

They tell me I'm not too bad with it now, but I have no real sense of when is too late to start, but I do know that if we stick rigidly to the old rules I won't have enough knights in another ten years. If Lucinda wants to try out for a position as a page or squire, have her talk to Adam or Tim."

Genevieve sighed. "Again, you put yourself down for no reason." She looked at Tomas directly. "We don't want his skill noised about – it's one more level of protection if potential assassins don't know Damien can defend himself as well as relying on his guards."

The duke allowed as how that made sense.

"Damien can out-fence any of his Royal Guards with the possible exception of Tim," Genevieve said forthrightly. "He's just used to practicing against Adam and Jason, so his perspective is skewed." She gave her husband a sweetly challenging look.

Damien shrugged, but felt warmed by her confidence. "I can't even stand up right now, so it hardly matters." He swung one dangling foot illustratively.

Tomas gave Genevieve a shrewd look. "And you?"

She lifted her chin. "He can't beat me either. You know that's why Harald wouldn't spar with me, and that he sent the men-at-arms you'd seconded to him back to Siovale so they wouldn't see that I was the better fighter."

In the practice-ring or on a battlefield, anyways. When she'd had a sword in her hand and a clear enemy to fight. Not in the bedroom, where it had come down to brute strength on his part and reluctance on hers to risk an alliance that the Rebellion so badly needed. Not to mention that Harald had managed to convince Genevieve that what he was doing to her *was* love.

The duke leaned back against Damien's dangerously over-papered desk and folded his arms. "So, if it's such a big secret, why tell *me?*"

"We've changed everything around in the last week, Tomas," the king said seriously. "A new Heir and Duke of Emeralsee, a new Champion, a new Captain of the Royal Guard. Genevieve is pregnant again, and we're *not* going to send her back to Elendria. We're going to try to keep her as quiet as we can.

"And now... this ice-storm and probable invasion. Quillian's province got nearly as blasted as Emeralsee. I'm – *we're* – going to need allies." Damien bowed his head. "If Jason becomes king this year, *he's* going to need allies..."

"Damien, love, will you *please* stop trying to terrify everyone?" Genevieve said in exasperation. "Tomas, he just... goes down this rabbit-hole. There's no reason to worry."

The duke looked at her skeptically. "By all reports, Genevieve, you nearly died in Elendria with the last miscarriage. And the king, Jason Solway, and Adam Loveress spent the entire Autumn jumping all over themselves to keep you resting. I know enough about soul-bonds to know that he won't outlast you by very long... and now he's telling me you're pregnant again. Granted it's been longer, but should you be trying again at all? How far along are you anyways?"

Genevieve blushed. "Only just. An advantage of having a husband who's also a Healer is that we know right away."

"What choice do we have, Tomas?" Damien asked, allowing a little of his desperation to show through. "Jason is the only person I've found in five years of searching who can legitimately bear the Alsterling name. And he's the only person in the Realm for whom the Sword will speak – whether of noble birth or my grandfather's bastard scions. And *he's* not exactly going to be creating any Heirs of his own." He kept his eyes on Tomas' face, making sure his gaze didn't waver as he stated that... extreme prevarication. "His best hope would be to name a niece or nephew – and until just now I'd seen no sign that any of Countess Alexa's grandchildren were even worth considering."

The duke's eyes narrowed and he nodded thoughtfully. "So that's why you made sure to make that wedding so public. Not just because it was the right thing to do," Damien felt himself warmed by the older, and still-far-more-experienced, ruler's approval – not to mention the likelihood that the change would be accepted in Siovale. "But so that Adam Loveress' siblings could also be named in the line of succession."

Genevieve nodded. "Or his nephews, who are young enough to train up early. We tried giving the Heir's Ring to Rosa, but as you know, she gave it back. And clearly Zachary won't take it for the same reasons."

"I'd have named *you* as Heir, Tomas," Damien went on, "so long as we're going outside the Alsterling line. But I can't even get the Royal Council to agree to appoint you as Envoy to Elendria. I could force the issue, but it would just mean an unending string of power struggles – for me and then for you."

The duke huffed. "Not sure I'm diplomatic enough to be an envoy, anyways."

Genevieve sighed. "And whom else is there? Laura, who grew up half Mercasian? Quillian, who has opposed everything we've tried to do? Tariana, whose title as Duchess is still so new it's shiny? Especially," she fixed her husband with a gimlet eye, "when Damien seems intent on convincing everyone that he'll be dead in less than a year."

"I see your point." Tomas looked thoughtful. "You could adopt someone from one of the lesser Houses – or a younger child of... no, I suppose *I'm* the only duke with a child old enough not to need a regent in the worst-case scenario." He blinked. "How did *that* happen...?"

The duke considered. "I suppose there's still Aldred. And his..." He paused, looking for a way to say it delicately.

"My unborn half-sibling?" Genevieve asked dryly. "First, the child hasn't been born yet. Ciriis is the same age as I am, and *she's* never borne a child either. Second, Papa is old enough that there's no guarantee *he'd* live long enough to see the child to maturity. We're from a long-lived family, but given all that he's been through, he's probably only made it along this far because of Damien." She flickered a glance at the king, who nodded confirmation. "You'd likely be ending up with Ciriis as Queen-Mother-Regent."

Tomas winced. "That one is too used to manipulating things behind the scenes," he agreed. "And... I'm not sure I want to see my old friend as Regent either."

The duke nodded a little apologetically to Genevieve. "I've no doubt as to his abilities, my lady. And his ambitions *should* muted in such a case, by obtaining what he has sought for half his life. But he's given us recent reason to doubt his judgment, and coming in as a Regent after Damien's death, would he be Bound to the Realm's best interests? Or simply to what he perceives as best for his child? And the same for Ciriis Cellavel."

"The Sword spoke for Lord Aldred once..." Damien mused.

"Would it still?" Genevieve asked sadly. "He was an innocent child when Princess Alexandria stole it away from Elaarwen. He's had over sixty years to change. It's not merely a matter of Alsterling blood, or Prince Anthony and his siblings would have been acceptable."

"Nor of sorcerous potential, or King Reginald would have been," Damien agreed. "I've no idea how the Sword would feel about Lord Aldred now." He shook his head. "It's all moot for the nonce. We followed the midwife's advice to let Genevieve rest, and pushed the soul-bond as far as it would go to let her do it. She's pregnant now, and Jason is Heir – if he becomes king, the mess is his problem to sort out. I've given him what options I may."

Tomas looked thoughtful. "I'd forgotten that the soul-bond would also be placing demands on you."

The king waved it off. He hardly wanted to discuss this aspect of the problem – or their lives – with his Duke of Siovale. "We have other problems to solve, and they are rather more urgent. You two are the Realm's top strategist and battle commander... as evidenced by the fact that my grandfather's generals never managed to do more than put dents into the Rebellion. Tell me what I need to know."

They were interrupted by a knock at the door. Marianna and Elaina carried in trays of breakfast themselves along with Lord Aaron, one of the new gentlemen-of-the-chamber, with Sir Marcus holding the door and Sir Rodney falling all over himself to help. Past them, Damien could see Sir Angelos glancing back with a grin and a shake of his head before returning to a watchful pose at the door. He wondered if Tim would be open to the idea of replacing Marcus as his second-in-command with Angelos. His cousin of Elderwyld just seemed... more flexible-minded.

Of course, it *could* be that Sir Marcus and Sir Rodney were simply overwhelmed by Adam's dynamic and pretty sister... but the problems between the Secret Cadre and the Royal Guards had been going on for some time. If Genevieve had been home more and not so ill when she was, the newer Guards would certainly have had their presumptions beaten out of them. Or if Damien hadn't had to claim increasing amounts of Adam's time to cope with his own work. Marcus was an able administrator and a fine fighter, but it was clear to the king that even after years of more 'seasoning' he would never make Captain. It was why they had side-stepped the issue by bringing Tim back.

Elaina looked like she had taken the younger woman as her model. Given how all the ladies-in-waiting adored Jason, it was probably just as well. Marianna – despite her newness to the Secret Cadre – would be able to blunt the unavoidable distrust of Jason's niece better than anyone else. Right now, Elaina seemed too shy to respond to Marcus and Rodney's fumbling attempts to be gentlemanly, but her eye sparkled when Aaron made some witticism that the knights were too far away to catch.

Damien nodded his thanks to all three, making sure to particularly catch Aaron's eye. Neither he nor Genevieve particularly wanted or needed help dressing for anything but the most elaborate functions – finding ways to incorporate the members of the Secret Cadre, but especially the *male* members, seamlessly into their lives was a constant challenge.

So far there was only Aaron, Lord Devin, and Master Xavier. Each one of them would have tried for his shield, but their families had been members of the Rebellion and they had been too old when Damien took the Throne. If the knights of the Royal Guard didn't take the young gentlemen – or the young ladies – seriously, they deserved to be knocked on their rears in practice.

Xavier and Devin had both served as mounted warriors and fought in major battles with Crown troops – as had Lady Alanna and Lady Emily – which actually made them *more* experienced than the green young knights of the Royal Guard. Lord Aaron's skills were more subtle – he was a trained assassin – and he was more slightly built and gave off a 'Court-fop' vibe that Damien suspected he exaggerated because it amused him to irritate Sir Marcus.

The young women and Aaron made sure that the king, queen, and duke were settled with cups of tea and a first serving of sausage and porridge, then took themselves out, and the door was shut firmly behind them. This time Genevieve put all the wards into place.

"Would you consider Mark as well, for this group of secret guards of yours, Damien?" Tomas asked thoughtfully.

The king shrugged. "There's only three men in it so far. And none who are Heirs to their province."

"I think it would be good for him to see that there are other paths to honor than knighthood." The duke looked at both his sovereigns seriously. "We have a generation of young men who weren't able to earn the shields they should have done. And going on *five* generations of young women. You are both an inspiration – but you are the exceptions to all other rules. These secret guards of yours include men and women who aren't just exceptions."

"Of course, they *are* secret," Genevieve pointed out. "No glory in the position."

"No," the duke agreed, "but that, too, is a lesson the young can stand well to learn. To see men like Lord Devin and Master Xavier – who are both well-known and redoubtable warriors – take the position should be a message to others. To see Lord Aaron doing the same... should imply that there is more to him than meets the eye. Mark and Arabella could use that kind of understanding."

Damien made a gesture of acquiescence. "Have them apply to Aryllis Ancellius, then. She is Captain of the Secret Cadre."

They ate quickly before turning to the maptable. Genevieve and Tomas were done, but Damien continued to eat as they began to look it over.

"The enemy fleet is here," Tomas indicated the seaward curve of the peninsula, known as the Cape, that embraced Emeralsee Bay. "We have numbers, but not good ones, and no word on what flag they're flying. The watchtower there sent their boat across with the message, but the messenger only made it into the castle moments before the storm struck."

Damien swallowed a huge bite of porridge. After the magick he'd poured out against the storm and then two days in the tower with only Genevieve's old emergency supplies of dried meat and fruits stashed in a desk drawer to feed all four of them, the king was ravenous. "I can solve both of those things, now that the storm is gone. But I'd like to get a complete idea of what we need to know first."

Genevieve nodded. "We know that they're deep-keeled ships. They can't go up the coast and come ashore at Seasbourne. The watchtower commander's guess was that they'd need to anchor a good two miles out just to send in their landing boats. So, we're unlikely to be outflanked."

"At least from the sea," Damien said grimly.

She nodded. "Obviously we don't have word about what's going on in Flowerdell... or across the border into Elendria."

"You left your troops bivouacked there when you and Jason came home," Damien frowned. "I should remember what plans we had made for them for the Winter."

"Maybe not," Genevieve answered. "Or at least it wouldn't stand out. We've had a division of the army on the Elendrian border for ten years. They're not so much 'bivouacked' as dug-in with solid facilities and their own local supply-chains. It would be madness for Queen Estelle to nail Elendria with an ice-storm and then try to invade that way."

"Even if she expected Flowerdell and the rest of Dalzialest to be just as devastated?" Damien asked. Genevieve paused to think about that, and he pointed north. "What about Vindalia? The way is still clear through from Minglemere. No ice until you get close to the capitol. If we were considering the possibility of the ships bringing people as far out as Seasbourne to attempt to outflank us, shouldn't we look that way as well?"

Genevieve shook her head. "Vindalia almost tried to give us *back* Minglemere, if you recall. We have excellent relations with them. And Minglemere is a mess to get through at this time of year. Not as swampy as the Spring when they have the excess runoff from the Alpinsward mountains, but really the only time you'd want to bring an army through Minglemere is late Summer after a significant dry spell."

"What about through the western hills, farther into Embervest?" Damien asked. They'd had pieces of these conversations before, but he wanted a refresher to remind himself of the details of lands he *knew* from being Bound to them but had only briefly seen in his one visit nearly five years earlier.

Genevieve shook her head again. "That would require collusion with the locals. The Embervest hills are karst – they're rotten with sinkholes that appear without warning in new places. Not to mention all the caves that make it both a great place to defend, as well as a haven for smugglers."

Damien sat up a little straighter. "I thought we were dealing with smuggling more effectively. Don't we have all the same laws about illegal substances as Vindalia does?"

Tomas chuckled. "There will always be smugglers, lad. Some of it may be flow from Deltheren or Mercasia, and they're just using us and Vindalia as a route to somewhere else. Some of it will be people or stolen goods. I've a similar problem in Siovale. With the mountains to the south there's just too many hidden ways for people – and even caravans – to make it through."

Genevieve nodded. "I'd see more in Elaarwen if it weren't for some of those deep canyons – but every now and then someone manages to get a rope bridge across..."

Damien shook his head. "It seems like a lot of trouble to avoid a few simple rules. We'll need to look at the economic incentives at play a little better and see if we can bring this stuff into the open – yes, yes, later." He waved at his wife's objection, looking back at Emeralsee.

"Am I right," he asked slowly, tracing the graceful curve of the Cape with one finger, "in thinking that the ice-storm actually did us a favor? It's keeping those enemy – presumed enemy," he corrected himself, "ships out of the Bay."

"It's also preventing us from preparing our defenses, communicating with our people, and our best guess is that it's boxed our own fleet in," Tomas said dryly.

Damien looked at him. "How effective is our fleet at naval battles anyways? We aren't a maritime power like Dawil."

Tomas shrugged. "Not my specialty, but I'd assume that they're prepared to defend the Bay. If their boats can move."

"Ships," Damien corrected absently. "Don't we have a map that shows the Bay and the Cape more closely?"

"Right here." Genevieve unrolled it, and Tomas helped her move the weights to hold down the corners.

Damien nodded approval. "I think I have enough to get started. I need to know how many ships, what kind, and what flag they might be flying. I need to see what shape our fleet is in, and what the ice in the Bay is doing. And, more generally, I need to survey the city to see what we can do to get people out and moving again."

Genevieve considered. "I think that's about it for now."

She looked at Tomas, who nodded.

The king looked at the map. "We'll need markers of some kind for the ships. I'll make sure they end up in the right places. There's a basket of pebbles over in the corner. Spill some onto the map – well onto the land, please." He vanished himself onto the couch. It was a much more stable position, meaning he was less likely to fall off and injure himself while his mind was elsewhere.

Briefly he shook his head. "We may have to do this again with Jason's help. I can't see normal things the way he can. There's usually enough magick in things for me to get what I need, but this time... flags and such... we'll have to see." He paused. "I'm more likely to be able to report numbers of people on each ship than details of what the ships look like. You're going to want to take notes."

It wasn't as simple as closing his eyes, but that was all Tomas and Genevieve would see. Damien took a deep breath and began.

Chapter TEN

First Meeting

THE ICE THAT COATED EVERYTHING in Emeralsee glittered maliciously at him, and he stayed well up and away from it. Somehow it was still Bound with the *intent* to do him harm. Damien wondered how he could possibly melt the ice and if it was going to let that angry, *intent* water into the Bay.

He also wondered what could work to unBind the *intent*. It had been clouds, then an ice-storm, and now an ice-coating. How many more transformations could it go through and retain its *intent*? It was just water, wasn't it? And one bit of water should be just like another bit...

The Bay of Emeralsee was a sheet of ice. It didn't sparkle at him quite like the smooth ice coating the city, however. *This* ice had formed while the underlying water of the Bay fought back, so it was choppy, with ice piled up higher than he would have believed in some places – higher than the height of two men. The home fleet – naval vessels, merchantmen, fishing boats – and those foreign ships unlucky enough to be in the harbor when the ice-storm struck were bound tightly, not even bobbing.

The ocean was a great repository of magick, and right here, enclosed by the Cape, it was part of Damien's Realm. He sent his awareness deep to see how thick the ice was.

Feet. *Yards* even. There was three times as much below the usual depth of the water as there was above it. He sensed disturbances near the city, and discovered that the Emerald River still had water flowing under its own thick crust. And the sewers, which weren't supposed to be dumping into the Bay at all, were seeping much, much warmer fluids.

It hadn't been on his agenda, but he sent himself rushing back along the Emerald River. It made its way through the duchy, then served as the dividing line between Siovale and Emeralsee. It was iced as far back as Cedarwen where the Sapphire River joined the Emerald... farther. That small, tortured barony would need help yet again when the rivers burst their icy bonds. Perhaps even later today. He cringed at the idea of having to tell Baron Raphael.

But right now – the ships.

Back to the Bay. Back and beyond the encircling Cape.

As he'd feared, Damien couldn't see the ships themselves except for the vague sense of the wood nymphs whose trees had gone to build their masts and hulls. He could sense the *people* on board, however.

He activated the spell he'd set on the stones long ago in some of what Genevieve would doubtlessly have referred to as his 'paranoid' preparations for a day such as this. The king focused on one locus of people – a ship by inference, to have so many humans surrounded by that much water – and one of the pebbles slid into position as he gave his listeners a number.

Then he moved on to the next. And the next...

He was beginning to feel the strain of the magick, of being so far from his body for so long... of not having had nearly enough breakfast.

Seen enough, sorcerer-king?

The voice spoke into his mind, startling him out of his count of the last ship. The voice was... seductive. Suggestive.

You turned the storm against us. I'm impressed.

The tone invited him into a joke, invited him to... delights beyond mortal imagining seemed like it should have been an exaggeration, but somehow it wasn't.

Not ready to play? Don't worry about all those things you've Bound yourself up with. I can take care of that when you're ready. I'll be waiting.

Damien shuddered and scurried back to his body.

"I didn't get you a number on that last one," he gasped, opening his eyes to the familiar office and the reassuringly familiar faces of his beloved wife and good friend. "I was interrupted. I counted just over forty. I'm not sure how many more."

"It could be worse," Genevieve was looking at the map.

"It's bad enough," Tomas disagreed. "They're mobile and our boats are not. And when the ice breaks up, it's likely to damage our fleet. They can just wait it out and come in as half our boats sink."

"But, Tomas, those numbers and this placement. This isn't an invasionary fleet from another country." Genevieve looked up. "These are pirates. They have to be."

"Pirates?" the Duke of Siovale was clearly skeptical. "I've always heard they're solitary, not pack animals."

She shrugged. "If *you* were planning to invade the capitol of a sovereign nation, would you try to do it with a force this small? *I* wouldn't. I'd want double this number. Five times, if I could find the men and transport them. This isn't an invasionary force, it's a *reiving* force. They aren't here to conquer – there's not a chance they could succeed."

"*I* conquered this castle with less than fifty men," Tomas said dryly, standing with his arms folded. "And I wasn't even in my right mind."

Genevieve waved that off, not bothering to note that she and Damien had captured it back from him with just the two of them... by freeing the soldiers he'd confined and arming the servants.

"That was an inside job." She looked much more relaxed. "And even you couldn't *hold* it. Look, the ice will begin to break up, and you're absolutely right, I can't see how we're going to have much of a fleet left. But the ice floes will keep the pirates out of the Bay while the city melts. We just need to get enough men-at-arms down to the harbor to defend against anyone trying to come ashore."

"That can't be their entire plan," Tomas stated flatly. "It's doomed to fail."

"They didn't plan on it turning out like this, I'm sure," Genevieve argued. "They anticipated us getting smashed by the storm, but that it petered out as it hit the city. We were supposed to be sealed in by ice, with no hope of getting help from outside Emeralsee, but the Bay wasn't supposed to be iced in. Damien changed those things by hurrying the storm off of Dalzialest so that it still had so much ice left to throw at us. Right?" she turned to the king.

"Erm... *yes*," Damien half-agreed. "Actually, it had *more* ice to throw at us because of the tropical storm that I used to protect Flowerdell. It took all that moisture and converted it into ice," he admitted.

His eye wandered over the map of his city... *his* for all that Jason – and Count Antonin – were Bound to it. He'd grown up here, had spent the last five years learning everything he could about it and walking every street he could persuade his Guards to go down with him, talking to every person who would take the time. Jason... still considered himself a son of Brindlewell's rolling hills and dales and always seemed vaguely uncomfortable in the confines of cobbled streets and screaming fishwives.

Doubtless that would solve itself as Emeralsee made Jason its own through the Binding, though he might always feel more connected to the fertile countryside past the city limits.

But for now, Damien wasn't certain even the Bound Duke and Count felt the city calling out for help the way he did. And certainly, *they* had no reason to feel the guilt of having made it all worse...

Genevieve folded her arms and stood back from the maptable with a look of vindication. Then she frowned and looked at it all again. "Gah. *You're* half-right, too, Tomas. I still don't think their plan was a full-scale invasion, but this was far too much effort for a normal reiving run, and pirates *don't* work together as a general rule. They're coming here for some very specific reason." She shook her head. "Pirates. Bandits. They don't make sense... and they *don't* make grand strategic plans like an invading nation would."

"If they could make it to the castle across all the ice, they'd have the entire ruling class of the Realm in their hands," Tomas argued. "They planned for *that*."

Damien frowned. "Maybe... not. They planned the storm to hit the evening after Jason's investiture, yes... but if I'd been less... scattered... if I'd been my normal self in the days leading up, we'd have finished all the meetings beforehand. At least half of you were planning to leave the following day – but how many put off their departures simply because I'd called a meeting?" He paused and swallowed. "And *who?*"

He'd had the feeling the wizards had started and aimed the storm much earlier and he had no idea how one could plan a *storm* that finely... but the date of the investiture had been known for some time. Damien's first thought that trapping the Realm's nobility here had been happenstance... might have been wishful thinking.

Tomas frowned as well. "Those who have farthest to go, I'd imagine. The Alpinsward and Embervest contingents. Dalzialest... although one might assume that Rosa and Zachary themselves might stay longer out of friendship and family feeling. Sildra wanted to spend more time with their babies, so we were going to stay on a bit. Quillian's vassals might have stayed, but once Tariana was gone, he never stays long himself. My people close to the mountains..."

"The handful who came down from Elaarwen." Genevieve looked at Damien. "You're not thinking they're working with someone *here*? Which of our people could possibly benefit from the Realm being devastated by an *ice-storm?*"

Rebellion... Usurpation... Treason...

The words hung unspoken.

But not unknown.

"That would be the question, wouldn't it," Damien said grimly. "But as Tomas has pointed out, it's entirely believable to take the Castle with a handful of people if it's an inside job. Or if we're unprepared. *One* of those ships has as many people – or more – than he had, Genevieve. Even if they can't land them all... that was *how* many ships?"

She glanced at the map. And paled. "Eighteen."

The king looked at Tomas. "Could they possibly hold the city if they took the Castle with nine hundred or a thousand fighters? Under the original scenario where the citizens are largely sealed into their homes by ice, most of the nobility has left – and taken their excess men-at-arms with them, and we can't get help – or even word out to *call* for help?"

The duke pursed his lips. "Not... for long. Don't you keep a division of the army here? That's five thousand right there. But if they had the two of you under their control... and potentially Jason and Adam as well... the army would be in a difficult place."

Damien looked at him. "Assuming you, Rosa, and Zachary were likely to have stayed another week... who does that leave in charge of the country?"

Tomas and Genevieve looked at each other. "Quillian?" the Queen suggested. "He'd be the most senior person left except for Father." Not that the young Duke of Reyensweir was a great deal older than Duchess Tariana of Embervest – who seemed to be in love with him. Or than Duchess Laura of Alpinsward... who had no real power-base in the country her parents had changed allegiances away from.

They all stared at each other for a few moments.

"This doesn't even deserve the name 'hypothesis'," Damien said softly.

"'Yet'?" Tomas asked sardonically.

"Let's hope 'never' is the operative term," Damien replied. "We've had enough of... this sort of thing... to last a lifetime. And right now, *everyone* is trapped here together. I didn't see anyone try to flee before the storm hit–"

"Flee into the teeth of an ice-storm? That would have been suicide. If we're looking for more reasons to put this... *not-hypothesis* to bed." Tomas shook his head.

"Nonetheless. Right now, if these pirates *do* manage to make their way in, all of us are here. With perhaps twice the usual number of men-at-arms in the Castle – but also a huge number of potential hostages." Damien saw Tomas' face go white, and hated that he'd had to say it. "We need to determine what they're likely to do and how to counter them."

Genevieve was looking at him oddly. "You said the storm targeted *you*. And when you 'came back' just now you said you'd been *interrupted.*"

Damien stared at his stockinged feet stretched out before him on the couch.

"When it was far from Emeralsee and I was fighting it, I could tell it was targeted to Emeralsee... at that point I wasn't sure it was after *me*, personally. It was after you and Adam made me quit fighting it – they were quite right," he answered Tomas' surprise. "I'd run out of ideas, and I was digging into a dangerous level of Power. Dangerous for me *and* for the Realm. Even if I'd survived, killing off our harvests for the next several years to beat this ice-storm would be... a Pyrrhic victory."

The duke looked even more startled, but nodded.

"It was in the early morning, when I tried to sense how much longer the storm would go on... it gathered itself to attack me directly. We got the top level of my wards up just in time." He looked at Tomas again. "I didn't dare take them down after that until the storm ended. Even if I could defend myself, there was still Genevieve. And the baby..."

He saw understanding in Tomas' eyes.

"When I just 'went out'," the king went on, "I could feel that same malice trapped in the ice that covers everything." He shuddered. "I have no idea what will happen if I try to melt it. And then while I was counting that last ship... someone talked to me. Tried to... *seduce* me to join them. They made it clear that they are helping the pirates – whoever they are."

Genevieve's brows went up. "Seduce you to act against the interests of the Realm you're Bound to? That seems pointless."

Damien gave her a pleading look. "She seemed to suggest that she could break that Binding... *and* ours."

"'*She*'?" He watched his wife's face go through a range of emotions, settling between fear and disbelief. "Is that even possible?"

Damien shrugged helplessly. "I didn't think so... but she sounded... *ancient*. Knowledgeable." He sighed. "*Sexy*. She wasn't just offering to free my *Power* from its Bindings."

Genevieve's brows went up again. "Ancient *and* sexy. I didn't think that was a combination that worked."

The duke's face was... suffused was the only way to say it politely.

"Well, it *didn't*," Damien pointed out. "I wasn't tempted in the least. But my grandfather and Lord Prydeen had the Realm eating them up from within, or they'd have been able to fend off old age themselves. According to my reading, most Evil Wizards do. She could look eighteen and be – I don't know – eighteen hundred?"

He didn't want Genevieve to that see he took the mysterious sorceress' threat – or promise – seriously. He didn't want her to see how much the idea that this woman could break their soul-bond terrified him.

Damien's connection to Genevieve was at the core of his being. He'd scoffed to Jason and Adam about how she'd made up a Grand Destiny that they had been Meant to Be... had also suggested that his dreams of Genevieve had been a fairy-story *he'd* told himself to cope with years of loneliness. But he'd *felt* that bond since their eyes met when he was eight. And while *she'd* built up a mythology of a Grand Destiny to justify her actions, *he* hadn't needed to. He'd felt it to be true with every bone of his body.

When Damien had suggested to her and Jason both that they might have had a soul-bond *if only Damien hadn't come across her first,* he had been smugly certain that the timing had been the Hand of Fate. The fact that they actually now *had* an active soul-bond had shaken the king deeply.

"Hmmn." Genevieve was clearly distracted by this notion of an ancient and *sexy* sorceress trying to seduce her husband.

Damien wanted to get her brilliant strategic mind back on the problem at hand, but wasn't sure how to do that without making the whole thing sound even worse. Tomas' smothered laughter on the side wasn't helping.

"Can she get that fleet into the Bay? And their crews up to the Castle?"

Oh. Apparently, she wasn't *that* distracted.

Which suggested that *he* was...

That was... not good.

Damien tried to concentrate on the problem. If he were out there on the ships, could *he* do it? Could he melt the pirates a sailing corridor through the yards-thick ice of the Bay, clear docking for eighteen ships in the harbor, then a walking path through the city?

"Probably," he admitted after a moment. "If she's powerful enough to create that ice-storm, she can probably generate enough heat to carve them a pathway to sail into the harbor. That's going to take a lot more Power than melting the ice on the streets to make them a path to the Castle." He hesitated. "I can't imagine she'd have much left after all of *that* though."

"Can we be sure that this is the same evil sorceress who created the ice-storm?" Tomas asked.

"Evil wizards don't tend to work together any more than pirates do, Tomas," Damien told him, dryly. And yet the pirates notably *were*...

But Genevieve had a *look* in her eyes that he recognized as her mind strategizing almost faster than she could speak. If this part of her engaged more often when she was playing chess, she'd be utterly unbeatable... instead of just occasionally beatable.

"But she could be using them. As your grandfather used Lord Prydeen. Or even without their knowledge." The queen looked thoughtful. "Adam said you told him you thought the storm had been *sent* from Deltheren, but that it had been *summoned* to Emeralsee."

Damien couldn't argue with that. It *was* what he'd said. It was what he'd *felt*.

Genevieve turned away, the pale blue skirts of her Court gown swishing out around her.

"There's something we're missing. Something *big*." She began to pace. Damien itched to join her. He always thought better on his feet. Bedamned frostbite. "The storm was *sent* from Deltheren. It was *summoned* to Emeralsee. Presumably by someone on that pirate fleet. But not necessarily."

"Don't add complications we have no evidence for," Tomas told her. "Remember that the simplest answer that fits everything we know *is* most likely to be correct."

"That's only true if we have most of the pertinent information. We're missing something *big*. I can *feel* it." Genevieve frowned.

"We still need to figure out how to deal with them if they *do* make it here," Tomas reminded them both. "Or, preferably, how to *avoid* them getting to the Castle in the first place. That seems rather more urgent than trying to suss out some potentially non-existent Grand Scheme." His tone suggested that they might be operating out of paranoia.

Genevieve shook her head. "We can't plan to stop them if we don't know what they're after."

Damien felt cold. "Me. I don't know what the pirates want out of this, but that sorceress wants *me*. I think that's why she's involved at all." He shuddered. "Oh, Gods. That's why this is happening *now*. Jason's investiture and the nobility gathered here – that could all be a coincidence. But it's the cusp of Winter. She knows I can't fully access the Power of the Realm right now. Unless I can actually get her into the Throneroom somehow, I'll be facing her with little more than my own Power." He looked at Genevieve with dread. "And she is much, *much* more Powerful than Lord Prydeen."

His grandfather's Evil Wizard Apprentice had been a gnat before the Power that the Realm had given Damien. But he'd never faced even Lord Prydeen with his own newly-awakened magick alone.

"What can she do if she has you?" Tomas asked.

Damien shivered. "If she truly *can* break my Bindings to the Realm – and to Genevieve… If she can break *me*… my Power would be at her disposal. If she can break me *without* dissolving the Bindings… she could use me to drain the Realm to a withered husk of a land."

He couldn't say what would happen to Genevieve in either of those scenarios. By the expression in their eyes, he didn't have to.

Nor, Damien expected, did he have to say that if the sorceress got her hands on Genevieve, she could break him that much more quickly.

Tomas sighed. "So, you don't have the magick to fight her unless she's in the Throneroom – assuming she has any magick left after cutting them a path through the Bay and up to the castle. But if we let her get *that* far…" His jaw clenched, and a muscle ticked beneath his beard. Doubtless he was thinking about his wife and children, trapped in the castle with them.

Damien wished he could reassure the man. "She *should* use up a lot of her Power melting their way here. It might be enough… What I have on my own might be enough."

Genevieve had gone back to pacing. "We're still *missing* something."

Tomas watched her for a moment then turned to the king. "We're supposed to meet with the other dukes and duchesses after lunch. And we're getting perilous close to that time. What are you going to tell them?"

Damien looked down at his hands. "Love? What do you think?"

She paused to give him a distracted look. "Well, we *can't* imply that we think one of them could be colluding with these wizards."

"Of course not," Tomas said impatiently.

"And we have no evidence – yet – of any other invading force than this one." She looked at Damien. "Right?"

"I *think* I'd be aware of such a thing," Damien replied. "But… I'm not entirely sure. The Realm is half asleep and as far as its concerned, humans belong here. I'm not sure if it will discriminate between our armies and someone else's." He sighed. "I need Jason. He'd be able to actually *see*." Tomas gave him an odd look, but didn't say anything. "So, you're thinking we only tell them about the pirates. And the sorceress?"

Genevieve nodded. "The rest is sheer speculation. We don't actually have anything else *to* share. And this will be quite enough."

Their eyes met. Jason and Adam would get the full story as soon as possible. Through her new soul-bond to Jason if there were no other way.

Damien nodded grimly. He'd anticipated something like this happening. It didn't mean he was happy about it.

Chapter ELEVEN

Preparation

THE MEETING WITH THE DUKES and duchesses went about as could be expected – which is to say, poorly.

"Is there any way at all to get the children out?" Rosa asked. Genevieve's heart broke for her. She wasn't asking about herself... and baby Betha wasn't even six months old.

But it was also *Rosa* asking for a reason. She, like Jason, like Adam, like Damien and Genevieve, knew about the secret passage through the walls. And she also knew that there were only air-filled pockets along the way – that part of the 'passage' involved King or Heir physically *pulling* anyone else through the solid stone. Genevieve had done it when she wore the Heir's Ring, and Damien had been able to even though he'd given up the Ring and had not yet found the Sword. The Queen might still...

But there was nowhere to take them. The passage ended inside the city wall, and the ice extended for dozens – *hundreds* – of miles in every direction.

Possibly they could stash the children in the pockets... but then if Damien, Genevieve, and Jason were all unable to return for them...

She didn't even need to shake her head. Rosa read it in her eyes.

"We have a few warded rooms," Damien volunteered. "We can put as many of the children as possible in them. Once the last level of the ward is set, nothing should be able to get in."

He met Genevieve's eyes. She knew he was asking her to stay in one of those rooms also, but he wasn't sending it down the bond so as not to pressure her... so as not to ask the Commander-General of his Armies to hide away like a civilian instead of standing at his side as the Warrior-Queen she was. If either of them should be in hiding, it should be Damien – but they needed his magick.

She lifted her chin, and he dropped his gaze.

"Tell me where. I'll see to it," Zachary volunteered. He gave his wife a wan smile. "You're the warrior of the family anyways."

"Warrior of *words*, maybe," Rosa muttered.

"Tell that to Prince Oskar."

Genevieve saw Jason cringe slightly.

Tariana and Quillian had stepped close together at Damien's news. They were whispering heatedly. Her voice began to rise. "–*not* going to hide in some hole!"

"Tari–"

"*You* may have your shield, Quillian Mirion, but *I've* been chasing bandits since I was fifteen!" Her springy, dark curls bounced angrily from her elegant chignon, and her dark eyes flashed.

"Tari-*ana*–"

"If you don't want someone who'll fight at your side, Quillian, then–"

"Tariana Eledor!" Duke Quillian grabbed both of her hands and fell to one knee. "If you're going to insist on risking your life at my side, will you at least marry me *first?*"

"Oh, Quill! Yes!" The young duchess threw herself into his arms, completely overbalancing the poor man. Everyone else looked away to give them some privacy.

"The pirates don't stand a chance," Jason chuckled close to Genevieve's ear.

She gave him a startled look.

"She's not exaggerating," he explained. "Duke Istvan had her in the field on bandit patrol until he died last year because her unit consistently captured and killed more bandits than any of his others. And you remember what that territory is like from when we were negotiating for Minglemere. Bandit haven. It's probably why we didn't see much of Tariana then."

Genevieve looked at the delicate-seeming young woman with more interest. She had always seemed too merry and impetuous for the queen to take seriously, and she had wondered why the old duke had chosen her instead of his older son, the serious Robard, as his Heir. Clearly there was more to the girl than met the eye.

"Quillian's a knight," Jason added quietly, "but he earned his shield just months before Damien took the throne. He's probably never been in a real fight – unless it was while he was in Embervest to court Tariana. Come to think of it, that *might* have been how he caught her attention."

They had come up for air and picked themselves up off the floor. Duke Quillian approached the king, for once looking breathless and happy and as young as he truly was. He was also clearly unwilling to let go of Tariana's hands.

"Your Majesty," he began, then stumbled to a stop, unsure how to go on.

Damien grinned at them. "It *is* going to be a mess, but we'll deal with it. You have my blessings, Quillian, Tariana. Never let it be said that I came between true loves."

His smile migrated, as it always did, to Genevieve, and she returned it warmly. But she wasn't sure he could tell, because his eyes flickered past her and returned to the newly affianced couple without him having to pry them away from her as he usually did, though his smile never faltered.

Behind her, Jason sighed, and Genevieve's heart twinged. Damien had seen Jason when he looked at her.

"This is just lovely," Duke Tomas said dryly, "and all due congratulations to you two, but if everyone would like to come back to the topic at hand, we still have a battle to prepare for."

Tariana shrugged. "It's no great thing, Uncle Tomas. Pirates are basically sea-bandits. Which means they're cowards and they'll run once they see the main chance has shifted away from them."

Uncle? Genevieve wished she had the Realms genealogies memorized like Damien did, though she thought she recalled someone saying something about that a bit ago.

"There's nearly a thousand of them, Tariana," Tomas reminded her. "And a sorceress. And we have to either let them come into the castle so that King Damien can battle the sorceress after she's hopefully worn herself out melting their way up here, or else we have to have him wear *him*self out melting us a path down to the waterfront and then battle *both* pirates and sorceress. How many people do we have under arms in the castle, Sir Loveress?" he asked the Champion.

Adam regarded the duke of Siovale for a long moment from his post behind Damien's chair before answering. "One hundred Castle Guards. Each of you brought as many as five of your own men-at-arms, and each of the Counts was permitted two. Some of the lesser nobility brought one. Counting in the Royal Guards and those nobility who are willing to fight – perhaps three hundred."

Genevieve had worked out the numbers in her own head, but somehow hearing them from Adam made their situation seem much more stark.

"They have to get in past the Castle wall, though," Damien pointed out. "And with the city coated in inches-thick ice, the pirates won't be able to use their favored tactics of arson and hostages."

"Um, Damien?" Jason interjected. "The Castle gate... is iced open."

The king rolled his eyes. "Of course it is. Well, I can fix that." His eyes met Genevieve's again. "In fact, I should probably de-ice all the areas where our people may want the footing to stand and fight."

She nodded. Then a thought struck her. "Unless you can set it up to leave a thin layer – in the mountains we call it 'black ice' because you can't see it until you slip on it – and just narrow paths through... we could probably mark them in some way so *our* people know..."

"That could get dangerous for both sides in a fight," Adam warned.

"But we'd *start* with an advantage," Rosa commented. "At a three-to-one *dis*advantage, it sounds like we'll need every trick we can come up with."

"How many non-combatants do we have?" Tomas asked.

Damien sighed, "Too many."

But Genevieve found herself bursting out laughing. "Not as many as you think. Remember pretty little Maree and her frying pan?"

"*Genevieve...*" Her handsome husband blushed so prettily.

"Do I want to know?" Duke Quillian eyed his red-faced king.

"It's nothing," Damien muttered, looking away from everyone.

Genevieve went over and sat on the arm of his chair, and draped an arm around him. He leaned into her, despite his embarrassment.

"When Damien and I re-took the Castle five years ago, we first had to free the Castle Guard – who'd been locked in the food storage cellars off the kitchens," she explained. "The cellars were being guarded by mind-controlled Siovalese men," she nodded ironically at her former brother-in-law, who gave her a look of long-suffering, "and a handful of Lord Prydeen's bullyboys, who were terrorizing the kitchen staff. The kitchen knife-sharpener, a girl named Maree, helped get the staff involved in distracting the bullyboys so that I could fight them while Damien froze the Siovalese men with his magick. All those men recovered, didn't they, Tomas? Well, Prydeen's bullyboys not so much, but we weren't trying to save *them*. We ended up using the Siovalese swords and the various knives, pokers, pot-lids and such to arm the kitchen workers as well as our Castle Guard."

"And the frying pan?" Duchess Laura had been mostly quiet, but her eyes were sparkling as if she'd already heard this story from someone.

"Pretty little Maree brained one of the bullyboys while he was fighting Damien. It wasn't a fair fight – the bullyboy had no chance against my lord. But the girl didn't know it. She was sure she'd saved the king's life and was a Hero of the Realm."

"Genevieve, can we *please* end the story with that," Damien begged.

She was about to relent, even though Tariana was laughing and saying "Oh, tell us, do!"

"She wanted to pick her own reward, it seems," Rosa filled in as Genevieve hesitated. Damien groaned, and put his arms on the Council table and leaned into them to hide his face. "She decided her reward should be Damien himself."

The king looked up. "Zachary, make her stop. Please. I swear, I'll grant you anything you ask for."

The Duke of Dalzialest shrugged without much sympathy. "Most men wouldn't complain to have these problems, Damien."

"Wouldn't *you?*"

Zachary paused, considered. Looked at Genevieve and Rosa. "You have a point."

"*What* problems?" Duke Quillian still seemed confused. His new bride-to-be pulled him close and whispered in his ear. "Oh. Hmmn."

He eyed the king speculatively, and Damien buried his face in his arms again. "This happens to you a lot, Your Majesty?"

The duchesses exchanged an amused look, and it suddenly occurred to Genevieve to hope that Adam and Jason could control *their* expressions.

Genevieve let her smile grow slightly vindictive. "Not any more. *I* made sure of that." She paused. "Our good Castle Chatelaine made sure the girl found fair employment elsewhere. Her nerves weren't up for working here after I was done with her."

Tariana gave her queen a curious look. "I'll have to get details later. Just in case." She tweaked Quillian's nose, rather to his disgruntlement, and gave him an arch look.

"Can we *please* go back to discussing how to defend the Castle?" Damien's voice was somewhat muffled.

"That's what we *were* doing, love," Genevieve assured him. "My point was that a number of our 'non-combatants' are going to be more than capable of defending themselves – and others. And," she said more soberly, "at these odds, we're going to need them to."

Damien sat up again. "Lady Aryllis and Madame Elista will probably have the best ideas on how to do that and who. The pages should go into hiding with the other children... Adam, what about the squires?"

"If we add the squires in, that boosts our numbers by another seventy," said the Champion – who had so lately been Captain of the Guards and thereby in charge of the squires and pages. "The ones in their last year are practically knights anyways, and they get most of their full-growth a year or so before that. The youngest ones, though... they'll be offended to be put in with the pages, but they aren't big enough or strong enough to fight adults."

"Messengers, then, and supplies," Tomas said promptly.

Adam nodded.

"So, my first priority needs to be to get that gate closed and the courtyards and battlements de-iced," Damien summarized. "The Castle can withstand a siege, so our first goal is to keep them out unless we need to bait a trap for their sorceress as a last resort. Zachary is going to organize getting the children and as many of the other non-combatants into the warded rooms as possible. Adam, you can give him locations on all of those? And then you can organize the squires. And break the news to the pages that they are going into hiding. Don't give me that look. If *I* didn't ask you, Tim would."

He looked around. "Captain Ancellius will be in charge of the Castle's defenses. Please have your knights and men-at-arms report to him for assignment. Prince Jason will give out assignments to the nobles. My Queen will be planning the strategy. Duke Tomas is the only one of us here who has actually commanded a full-scale battle, so once the enemy is upon us, *he* will be our field marshal and decide what is to be done and when."

Damien took a moment to focus on each one of them. "I'm going to be fighting the magickal battle, and the Queen will be with me. The Castle should be able to withstand a siege until the army can get here if I can manage to deal with the sorceress.

"Should Duke Tomas fall, command of the battle goes to Prince Jason. Then the Prince-Consort." He nodded at Adam. "Then to Captain Ancellius."

Damien looked around grimly at the gathered high nobility of his Realm. "This is not about rank or seniority, my lords and ladies. This is about trying to keep the most of us alive that we can."

Melting the ice to get the gate closed was easier than he'd expected. The temperature of the air blowing in from Siovale – the way it was supposed to at this time of year – didn't match with keeping huge amounts of water frozen, though there was such a mass of ice that the meltwater immediately refroze when it dripped away. Creating patches of black ice in the main courtyard turned out to be ridiculously easy for that reason – though marking it required some creative thinking.

The battlements and top of the wall were another matter. Luckily there were interior stairs to reach the top of the wall, but Damien felt drained by the time he'd de-iced and dried the walkways such that he could be sure they would provide safe footing for the defenders. Since he stayed in his chair and off of his feet the whole time, it was hard for anyone else to tell how tired he was – a small mercy at least.

The king had taken the time to review the status of their supplies with Madame Elista. The Castle was now feeding and housing close to double the population she had planned for, and the usual daily deliveries had, of course, come to a halt. The situation wasn't dire – apparently planning for a siege was part of the job of the Chatelaine that he hadn't been aware of, to her amusement – but there was still a limit. The Castle had become more dependent on the surrounding city as the city had become so vast and the Realm hadn't suffered any real external threat in over a hundred years.

Worse was the situation of the population of Emeralsee city. The people were sealed into their homes, some so thoroughly that asphyxiation was a real concern, some simply without food or heat or light... or a way to dispose of waste. Some were sealed into bad family situations. Jason could now feel it all as well, and every time the newly-made Duke passed his king, he looked more wan and anxious. Finally, Damien snagged Jason's sleeve and told him they'd do what they could after dinner.

Because *before* dinner he had to give the bad news to the rest of the Peers of the Realm.

At least by then the rumors had spread, but the dukes and duchesses had spoken to most of their vassals. Damien had plans to offer them, and real numbers. For once, he brooked no argument and entertained no questions. They were each to send their men-at-arms to Captain Ancellius, nobles who could fight were remanded to Prince Jason Alsterling, children to Duke Zachary Miramar. Duchesses Rosa Miramar and Tariana Eledor unexpectedly volunteered to teach simple self-defense to the non-combatants who could not be fit in with the children, and to help Lady Aryllis and Madame Elista.

Damien took the time to fashion more red cords to complete the magickal wards – but without the twist that required the same person to set the ward as to break it from the inside. And he took that twist *out* of the ones that Adam and Genevieve already had.

Back in his own room, Damien was ready to sleep – even vanishing himself and Genevieve to the top of the tower had been an effort for once. But when Jason knocked on the door looking even more tired and sick, the king was not willing to turn him away.

"There's people *dying* in the city, Damien," Jason said in a broken voice as he sat down and put his head in his hands, elbows on knees.

Damien wanted to make it better. But he couldn't. And it was only going to get worse.

"There are *always* people dying in the city, Jason," he said, not unkindly, but without great sympathy. "There are close to three hundred thousand people in Emeralsee. The average age at death is close to sixty, so roughly one sixtieth of the population dies each year. That works out to almost fourteen people a day."

Jason's head came up in consternation. His eyes were red-rimmed, and Damien's heart twinged. "How – why do you just *know* that?"

"I worked out the numbers because it was driving me crazy the way it's doing to you." The king sighed. "There's half again as many people in the rest of the duchy. That's another seven people dying each day just in Emeralsee province. We have seven duchies, though Elaarwen and Alpinsward aren't as populous. That's over two *million* people in the Realm, Jason. Or close to a *hundred* people dying each day.

"And that's not counting the livestock being slaughtered, the wild creatures being hunted by humans or other animals... or just dying for other reasons." Damien paused. "I *feel* them all. And every oak tree that is logged – or struck by lightning, or felled by beavers, or... I realized early on that I should count myself lucky that the *grass* doesn't think of itself as separate organisms..." He shook his head.

Jason was staring at him. "How can you stand it? All I can feel are the humans, and it's overwhelming. It's not just that they're dying, it's that they're starving for food, for light, for a clean space. That they're *hurting* each other... on *purpose...*"

"There are fewer humans, but they're harder," Damien agreed. "Animals aren't cruel, and plants... are so alien to our ways of thinking." His eyes unfocused, and he had to work to pull himself back. Telling Jason he was lucky not to *feel* the insects and even smaller life... would not help just now. "At first... those first few days I simply didn't have time to realize what was going on. *What* all I was feeling. Everything was so *immediate*. After that..."

He sighed again. If Jason weren't so twisted up with his own new set of perceptions, he'd likely remember how Damien had nearly starved himself to death a year or so into his reign. The *feel* of all the tiny living things dying constantly had made him unable to eat meat – which they had understood at least somewhat – or *plants* – which they had not – or even *bread*.

He and Adam had finally taken the severely weakened young king out to the grotto and forced him to exercise until he had been willing to eat *anything*. After a week of that, Damien had been back to eating enough – mostly freshly cooked plants and honey and the centers of hard cheeses – that his keepers had let him come home.

It had taken another year before he worked his way back up to eating the foods that everyone else found normal. And in the meantime, he had slowly managed to convince the Castle cooks to switch to making breads using a special kind of salt mined in at the border between Embervest and Alpinsward... which had luckily been restored to the Realm by then.

The mountain salt made bread rise faster than yeast, couldn't unexpectedly *die,* and lent itself to a variety of experimentation. The fashion – and convenience – had spread down to the City and was becoming popular out in the countryside now. It had stimulated the mining economies of the two mountain-provinces as well as expanded the baking industry in Emeralsee.

And Damien didn't have to feel all the yeast being killed every morning.

So, it worked out for everyone. Rather like what he'd done for the rats of Emeralsee last year.

"The others don't seem to be affected like this," the tall knight half-complained. "My mother, Tomas, Rosa, the rest."

Damien gave him a half-smile. "I've been telling you for awhile, Jason. Your magickal gifts are at least as powerful as Genevieve's. Most of the others simply don't have as much of a gift as either of you – thanks to your

Alsterling heritage. You might ask her how *she* dealt with things... though she was also rather incredibly busy those first few days. And neither of us had a crisis then like you have to deal with now." He chuckled. "She was also newly pregnant and I suspect a woman's psyche is constructed to protect the baby as much as her body is... or is supposed to."

The shadow of her many miscarriages still hovered over everything.

"I... don't want to tell *Genny* I can't handle this," Jason said a little abashedly. "I didn't want to tell *you,* after you've put so much trust in me, but I didn't know what else to do." He winced. "I was hoping you'd be able to tell me it wears off or there's some way to block it off. Or... *something.* I know I can't save *everyone...*"

Well, Jason's heart was in the right place – as always. And he was clever enough to realize he had limitations. Although, apparently he was still at the stage of falling in love where he thought he could hide his vulnerabilities from the person he loved.

"No... you can't, and it doesn't wear off." The king shook his head. "Ask Adam's mother. They have different gifts in that family, but she might have some valuable advice."

Jason tried for a wry smile. "She *always* has valuable advice. I'm just not sure I can take any more *valuable* advice right now."

His smile was still rather wan... but it was genuine.

Damien laughed. "I'm sure she does. No lofty illusions, that lady – but I suppose a baronetcy is barely more than a handful of farms. They're more connected to the land than most of the rest of us." He looked at his oldest friend. "Are you ready to try to *do* something about all that suffering you're feeling?"

"What *can* we do?" Jason asked, an unaccustomed note of hopelessness in his tone.

Damien shrugged. "Whatever we can." He swung his legs off of the couch, setting his feet carefully on the floor, and patted the seat beside him. "Sit here. I think we'll need to be in physical contact for this to work. You're going to show me where people are suffering, and I'll see what resources I have to help."

Jason stood up and walked around the low table, then stopped, staring at the spot on the leather couch beside his king.

Damien sighed. He was tired, and he wanted nothing more than to go to bed with his wife – even if he didn't have the energy to do more than hold her. "What's wrong *now*, Jason?"

"Are you sure you want to do this? It sounds like this is going to require our minds to be..."

"Intimate?" the king suggested. He raised his eyebrows. "A little late to complain about that, isn't it?"

Jason flushed. "It's not quite the same thing... and... you've been acting uncomfortable around me all day, Damien."

Well, and so he was. But this still needed to be done. And he didn't feel like talking about Jason's soul-bond to his wife right now. Perhaps some humor...?

He flashed a grin. "And I suppose you were perfectly *fine* when Quillian asked if I have *problems* like 'pretty little Maree' all the time?" His grin became genuine at the expression of chagrin on Jason's face.

It broke the tension enough for Jason to thump himself down beside the king. "Gods. What was Genevieve thinking to bring that up? *Today,* of all times." He leaned back and stretched an arm behind Damien on the couch back, and a note of true humor lit his blue eyes. "Adam told me about your long list of 'offers.' You *could* have just told Quillian 'yes'."

"I was *trying* to get us back to the topic at hand, if you recall," Damien said dryly. He was hyperaware of Jason's arm behind him. "Speaking of which..."

Jason offered him his *other* hand. "What do I have to do?"

The king took a slow breath and accepted the hand. He could ignore that arm. "Just what you did before. Go look at your duchy. Just... this time I'll be with you. Find the worst places first."

He didn't want to explain that his energy was flagging. A night's sleep with Genevieve and he'd be fine.

"All right." Jason closed his eyes and so did Damien.

He could feel Jason trying to 'go out' and he tried to lift himself 'out' as well... but somehow they were each tied down. It was ridiculously frustrating, since Damien didn't have to do this consciously most of the time. Sometimes, in fact, he had to intentionally hold himself to his body because it had become so natural for him to do this.

After several moments, the king gave up and opened his eyes. When he saw Jason do the same, he re-claimed his hand. "You go, and I'll join you." he said grimly. "I must have been wrong about needing physical contact."

Jason shrugged, but there was something in his eyes... Then they were closed and Damien was just as grateful. If this worked, he didn't need to worry about it.

Unfortunately, it didn't. Again, they were anchored. *Both* of them.

He wanted to scream. He wanted to get up and pace. Between his feet and the fact that he *never* lost his temper like that, neither was likely to provide the release the king needed.

Could this be a spell from that unknown sorceress? Or was he really that tired? And why was it affecting *both* of them?

Genevieve stepped out of the bedchamber, a silken robe over what he could only hope was nothing else at all. "What is going on out here? I can *feel* both of you and it feels like you're... fighting each other?" She was clearly puzzled.

"I *thought* we were trying to work together," Damien muttered in frustration. He avoided Jason's baffled blue eyes.

Genevieve folded her arms and looked at him. "Hmmn."

He studied his own hands, but didn't say anything.

She waited.

She was going to make a wonderful mother. She could out-wait the Gods themselves when she wanted to, despite her personal lack of enthusiasm for patience.

Jason squirmed beneath that turquoise regard before Damien did, to the king's surprise.

"It's my fault," he admitted heavily. "They say guilt weighs you down. I guess it's literally true in this situation."

"Guilt?" Damien was baffled. "What do *you* have to be guilty about?"

Genevieve sighed gustily and took a seat on one of the chairs. "I can see *this* is going to take awhile."

The robe slipped back from her long, lovely legs as she crossed them at the knee. No, she *definitely* didn't have anything else on.

She met his eyes with irony when he was able to raise them to hers.

Damien swallowed and turned back to Jason.

"I shouldn't have a... a *bond* with Genny," Jason said miserably. "Not like this. Not more than *friendship*."

Damien stared at him. "But it's not *your* fault. If anything, it's *mine*..."

"Men!" Genevieve snorted. "Adam is the only sensible one of the three of you, and *I* get stuck with *you* two. This isn't anyone's *fault*. Unless you want to blame *me* for not being able to carry a child to term." She waved down their immediate protests. "The world is what it is, loves. We are who we are, and we have the gifts and challenges and blessings that we do. It's like snow in the mountains," she explained. "You can choose to enjoy it and embrace it or you can complain and hate it. Either way, there will be just as much snow and the only difference in the end is how you feel."

She stood up. "*I choose to believe you are both – all – blessings given to me. Now kiss and make up and do whatever you need to do so you can both go to bed. Tomorrow will be another too long day.*"

Genevieve walked around the couch, kissed each of them on the top of their heads, and then vanished back into the bedchamber.

Damien stared after her, and sighed. "She's right."

"She usually is." Jason's voice was chagrined and amused at the same time. He sighed. "I suppose I was feeling guilty because I *do* love her as much as I do. Part of me has been in love with her since I was thirteen. But *she's* supposed to be *yours*. And I'm supposed to be *Adam's.*" And his voice became a little forlorn as he said that.

Damien looked back at him with a wry smile. "Adam says you love rarely but fiercely... and that you never let go." He paused. "He says *he's* come to terms with the idea that you loved – and *still* love – Prince Oskar."

Jason's eyes were startled... and relieved. "And you?"

Damien felt himself blushing. "I've always known you – care – about me. Adam said you're *in love* with me... I hadn't thought about it that way before." He hesitated. "I didn't think it was *possible* to be in love with more than one person before... I..." Damien swallowed. Why had this felt so much easier when they were all stuck in the rooms downstairs for two days? "I love you, too. *And* Adam."

Jason's wry smile warmed his blue eyes to near violet. "'Before'? And... actually, I had meant to ask how you're doing with how I feel about *Genny.*"

"Oh." Damien looked down. "That's... I've... I..." The day had been too long. He had simply run out of energy. *That* was why he was tearing up. That was *all*. "I'm afraid I'll lose her. And I never thought I had to... before."

"That word again." Jason's tone was understanding.

Damien nodded.

"You know..." Jason said thoughtfully, "I thought you embarked us all on this... *path*... a little... *blithefully.*"

The king's head shot up, "What are you talking about? I've been thinking this through for *five years!* Thinking about it, looking for alternatives, discussing it with Genevieve."

"Thinking things through and stewing about them can look awfully similar, Damien. One is productive, the other is not. And I've watched you do both often enough as a youth – and as a king." Jason's face was slightly amused. "I can't honestly say I *mind* the results, my sweet prince, but you're just now feeling the kind of fear that Adam and I – but particularly Adam – have been dealing with since you first proposed this scheme."

There was nothing Damien could say to that. It was true.

And... perhaps he *had* been stewing about this. Genevieve had avoided the thought at all, but he had been unable to avoid bringing it up over and over... perhaps he should have spoken to Jason and Adam early on. Perhaps their four heads together could have come up with a better plan. Or at least had the time to make it a less emotionally tortuous one.

"I'm sorry." He dropped his gaze again. His sight was blurry with tears anyways. "You're right."

Jason lifted his chin. And Damien was surprised to see him smiling.

"I told you, love, *I'm* not sorry with how things have turned out. And I don't think Adam is either. Or Genevieve. Are *you?*" Jason paused, then unexpectedly leaned forward and *licked* the line of tears off of Damien's eyes, first one and then the other. "Those beautiful silver-grey eyes of yours should always be clear."

"Jason..." He'd – *they'd* – agreed, that the last time was *the* last time. And he only wanted Genevieve, *really* he did...

Jason's eyes sparkled. "She *did* say to 'kiss and make up'."

"And... Adam?" Damien breathed.

"You said he told you I love fiercely and never let go. I think he'll understand." Jason chuckled. "Right now, I think he'd be relieved that I'm kissing *you* instead of Genny."

He fit action to words, the arm stretched along the back of the couch coming down to pull Damien closer. Damien felt his own arms automatically going around Jason as he gave himself up to the kiss.

"So much for a 'last time'," he murmured at last, resting his head on Jason's shoulder.

"Mmmn." Jason brushed the lock of hair that always fell across Damien's face out of the way and kissed his forehead. "I'm not going to pretend this is going to be easy... but..."

He paused, and Damien looked up to see Jason's eyes go unfocused.

The tall knight shook his head as he chuckled. "Adam is *laughing* at us. At *me*. How do you ever get used to someone else's feelings inside your head? How is he so easy with this already?"

Damien relaxed. It was... more than nice to be held by someone that for so long he had thought could make everything in his life safer and better. Who *had* made everything in his life safer and better.

"Adam is a fairly powerful empath, Jason. He's been aware of your feelings since–" He caught himself. *How* long was Adam's to tell. Or not. "For a very long time. For me and Genevieve... the soul-bond kind of drowned out everything else until we sorted it out."

"An *empath*..." Jason's eyes were speculative, and Damien had no idea what he might be thinking but it clearly pleased him.

The tall knight shook himself back to the present. "Should we try again? To *See* the city, I mean."

His eyes sparkled at what had surely been an unintended *double entendre*.

Damien sighed, and pulled himself up off of Jason's shoulder. "We have to. But... I don't know how much energy I have. Melting that ice took more out of me than I anticipated." He paused. "Normally I'd tap into the Realm, but there isn't much there right now for me to touch, and I want to leave as much as possible for the battle we know is coming. On occasion, Genevieve has shared her Power with me, but I don't want to touch anything that might disrupt..."

"... the pregnancy," Jason nodded. He hesitated in his turn. "Have you been able to tell if... if there's the same sort of problems as before?"

Damien shook his head. "I'll be able to tell soon, though. Another week or two." He sighed. "It doesn't make any sense. We're not such close cousins that we should be having these troubles. And you're only slightly less closely related – one extra generation, by virtue of the long length of my grandfather's life."

Jason's eyes were startled, and his lips moved as if he was counting something. "I guess that's true. King Reginald was your grandfather, but he was... *my* great-grandfather." The golden-haired knight shook his head. "I'm still having trouble wrapping my head around this. I didn't even know who my *father* was until last week..."

"In some ways, it's more of a surprise that no one figured it out sooner," the king told him. "You *look* like an Alsterling. If you'd stood next to my father, they'd have assumed *you* were his son, not me."

"I suppose we all see what we want to see," Jason said philosophically. He smiled. "Speaking of which..."

"Oh, yes..." Damien took a breath in preparation to step 'out'...

"I see my very handsome sweet prince, and I'm claiming another *kiss* before we do anything else."

...and Damien needed that breath for other reasons entirely.

The kiss ran tendrils of energy through Damien's entire body. Energy, he knew, had to come from *some*where. He still hadn't figured out how emotions translated into magickal Power... but he couldn't argue with results. Or disagree with what gave him the ability to help his poor people.

This time it was easy to fly up and out. He sensed Jason beside him as a magickal entity, though he couldn't *See* him. There were three hundred thousand *other* people to sense after all...

Jason led him first to those whose air was running out. Damien showed him how to use raw Power to melt air-holes through the thick, hard ice. Two holes for every place where the air was growing stale, and wide enough that, as the ice eventually melted, they wouldn't clog up again immediately. There weren't as many of those as he had feared, but the downside was that the ice had actually served as insulation and as the trapped people could breathe, they also began to lose their precious heat.

Food next, he told Jason, *and fuel.*

Food, after all was fuel for the body. A person who could eat might keep himself warm. Damien knew which warehouses and shops stored different foods and began vanishing sacks of lentils and flour, sausages and cheeses to the places Jason identified for him. He'd pay for it from the Royal Treasury when this was all over.

Fuel was more difficult. Coal had become more popular recently, and it was easier to transport – weight for weight and volume for volume. The king had been advocating its use, since it generated less smoke than woodfires and was far less flammable when stored, although the odor was far more objectionable. But in a city the size of Emeralsee, smoke and soot were serious concerns, and though much of the city was good solid stone and brick, the newer areas relied heavily on wood construction.

Unfortunately, not all of the citizens had stoves that could burn coal. Damien had to hunt – using Jason's eyes – to find wood for those who needed it. *Those* warehouses were outside the city walls, it turned out, and walled sensibly in stone with slate roofing to keep the firewood dry.

You've brought a friend this time, sorcerer-king?

They were so close to done, and he was trembling with fatigue, even in his magickal form. He really didn't have time to deal with this.

Ah, not a friend so much as a lover.

Go home, he told Jason, and felt his *friend* speed away. Damien couldn't. Not yet. He needed to know something about this witch.

Sorceress, the voice insisted, *you know better, sorcerer-king. A* **witch** *is something else entirely.* There was no irritation in the voice, merely vast amusement. *I think you want to use a different word, but you are too much the gentleman for that. This will be interesting. My apprentices are usually younger and much... rougher. Your morals and ideals are already well-formed. Working with you will be a challenge.*

He didn't bother to reply. All he could say would be a denial that he would work with her, and she already knew that.

You've done good work. You and your lover. Shall I take him, too?

Damien was hard put to not reply to that one.

Stubborn today, aren't we? You've surprised me again. You've chosen to use your Power to protect those in your care, rather than hoarding it against our confrontation. Perhaps I'll give you another day to recover.

That... seemed like too good to be believed. A list of all the things they could accomplish in one more day instantly began to run through his head... of all the things he could add to their defenses...

But then you'll likely squander yourself again. Go get some sleep little sorcerer-king. Tomorrow I will send for you.

And Damien found himself back in his body, shivering from head to toe. It was no longer from exhaustion – the unknown sorceress had given him a boost of Power that had filled him near to bursting. And it wasn't from cold – she'd dealt with that as well.

It was pure fear.

If she could – and *would* – warm him and give him Power to replace what he had used up in advance of her own coming battle with him... she must not care what he would do. What limitless Power-source must this woman *have* to behave like this?

Jason, she had not replenished, and his dear friend looked completely exhausted.

"That was her?" the tall knight – the Crown Prince and Duke of Emeralsee – asked, his voice rough.

Damien nodded. "And she gave me – *us* – a gift. Here."

He took Jason's hand and carefully, slowly, seeped some of the excess Power into him. It was like watching a plant un-wilt as you watered it. Energy came back into Jason's posture, his face smoothed out, and his eyes had sparkle and alertness again.

And with alertness, suspicion: "Why would she *give* you this Power before a battle... with *her?*"

And dawning understanding. "She knows she can't lose."

Abruptly Jason realized that Damien was shaking like an autumn leaf, and pulled the king close.

It didn't help.

"Genny!" he called in alarm.

She was squeezing herself onto the couch on Damien's other side in an instant, but he still couldn't stop shaking.

They were going to *lose* tomorrow. *He* was going to lose tomorrow. He couldn't protect his people, his city – his *wife*, his *friends*. His *child*, still too small to be seen by the naked eye if it were possible to see inside Genevieve's womb.

Jason pulled himself away as there was a pounding at the door.

"What, in the name of all the Gods, are you people *doing* up here?" Adam demanded as he came in and shut the door on the curious gazes of the Royal Guards.

He caught sight of Damien before Jason could begin to answer and swore with exasperation.

"Again?" he complained and threw himself onto the seat that Jason had just vacated and wrapped his arms around the younger man.

"He's not cold this time, so what's wrong?" Adam demanded, finally waiting for an answer. "What were you *doing* that would put him into this state?"

Jason raised his eyebrows at his husband. "We were bringing air and food and fuel to the trapped residents. Then the sorceress intercepted us. Damien told me to come back... but he delayed for some reason. And the sorceress *gave* him enough magickal Power to refill him – and me, too, when he came back."

"It's fear," Genevieve said with a sort of controlled calmness. "He's utterly terrified, but I can't get through to figure out *why.*"

"It's because the sorceress could afford to give us her Power, even before she faces him in battle," Jason said morbidly. "If she has the resources to do that, there's no way she can lose. We're doomed."

Damien managed to nod and felt Genevieve pull away, curling around herself in automatic reaction. Not that such a physical response could protect the unborn baby.

Adam shook his head. "Honestly, the lot of you. Genevieve, quit acting like a – like *that* – and put your strategist's hat back on. Your mysterious sorceress isn't telling you she has limitless Power. She's telling you she won't *need* her Power because they're going to attack in a way that nullifies Damien's advantage there. Think, woman! What could that be? If we can figure it out, we can try to find a way around it!

"And as for our own sorcerer here..." He sighed. "Shock therapy seems to be the only thing that's ever worked on this one when he gets himself into a state."

He glared at Jason. "Which *you* should know, having dealt with this *how* many times when we were getting him out of that bloody Library? Nevermind," Adam shook his head as Jason stared at him, "at least I have something less messy to try than dumping him in the horse trough this time."

Soft lips on his and a sense of love and security that enveloped him... Damien felt his muscles relaxing and he collapsed into safety – temporary though he knew in his heart that it was.

Safety had *always* been temporary for him. It was all the more to be cherished when it was available.

"*You* could have done this, Genevieve." Adam's voice continued on. "Either of you, really. You just let yourselves get sucked into his emotional tornado instead of thinking..." The rant was going on, Adam's voice berating the other two, though none of it was quite connecting for Damien.

He should apologize. This, too, was all his fault. The sense of warmth and security bopped him on the ego. It was *not* his fault.

"Adam," he whispered, and the half-argument he hadn't been able to focus on around him stopped. "You're a *projective* empath, too."

Adam snorted. "If that's what you want to call it. It's whatever it needed to be to teach you not to do this sort of thing. I'd have gone mad if I hadn't."

Genevieve sounded slightly dazed. "I've never *felt* that... not in *five years...*"

"Like I said, I taught him to keep it under control. When he was *sixteen.*" Adam shifted Damien to a more comfortable position in his arms. "I suppose I should be glad this worked. There's no horse trough handy up here."

Jason's voice was quizzical and amused at the same time. "I never did understand what was going on between the two of you. We'd just barely managed to extract the boy from the Library and suddenly you were dumping him in the nearest horse trough every other day. Though he was *seventeen* by then."

Dumping him in the horse trough and then holding him tightly, sometimes for as long as an hour...

"Reinforcement," Adam said with grim humor. "I'd gotten him to contain it in the confines of the Library, but when we brought him out in the big wide world..." He chuckled. "He nearly got himself dunked a time or two in Lynncrag. But he pulled it in before I got to him."

Damien sighed. "Your brothers got to me before you did. I had no idea how they even *knew...*"

He was still keeping his eyes closed, face buried into the safety of Adam's shoulder. Making the world small enough to handle. Gods, but he missed the simplicity of his life in the Library sometimes.

Genevieve nestled in to his other side and *that* bad idea vanished. A life that didn't include her was not worth living. "I had no idea you had the capacity to *do* that, Damien."

He opened his eyes to see her glorious blue-green ones, and Adam sighed with relief. "It's usually better once he can open his eyes again. You need to make the world as small as possible for him, Genevieve, remove or swamp out as many sensations as possible. It's why the horse trough works. Being suddenly wet – or better yet, *cold* and wet – is so overwhelming that it cuts off his ability to take in more sensations and thoughts that he can't cope with. I suspected that sexual arousal would do the same... looks like I was right."

Damien shook his head, still looking at Genevieve. "It wasn't that. It was feeling *safe*. You've always made me feel safe, Adam. You and Jason." He smiled a little shyly at his wife. "It might be more... the other... with you."

She smiled back, more relief than understanding in her eyes for now.

He wasn't ready to leave this envelope of warmth and security... and he was grateful that Adam made no effort to move away from him.

He could almost feel the other man's eyebrows rising, however. "We make you feel *safe*? I feel like we've been the ones forcing you into dangerous situations for the last fourteen years."

"Maybe *safe* isn't quite the right term," Damien agreed. "Maybe cared for or *secure*."

Adam kissed his hair. "That we can agree on, right Jase?"

He leaned a little away without releasing his hold on Damien, and the younger man guessed that Jason was sitting on Adam's other side.

"Always," Jason agreed.

"Now," Adam said firmly, "can you talk about what happened with the sorceress without spinning out of control again? Speaking of *projective empaths*." Damien didn't quite startle at the semi-accusation. It... had to be true, for Genevieve and Jason to have been trapped in his own emotional downspiral. And *stronger* than he'd been at sixteen or seventeen – no one but Adam had ever noticed then.

Or rather Adam *and* his family... no wonder the Baronetta had tried to mother him. She knew exactly what he was going through. And Adam's brothers must have been used to helping the younger ones contain themselves...

136

Damien shivered slightly. "I have to, don't I?"

They needed to know about the sorceress, even if it was the last thing he wanted to talk about.

Adam shook his head. "It won't do us any good to have more information if you can't handle talking about it. It would be better to pretend it all never happened and move forward in that case."

The king struggled to sit up independently. "Genevieve, before I forget. I 'stole' food and fuel from warehouses and butcher-shops and cheesemongers. We'll need to reimburse the merchants from the Treasury when this is all over."

"Do you remember how much and which ones?" she asked. "Can you make a list? If we just let the merchants come forward, we'll end up paying out for two to three times as much as you took – at a low estimate."

Damien winced. "I'll try. I should have asked you to keep track as we went, like we did with the ships this morning. I suppose... we could call it a national emergency and declare that the goods were taken by King's Right," he winced. "I hate to do that. It hurts honest merchants and walks the very edges of that fine line between benevolent despotism and tyrannical dictatorship."

"Do your best, love. We'll sort out what we need to."

"I remember some of them," Jason said dubiously. "I think."

"Economics aside," Adam reminded them, "We have a battle to fight, perhaps as early as tomorrow morning. If we aren't going to hash things out about this mysterious sorceress, we should all get some sleep. Or... *not* sleep and then sleep, yes, Jase." The feeling of warmth around him intensified, even though Damien could feel it wasn't directed towards him at all. He basked in it, not even wondering if he'd actually *heard* Adam's last words or not.

"No wonder he responds to you both," Genevieve said in a wondering tone. "Your love is so inclusive... so... all-enveloping. Oh. Adam... that's mostly *you*..."

"Sorceress?" Adam said emphatically. "Or bed?"

Damien nodded. "The attack will definitely be tomorrow. *Late* tomorrow is my impression. That might be the practical side of just having to melt their way through the Bay... but I got the feeling that the pirates prefer to attack at night. And... she said she'd *summon* me." He hesitated as he went back over that terrifying conversation. "No, I have that wrong. She said she'd 'send for' me. And then she gave me that gift of Power and sent me back."

They were all silent for a moment.

"Let's sleep on it," Genevieve said at last. "It doesn't make any sense that she would 'send for' you and you'd go to her. So, let's all think about how she might be able to make that happen."

"It can't be a matter of simply overPowering Damien," Adam warned. "From everything I've read, there can't be more than a couple of sorcerers more Powerful than him in the *world*. And it's *not* just his connection to the Realm."

Exactly so. The sound of a woman's aged voice in three of their heads startled everyone but Damien.

Stop that, Queen Marian said sharply as the Crown Prince went stiff.

"I... can see her..." Jason said dazedly.

Of course you can, grandson. And you, Champion, you can hear me using your own gifts, can't you?

Adam nodded warily, and Jason said, "But I could never see – or hear – you before. *I* haven't changed..."

Actually, you have, what with your Binding to the Realm and these two new soul-bonds and all. But, you're right. The most important part was **knowing** *that you're my grandson. At several removes, yes. Once I knew that, I could tell the Sword. It... started listening to me since it was effectively in my hand for over fifty years. You're right, Damien, it won't speak for anyone not* **known** *to be an Alsterling. I don't know why the person offering the Blade has to know how the person being tested is descended from the Alsterlings, but they do. The Sword apparently can't sense the connection itself, so it relies on its bearer. You were the best person to do that, with your extensive knowledge of the genealogies of the Realm.*

"This isn't really the best time to have this discussion, Grandmother," Genevieve suggested. "The Sword is the least of our worries right now."

No. It's not. Damien needs that Sword to focus the Realm's Power to fight magickal battles – but you could do that, too, as Queen or Heir. It's spoken for you both. This sorceress – and I don't know any more about her than you do – wants **Damien** *for some reason.*

"As an apprentice, she said..." he murmured.

Be that as it may be. You've had some experience with mind-controlled people, all of you. You can't allow Damien to take the Sword to her. Without the Sword, even if he remains Bound to the Realm, **she** *can't access the Power of the Realm.*

"You're saying we're going to lose him," Jason stated. His tone was as devoid of emotion as it only became when he had closed himself down.

I'm saying no such thing. Queen Marian's tone was very tart. *But we don't* **know** *what we'll be facing tomorrow. I'm just telling you not to let that bitch get her hands on my Sword.* **Or my Realm.**

Damien found himself smiling faintly that the long-deceased Queen was willing to use a word he was not.

Or my great-grand-baby, she added with more gentleness but no less fiercely. *Grand***babies***. And I count all of you as such. Jason, Adam, I have more instructions for you before you go to bed. Go on with you now. I'll be down momentarily. I need to talk to Damien and Genevieve.*

"I suppose we've been dismissed," Jason stood up and stretched.

"Try to get *some* sleep tonight," Adam said dryly, as he followed his husband.

"Thank you..." Damien said as they exited, and got a wave as the door shut in response.

The ancient ghost sat down on one of the chairs opposite the couch. The one Damien had been using all day as he vanished himself around the Castle. *Good. Now I need to tell you a few things, both of you.*

First, this baby is fine. I know **you** *can't tell yet, Damien, but I have... other sources. Genevieve, guarding this child is your duty* **above** *and* **beyond** *holding the Castle. If need be, you're to take the secret passages.*

Damien approved of this wholeheartedly and knew to keep his mouth shut to avoid giving his wife more to argue about.

To his surprise, however, she didn't complain. "The exit is still iced over. And it's within the city walls anyways."

I'll help with that if and when it becomes necessary. It's... sort of a one-shot option, and I won't be available to help with anything after that, so let's not borrow trouble, shall we. I rather enjoy my time with you, and I look forward to more than the one great-grandbaby.

"That sounds more promising," Genevieve said dryly. "Much less doom and gloom."

Humph. I call them like I see them, granddaughter.

Now, Damien. It's not in any of the books and scrolls I'm aware of, but there was a Queen of our line who was separated from the Realm by an evil sorcerer. She survived, and so did the Realm. I'm not sure how... but even if this mysterious sorceress gets the upper hand somehow, don't give up.

"And... it's back to the doom and gloom." Genevieve sighed.

"Did this Queen return to rule?" Damien asked. "Or was her Heir Bound to the Realm?"

Silence.

I don't know, Queen Marian admitted. *It's... a story. Passed down from ruling parent to ruling child. There are others.*

"Decided it was time to break with tradition, Grandmother?" Genevieve asked. "By *not* telling Damien until now? Or by telling me also?"

Oh, child, the ancient Queen's voice was tired, and she sagged her ghostly body into Damien's old favorite chair. *There was supposed to be* **years.** *My father trained me to be Queen for* **twenty** *years after the Sword spoke for me.* **His** *father trained* **him** *for twenty-* **five.** *The first five or ten were just the basics. The rest... the stories, the magick, the history and secrets... I should have sped things up for Damien. But he's had his hands full learning to rule on the fly and to manage magick the likes of which our Realm hasn't seen in centuries. If ever. I honestly thought there would be time. And some of the lessons... some of the* **secrets...**

She met the king's eyes. *They might make more sense to you than to me. I'm going to have to drag them up – things I memorized and then forgot – or rather set away in the far back of my own memories since they were things I didn't need and couldn't use for myself.*

"Spells?" Damien felt like he'd been punched in the gut. If Queen Marian had held the keys to the things he needed to know... the things he needed right now to defend his people, his city... his child...

I don't think so. Most of it is detritus, I suspect. Meaningless after centuries of being passed down, none of it committed to paper, so who knows what mistakes between speaking and hearing and committing to memory? She gave him a worried look. *Don't get yourself killed tomorrow, grandson. Come back so we can sort it out together. Or I'll be stuck trying to teach it all to this little girl of yours.* She caught his expression. *No, not Genevieve.*

A gift. Had she given him the gift to know it was a daughter, just as Adam had been insisting, because she didn't believe he'd come back?

Don't be an idiot, grandson. It's to give you more incentive to come **back.** *Do you seriously want* **me** *more involved in raising your daughter than* **you?**

Genevieve chuckled. "She's got you there, love. I don't think you even want *me* raising her more than you." She paused. "Maybe Adam."

As Damien ducked his head in embarrassment, Queen Marian chuckled also.

There's no shame in it, grandson. Genevieve and I are more of a kind than we might like to admit. The ghostly Queen exchanged an ironic glance with the live one. *We'll love our children, but you and your Champion have what it takes to raise them and make them* **know** *that they are loved. I never had someone to give my children that sense. She added regretfully. When Arthur – Anthony's father – died, he left me with a pack of toddlers. I didn't have the… the* **initiative** *after that to find another husband. Eventually I had lovers who came and went, but none willing to be a parent as well as a consort. Alexandria's father was… chosen out of desperate need. Your Jason's grandfather, Robert, and his brothers might have had some potential, but Reggie wasn't even married when I decided I had to do something. I had no idea Lindrea would come so close to reforming him – or to producing children with potential. If* **she'd** *lived…*

The ancient ghost shook her head.

Go to bed, children. And live every moment knowing how much you love each other.

Genevieve smiled and stood, extending her hand to her husband. "I think that's wonderful advice."

Damien gave her a wry look. "If not for that gift of Power, my beautiful love, I'd be sleeping out here. Stupid feet…" He vanished himself into the bedchamber and she followed on foot, laughing. "Goodnight, Grandmother," she said softly, closing the door.

Goodnight, children… Queen Marian took herself down a level to have a serious conversation with those two handsome men.

MANGALA MCNAMARA

Chapter TWELVE

The Beginning of the End

IT TOOK ALL DAY FOR the pirate ships to melt themselves a passage through the ice of the Bay to safe moorings in the Emeralsee harbor.

Duke Tomas forbade the King and Prince Jason to use their magick to track the progress of the enemy vessels. "We've plenty of telescopes for the job," he told them. "And telescopes don't wear out for looking through them, nor use themselves up. Save your strength."

Damien itched to refreeze the water as the sorceress melted it – but water... didn't *like* him all that well. Even if a significant chunk didn't have that evil *intent* still somehow impressed upon it, water tended to do whatever it pleased rather than what he requested of it. Fighting *that much* water into doing his bidding would unquestionably exhaust him and not have any clear and predictable result that they wanted to see. He had a million clever ideas about what he *could* do – if the water would only obey or he had an idea of the sorceress' limitations...

Jason had plenty to keep him busy without adding in magick. He was wholly occupied with ascertaining the level of skill of the various nobles who were willing to fight. They ranged from the portly Baron Rivencour of Flowerdell to Duchess Tariana Eledor to heroes of the Rebellion... from both sides. It was important to make sure that old enemies with feuds that still raged not be sited next to each other with edged weapons.

Genevieve was likewise busy. Since their strategy was to withstand a siege, there were siege-tactics for their chief strategist to review, and everything that was known about pirate tactics. And consultations with Captain Ancellius – as well as Lady Aryllis and Duke Zachary – regarding what should be done if the fight did come within the Castle walls.

Damien created his list of merchants and made sure it was left where it could be found later. He cast a binding spell on his office to make sure that the papers would be undisturbed, since it was one of the five warded rooms that would be used to shield the children and as many other non-combatants as possible. He contemplated warding the Library to protect it from pirates... then considered that it would then be packed full of rowdy children as another warded space and wisely decided to use his energies otherwise.

He was sending little spits of Power to free the Emeralsee Home Guard – the division of the Army assigned to the province. It was usually considered a rest-and-recuperation assignment, not a fighting deployment. He'd vanished notes to and from the general currently in residence: General Direlien, Commander of the Armies himself. They were working to dig themselves out... but appreciated every bit of ice Damien was able to melt away. Their barracks were, unfortunately, located outside the city wall, where there was sufficient space for proper training grounds among other things. But it meant that even once they were free of their buildings, it was a long, long way to the Castle. The king's other task was to melt a path for them.

Once those five thousand troops were free, however, they could break any siege. And once the pirates were disposed of, they could be turned to the more important work of freeing the citizens still trapped in their homes.

It also did not pass Damien's attention that the ice-storm had done more than crush Emeralsee: he had half a *Realm* to see recovered from this disaster.

Indeed, how *could* he avoid noticing, when Baron Raphael Anvliyar checked in with him regularly for any updates on the situation in Cedarwen Valley?

The only bright note came when Lord David Solway stopped by to thank him for accepting his younger children into the ranks of pages and squires – and Elaina as a lady-in-waiting.

"She'll surprise you. In good ways, I think," he said. A quiet, serious assessment, not that of a doting father. "I wanted her – all of them – to serve some time aboard a merchantman, but Alexa wouldn't hear of it. So, I did what else I could." He gave the king a dry look. "They're neither so spoiled nor so entitled as they appear, I promise you."

"She's already surprised me in good ways," Damien admitted. Though that was mostly because his expectations had been so very low. He had honestly not expected Elaina to pass Aryllis' assessment – on either the matter of physical defense skills *or* loyalty to the Crown.

"My family makes sure all our children are trained to defend themselves from a young age," Lord David explained. "It was one area Megan and I could see eye to eye on... though for entirely different reasons." He paused. "I'm sure the Queen has told you by now that we – the Metreedi Family – helped fund the Rebellion. I came here originally with my older brother, who was Heir to our House, to assess whether it was either morally or economically viable to continue trade here. It's how I met Megan." He took a deep breath. "I kept the Rebellion's supplies of goods and money flowing through Brindlewell without Alexa's knowledge."

Damien regarded the slight man with more interest. "Genevieve mentioned something about that," he said. "Though I don't think she ever mentioned *your* connection."

"I doubt she knew," David replied. "My usefulness could last only so long as almost no one was aware of my personal involvement. I worked through other channels. My brother Veren found the whole thing rather amusing," he said dryly. "He has a strange sense of humor."

"Brindlewell could have been a bottleneck for the Rebels," Damien suggested.

"For physical supplies, certainly, though there are other routes for those," David agreed. "My larger role was to make sure they retained access to the banks – in Deltheren, Mercasia, and Vindalia, as well as across the sea in Dawil."

"But not in Sindala?"

"Nothing seems to move through Sindala, Your Majesty," David answered. "I've heard it was once a prosperous land, but it came upon dark times some hundreds of years ago. I've never understood why Farivera defected to them, even to escape from your grandfather's rule. It seems like it would be jumping from the frying pan into the fire." He paused. "We don't even hear much of the lands beyond Sindala, though that might be due to the mountains and the high cliffs. We have trade with nations much farther to the south along the Merutian Sea, but nothing in direct contact with Sindala."

"Well, if the Metreedi family doesn't trade there, there must be nothing worth trading for," Damien said graciously.

David shrugged. "I wanted to assure you of the support of my family, Your Majesty. When this is all over," he waved a hand to suggest ice, pirates, and all, "we'll be ready to help you rebuild." He smiled wryly. "Most of The Family thought it was foolish to bet on the Stellarines in your civil war, but my brother Veren – and myself – felt that the moral imperative was with the Rebels. We couldn't have anticipated Your Majesty's ability to salvage the situation, of course. Veren is Head of House now, and our investments in keeping Elaarwen and Siovale viable and their assets fluid have already been paid back because they were able to re-integrate into Ilseador so smoothly and because trade has grown so spectacularly under Your Majesty's reign after being suppressed for so long under King Reginald. I think it will be an easy sell to The Family to offer you loans and other assistance after this disaster."

"Thank you," Damien said automatically. "You understand, of course, that I'll have to look at the details of any offers."

David bowed fluidly – like the assets he managed, apparently. "Of course. We pride ourselves on doing honorable business, but we may not understand your needs and preferences as well as we think. Every offer is subject to negotiation." He hesitated, then added, "We have a common enemy in the pirates, Your Majesty. Every Metreedi in the world has fought pirates or lost someone who has. It's a dream of most of my younger cousins to find the so-called Pirate Isles and burn them out." The light in Lord David's eyes suggested it was not just his 'younger cousins' who shared that dream. "Keep us in mind when you seek to chastise the sea-rats."

It was one of the stranger conversations Damien had that long day.

His feet were feeling better, at least. The accelerated Healing had gotten them far enough that he could tolerate soft, indoor half-boots that looked rather like tall, somewhat stylish slippers. He could even stand briefly. He stayed off of them as much as possible, hoping that tonight he'd be able to stand on the wall and look down at the pirates as they approached. *And* on his personal nemesis.

At last, the word came, from those manning the Castle's telescopes, that the pirates had reached the docks. Lord David happened to be in range of the king's view, so he saw the man wince when it was announced that the pirates were burning merchantmen to clear moorage for their own vessels.

Damien wondered about David's own experiences with pirates.

"Missed opportunities," Genevieve muttered irritably from behind him. "We should have put barrels of flour on all of those ships and had you light them. I'm not used to thinking about naval situations... it didn't occur to me that those ships were doomed anyways."

"Flour?" Damien was startled.

She gave him a grimly humorous look. "Didn't you read that report about the flour mill in Embervest that exploded last year? When the flour dust gets into the air, a spark can set the whole cloud off."

"I read it..." Damien was thinking quickly. "Can I vanish a bag of flour over their heads and set it off?"

Genevieve shook her head. "It needs to be in a confined space. It's the heat that makes the air around the dust expand and break the container. It's the shards of the container that are the real problem."

"A barrel... flour..." Damien muttered aloud, thinking rapidly. "Adam!" he called out, knowing that the Champion was hovering nearby – he'd been barely out of the king's arms-reach all day – but that his eagle eyes were more focused on the mob of squires than on his king. For once.

"Your Majesty?" Adam appeared at his side.

"I need a barrel. Half-filled with flour. And a barrel of sand. The sand first, if possible. And someone who knows how to seal barrels."

Adam gave him a baffled look, but didn't argue, thank all the Gods at once.

"Damien?" Genevieve wasn't arguing, but she was curious what he was planning.

"I'm going to create shards of glass and add them to the flour barrel," he explained. "We'll seal the barrel and place it in front of the pirates. I set a spark in the barrel, and..."

"And with any luck, we'll cut down a few pirates," Genevieve nodded. "Just one?"

"Just one to start. I've never done this before. There's a zillion things that could go wrong. Start thinking about where you want it to go."

It took too long to find the things he'd asked for, but almost no time for Damien to create glass and break it into shards. They got the flour barrel sealed with the glass shards in it, and Damien vanished it onto the lead pirate ship and set the spark inside. Nothing happened.

The pirates, meanwhile, were not treating the mysterious arrival without suspicion. Damien vanished it back to the Castle just in time to prevent them from heaving it into the Bay. Frustrated, the king sent his awareness into the barrel, then looked up in alarm and vanished it right back to the pirate ship.

Shouts from the telescope-watchers on top of the wall directed everyone's attention to the plume of fiery smoke rising from the direction of the Bay. It had simply taken longer to ignite than he had anticipated.

Damien ignored the feel of the pirates in pain – none dying, that he could tell. They were in his Realm now, so the Realm considered them 'his' people.

Damien looked at his wife and his Champion.

"The glass shards need to be heavier," was all he said.

Adam was already ordering more barrels.

It didn't take half the time to prepare the next three as it had the first, but now they had a new problem. It was no longer possible to vanish objects onto the pirate vessels; some sort of spell prevented him. Genevieve quickly directed him to put the already-lit barrels among the disembarking pirates. They did some damage, but not as much as the defenders had hoped.

"Could you... drop the barrels on them from above?" Genevieve asked dubiously.

Damien frowned. "I *could...*"

"If the goal is to get glass shards into pirates," Adam suggested, "Why not the idea you told me about when we were discussing our visit to the glassworks awhile back? A large sheet, and someone shoots it with an arrow... except..."

"Except why bother with the arrow!" Damien exclaimed. Adam nodded.

The king got to work turning sand into glass and handing it to a pack of squires to break – carefully – into an empty barrel. When the barrel was almost full, Damien vanished the contents – but not the barrel – to the space over the leading set of pirates.

The men with telescopes reported that the deadly rain of shards caused a fair amount of confusion. Confusion was good – but it wasn't as *deadly* as they needed it to be. Damien could *feel* that there were only a handful of fatalities, if rather more casualties.

It was taking a lot of magickal effort from him – for very little result.

Worse, he could *feel* the blaze of Power that was the sorceress. Somehow, he'd missed her when he was surveying the ships, but once she'd begun melting them a passageway to the harbor, he hadn't been able *not* to feel her presence.

And worse still: that blaze didn't seem to be dimming at *all* as she came closer.

It *should* have taken a vast amount of energy to accomplish what she had done. Damien knew just how much, from his own experiments with melting airholes for his stranded people, and de-icing the Castle, and trying to prepare a path for the Army.

There was no way she should have been able to glow that brightly to his inner sense after using up that much Power.

None.

Unless the source she was drawing on was more limitless than his own vast Realm.

Was he preparing to fight a Queen Bound to her own land? Was this actually Queen Estelle of Deltheren, who had somehow outflanked them and was now attacking from entirely the wrong direction to mislead them?

There were no rumors, he'd had no *sense,* that Estelle had such abilities. Yet... if he hadn't had to reclaim his throne from Harald so dramatically, mightn't Damien have hidden his magick? To prevent those worried and speculative looks around dark corners that he caught... and that loathsome title of 'Sorcerer-King' that he shared with his unlamented grandfather?

Who *was* this woman? And *what* were her powers?

He wanted very much to 'go out' and take a closer look at his nemesis. Possibly using Jason's Seeing Eye to view her physical form.

But Jason was busy. And both Tomas and Genevieve agreed he should hoard his strength.

Glass... what other tools did he have from his migrations through the artisans of the city?

The trouble was that there was just so little to work with right now. Early Winter had everything battened down, physically and magickally both. And what little was left had been iced in place. There was nothing to weave, to forge... No animals to call to the city's defense, no plants to spur to sudden, wild growth.

There were only the elements themselves: air and earth and water. And fire. He'd spent less time on those, feeling them the province of the priestesses and the Gods. He knew Earth best of all of those, but the living part of the soil mostly. The insects and snails and worms, right down to the tiny life that he had no names for that nonetheless made up the greater part of the soil and its fertility.

Damien's true role, he had always thought, was to *Heal.* To Heal the land. To Heal the people. To Heal the animals and plants. It was all he wanted...

But it was not all he was called on to do, clearly.

And a Healer... knew better than any other how to hurt, and hurt so deeply that there was no recovery.

The Realm claimed all humans within its boundaries, as he had been so direly reminded when he damaged those pirates with the first flour barrel. He could affect them. He could... *hurt* them.

What he didn't know was whether he would still be *himself* after such a dark act. Was saving his people right now worth taking a step down that path? Could he live with himself afterwards?

Could he live with himself if he... didn't?

"Damien? What's wrong?"

It was said in a low, quiet voice, to avoid alarming the nervous people all around them. Adam was squatting in front of him, and Damien realized he had leaned forward, head in his hands, curled around himself.

"Are you cold?" His Champion asked. "You're the only one sitting still... those feet... I should have guessed..." But the look in Adam's eyes said that he had picked up on the king's emotional turmoil more than any physical need.

At least... at least he wasn't projecting his own fears onto those around him. Adam had, indeed, taught him not to do *that*.

"It's not that," the king managed to croak. Slowly, in halting words, he managed to explain his dilemma. A haunted expression came into Adam's eyes as he did so.

"I... could probably do something, too, couldn't I? With this... *projective empathy* of mine." The tall Champion shook his head. "We had eighty-three years of rule by an evil wizard, Damien. I don't think it's worth risking. Even if..."

Adam swallowed hard, clearly thinking about his entire family here, his parents and siblings so long estranged from him. His little nephews that he'd never met before last week. *Jason*. Genevieve and the baby. Friends and rivals and students... Adam had bloody well *taught* most of the knights when they were squires... they were all his children he hadn't yet had...

The Champion tried again. "Even if everyone here died, even if the pirates wreaked havoc on the city... there's still Lord Aldred up in Elaarwen to rally the Realm."

Damien dropped his eyes and repeated the numbers he'd given Jason last night. "Three hundred thousand people in the city. Two *million* in the Realm."

None of them deserved another tyrant.

But... none of them deserved to die right *now*, either.

Adam sighed. "We need our *Healer*-King. And I... need my friend. My... more-than-friend."

Damien looked up sharply. It was almost too much to say in this public venue, even so obliquely, and despite the fact that everyone else was dashing around involved in their own tasks.

Adam's golden-hazel eyes shone with compassion... and understanding... And suddenly Damien realized just how much of the Champion's cynical, sardonic mask was just that: a way to hide how deeply he cared. He'd seen more of that side of Adam recently...

"Thank you..." Aware of the watching eyes – he had planted himself in his chair in the main courtyard so that he was accessible after all – the king added, "It *is* colder than I anticipated while I'm just sitting here."

The Champion nodded and stood up. "I'll see that you get something to keep you warmer, Your Majesty. We want you at your best." The sardonic glint was back in his eye; his mask securely back in place.

And Damien then had to put up with being swathed in a quilt and having hot stones placed by his feet.

It helped, actually. He *had* been cold and not realized it – Damien typically used a small stream of magick without even realizing it to see to his bodily comforts, and normally never felt the drain. Right now, when he was husbanding every last iota of Power, the seepage was noticeable and he'd halted it.

The sun was setting as the mass of pirates was reported to be moving again. At least the estimates of numbers from the telescope-watchers were slightly below the king's initial ones. Presumably crew were being left on board to guard the ships, although against what possible retaliation the scanty force of defenders could not imagine.

Nor did it make that much of a difference, since there were still close to eight hundred in the mob that was approaching. Well over double that of the defenders.

If this were a normal military situation – a normal well-built and provisioned castle facing a siege – there would have been no reason to fear. The walls were stout and smooth, the moat well-maintained. They had a force more than six times that of the would-be-besiegers ready to break any attempts to isolate them in the next day or two.

But a *normal* castle wasn't surrounded by a city the size of Emeralsee.

At least the ice was keeping his subjects off the streets and out of harm's way. It should even protect them from the pirates to some extent: the reivers should find it as difficult to set fires or chip their way *in* to assault the vulnerable as the Ilseadorans were having in getting *out*.

If this were only a normal situation it would all be fine.

But it was impossible not to believe that there was something very *abnormal* about the entire thing.

Pirates – even whole fleets of them, and how often did *they* ever work together like this anyways? – didn't, as a rule, attack large cities and monarchs. They didn't work together with unknown sorceresses.

They had to have some trick up their sleeves. Some secret lever that they intended to pull to sway the impossible odds in their favor. And to do it *quickly,* before the Ilseadoran Army was free to eliminate them as a threat.

Genevieve was pacing furiously, cudgeling her brain for what play the pirates might try to make. She'd drawn Lord David into her confidences now, and, as the shadows grew dark enough that lanterns were being lit, was quizzing him on what a former Metreedi ship's captain might know that a land-bound strategist might not.

It was at this point that Damien ordered that the children and other non-combatants were to be hustled away into the five warded rooms as planned. Duke Zachary Miramar carried baby Betha with him as he checked each room to make sure the people listed for the space were within, down to the last hyperactive page. There were adults in each room in charge of the food and the ward-cords – with instructions to guard the door to prevent anxious or excited children from undoing the wards to hunt down parents or older siblings. At the very last, he gave over baby Betha to her nurse, kissed little Talia, and stepped away to be warded out. He wiped his eyes, straightened his spine, and went to his assigned position; he was a trained fighter as well, after all, having come within a year of earning his own shield before so abruptly and unexpectedly inheriting his position as Count of Dalizell.

Ladies-in-waiting clustered by each of the warded rooms as well as the rooms where other non-combatants had been sent. They were supplemented by those nobles whose fighting skills were rusty but good enough to help, and those Castle staff who were ready to fight – and unable to fit in the protected spaces. Damien had long ago asked Madame Elista not to hire children, due to his own fears that the Power in the Castle might twist them somehow, but he'd asked Zachary to put as many of the younger staff into the warded spaces as he could. It was their sacred duty as nobles Bound to the Realm to protect their people after all.

The rest – men-at-arms and knights and nobles with more up-to-date fighting skills – were ranged around the Castle walls. Damien was surprised to see Jason's sister, Megan, dressed in what must be borrowed hunting leathers and carrying a borrowed sword.

His bemused expression must have given him away: Jason gave him a wry grin. "Who did you think gave me my first lessons with a sword?"

There was a shadow of pain behind that statement... had those been 'lessons' meant only to give her an excuse to thrash him? And had he kept going back because his mother ordered him, because he was desperate to learn *some*thing that might bring him honor and value... or because it was the only way to get Megan's attention?

Would Damien *ever* know the rest of that story? He resolved to ask – if they made it out of this tonight.

Lord David had found something closer to a pirate's cutlass somewhere and was staying close to his wife after apparently having satisfied the queen's questions as best as he could.

Damien relocated himself – *and* his chair, though he was getting Gods-awfully sick of sitting around, *and* Adam, who was on bodyguard duty – to the top of the wall just over the main gate. Tomas, Genevieve, Jason, and Tim were already there, their eyes focused beyond the moat, beyond the far side of the city's main market square.

The iced-over reviewing stand drooped sadly there, a remnant of the festivities of so few days ago, the abandoned ribbons and rosettes in the royal colors sagging heavily under their weight of ice.

They were watching for the arrival of the pirates.

They could hear them – chanting bawdy songs, it sounded like – and, as the very air seemed to turn blue with evening, the orangey glow of the torches they carried also marked their approach. Damien forced himself to stay seated; like as not he'd need his feet later, if only because he'd forget and stand up.

He didn't need to *try* to sense the sorceress. She was blazing with Power, and just as brightly as ever... *how?*

How became blatantly obvious as the mob began to pour into the market square.

They were led by three tiny creatures glowing as brightly – no, much, *much* more brightly – than all the torches put together.

"Salamanders..." Damien breathed. Not the timid amphibians he was familiar with, but the fire-elementals he knew only by legend. He *really* should have spent more time learning about the magickal elements...

The salamanders were clearly *leashed* in some way, but Damien could detect no Binding. Nonetheless, they wandered around the square, great gouts of steam going up in their wake. They never went beyond the limits of the square, nor interfered with the humans in their wake in any way.

Damien found it hard to take his eyes off of them – they were beauty and grace and Power of a caliber that seemed to be somehow *beyond* mere magick … at least as he understood it..

The attention of his companions, however, was quickly taken by the mob of pirates pouring into the square behind them. The king had estimated that on a busy market day that space held close to ten thousand people at once – it would have easily swallowed to insignificance the mere eight or nine hundred of the pirates if they hadn't all been wielding torches and bristling with weapons. And chanting bawdy, bloody ballads.

"'Ware their grappling hooks," Lord David had made his way to the side of the command group, presenting himself as their local expert on pirates. And rightly so. "If they get lines onto the walls, they'll swarm up them like the cockroaches they are."

Tim looked briefly startled when he realized who had spoken, then nodded sharply and passed the word along.

"Familiar with the ways of pirates?" Duke Tomas asked with a lifted eyebrow. He had probably never been introduced to Countess Solway's son-in-law, but he clearly knew who Lord David was.

Lord David shrugged. "I'm a Metreedi. And as His Majesty noted the other day, I gave up a captaincy to marry Megan."

"Wish you'd spoken up earlier," Tomas told him, perhaps not having noticed David doing precisely that with Genevieve. "We're land-fighters here, one and all."

Lord David gave him a fierce grin. "You're *fighting* on land, Your Grace. If I'd seen any chance at saving the ships at harbor... but against *eighteen* pirate vessels? Not a chance. At least our people were all ashore in anticipation of the ice-storm. Despite their preferences, I'm sure," he added. "A captain doesn't abandon her ship, as a rule."

"Hmph." Tomas turned his attention back to the mob of pirates. They seemed to be waiting for something.

Or someone.

And *not* the sorceress.

A tall man stepped forward from the mass, sensibly clad in a metal helm and breastplate against projectiles from the castle, though most of his fellows seemed to have no more protection than thick furs and perhaps boiled leather. It was a pity Ilseador wasn't much known for its bowmen... some of Genevieve's mountain hunters in remotest Elaarwen might have made the shot to topple even this better-armored leader, but not the knights and men-at-arms stationed in the Castle now. They didn't even have catapults, more was the pity, but the Castle had been morphing into a residential palace for too long. Likely they were simply lucky to have the walls and moat intact.

Long, pale hair and beard shone orange and gold in the shifting light from the torches and the salamanders. The sword he held casually in his hand was surely as massive as Jason's broadsword.

The crowd of pirates quieted at a motion of his free hand.

"Where's the scurvy dog who calls himself king of this land?" roared out the man – and despite the volume it was clear his accent was their own. He sounded less foreign than Lord David did after over twenty-five years in Ilseador. A man of *their own people* led this invading force, this bloodthirsty mob.

Damien could hear the unsettled muttering of his subjects along the battlements as he stood up and leaned onto the top of the wall in an embrasure, bracing his weight on his knee to keep it off his feet. At least the pirates had no bows of their own either.

"That would be me, I suppose," he called down.

"And are you not also the son of that damned lying bastard, Eric? The tyrant's own handpicked successor?"

The king frowned at that. He had never heard anyone speak of his father, save in respectful or even regretful tones. He knew Genevieve was giving him a worried look. "I am Crown Prince Eric's son, yes. And both of us were named Heir by King Reginald. You seem to have the advantage of me, however. Would you care to give us *your* name?"

"I'm known widely as the Scourge of the Sea, Captain of the Red Sails, and King of the Pirate Isles," the man returned, and the mob roared its approval.

He quieted them again, and continued, "But *you* would know me as Evan Alsterling – and rightful Heir to the Throne of Ilseador!"

Mangala McNamara

Chapter THIRTEEN

The End of the Beginning

D AMIEN BLINKED. HE *FELT* JASON to his left, gone numb with shock.

Genevieve laughed from the next embrasure down, the crown of a crenelation partially blocking her from Damien's view. "We have a tradition here – you may have heard of it. The Monarch's Blade chooses who will rule. You may – or may not – be Evan Alsterling, but you've no claim on the Throne unless the Sword gives its approval. Come back tomorrow in the daylight and we'll test out your claim."

"I've waited near thirty-five years to claim my throne, *Duchess,*" the Pirate-King roared back. "And to claim my bride. And *our son.* I'll *wait* no longer."

"If he wants Alexa, he can *have* her," Adam muttered behind Damien, bringing a small smile to the king's lips, "but he doesn't get *Jason.*" He paused. "*Or* the Throne."

"Agreed," Damien said softly.

But now there was a disruption, and running feet, and an incredulous voice shouting, "*Evan?* I didn't think you were still alive, little brother!"

Damien sighed. No point now in trying to bluster through with the idea that this man was not whom he claimed.

The Pirate-King didn't seem impressed. "Looked *that hard* for me, did you, Eugenio?"

Sir Angelos was pulling his father back from the wall, arguing with him about something. The older man shook his son off and looked back out. "We did what we could, Evan. We could find no trace of you." He paused. "The king – King *Reginald–*" Baron Eldridge glanced Damien's way, almost apologetically, "–ordered us to stop looking."

The pirates made a huge noise of booing sounds, until Evan settled them again.

"*You* were just as glad to see me gone, *I'll* wager," he roared out bitterly. "But I've made my *own* place and – by the Sea-Queen's Honor – I'll *take* back what should have been mine. The *Crown*. The *wife*. The *son!*"

"This sounds familiar," Genevieve said dryly, leaning back from her own embrasure to look her husband in the eye as the pirates roared their approval again. Harald's words of five years ago, when he had briefly usurped the throne.

"He's added a new twist," Damien replied lightly. He looked at Tomas. "Orders, Field Marshal? Keep him talking or just let the battle begin?"

Tomas looked at him with a fierce glint in his eye, but before he could speak, a smooth, feminine voice spoke. It filled the square and swarmed up the wall of the Castle without seeming to shout at all.

"Evan, my dear. Let's not bother with all this masculine shouting and pounding of chests. We know what we want. Let's claim it and be done."

A slim, figure glided forward, glowing a soft, white light.

She was short, the sorceress, and barely seemed a woman grown. The white light seemed to exist solely for the purpose of showing off her long, pale hair and her pure white gown. She looked up with eyes that Damien was sure were huge and a soft, pale color – straight at him.

You will come to me now, my sorcerer-king.

"It's her, isn't it?" Genevieve asked. Damien couldn't – *daren't* – take his eyes off the tiny woman. He nodded.

"And what do *you* want, little girl?" the Queen asked in a bored tone.

The waif turned her gaze to Genevieve, and Damien sagged, grateful for Adam's hand on his arm supporting him. "You would be the soul-bonded Queen. How quaint. I'll lift that burden for you, my dear. I would say you could rule in your own name as a woman should – but dear Evan wants your crown for himself, I'm afraid."

She turned back to the king. "Come down here, King Damien. And bring... what was your lady's name, Evan? Oh, yes. Bring Lady Megan Solway with you."

Megan? *Megan?*

Damien looked at Jason, then over to Lord David, standing just beyond Tomas. The man looked utterly unsurprised... but just days ago he had sworn that Megan had come a virgin to their marriage-bed – when Jason was some twelve years old. No... David hadn't *sworn*, Damien's always accurate memory clarified – the king just hadn't imagined anyone could be bold enough to lie to him in the *Throneroom*, and while Damien held the Monarch's Blade unsheathed, no less. David had simply *agreed* when the king asked him.

The Sword made sure it's *bearer* told the truth, the king thought wryly. It apparently did nothing for anyone else in the vicinity. Something it would doubtless be important to bear in mind for the future.

Lord David shrugged. "I lied, Your Majesty," he admitted candidly. "You'd do the same to protect *your* lady. You'd managed to rehabilitate Evan's history enough to help Jason. Neither you nor he needed the rest of the story, I thought... And since Megan wasn't ready to tell him..." David's eyes rested on the Heir regretfully.

Clearly Lord David Solway – the former *Captain Daffyd Metreedi* – was a man to be watched. And perhaps not entirely trusted, for all that Damien couldn't really disagree with the assessment. What this might say about the man's far-flung merchant family, the king couldn't begin to guess... though David's demeanor suggested that he might not be the *only* Metreedi to take crowned heads at rather less than what might be considered their due.

"Now why would my royal husband ever do that?" Genevieve called down to the would-be usurper and the sorceress in a scornful voice and ignoring the discussion going on immediately to her back and sides.

The waif looked at her again, amusement clear on that small, innocent-looking face, even at this distance. "Your husband will come down here, Queen Genevieve, and he will come away with me and do as I bid. Because if he does not, I will loose my salamanders upon the city and let my pirate friends here have their usual sort of fun. And he can choose to try to stop them... or to stop *me*. I guarantee he hasn't the ability to do *both*."

The threat the salamanders posed didn't need to be explained to anyone. Even after melting through the harbor and up the streets to the Castle... They were clearly still capable of setting the city ablaze.

"Yourself and my sweet Megan down here, *now*, Bastard-King!" the Pirate-King thundered.

More running feet along the battlements. Lord David caught his wife in his arms before she could be spotted from below and began whispering fiercely to her.

Jason turned to look at her, his face blank, disbelieving.

Damien looked at Genevieve.

"She's right," he said quietly. "I can't fight her *and* contain the salamanders – I don't even know how to contain *just* the salamanders."

He gave her an anguished look. "Love... maybe... maybe if I give myself up, they'll go away and leave the rest of you."

He looked at Megan and David, having their own tearful, quiet argument. "Well, myself and Megan, it looks like."

"Damien, *no*. Once they have you, they have no reason to leave..." Genevieve disagreed. "Tomas, Adam, tell him..."

But Damien was already leaning out again. "If I come down, magick is out of play in this? No salamanders burning my city? No spells attacking my people?"

The pale sorceress' honey-like voice filled the space again. She must be augmenting it with magick; it neither looked nor sounded as if she was even raising her voice beyond the sort of polite tone one would expect over a tea-table.

"You come down, Sorcerer-King, and come with me, and my pets and I will go as well."

"*Azella!*" The Pirate-King roared. "That was *not* the deal! You said you'd help me win my *throne!*"

The pirates began to clamor again as well, this time beating weapons on shields to make even *more* noise.

The waif turned her huge eyes on Evan, and the mob fell silent.

"You should know better than to assume any deal I made with you would last longer than was convenient for *me*, O 'Scourge of the Seas.' I promised to take the Sorcerer-King from his throne and to see your lady in your arms again. *You* claimed you could take it from there." She smiled silkily. "I am not called Azella the Unpitying for nothing."

Damien felt a spurt of hope. If he and Megan Solway went down there, it fulfilled the sorceress – Azella's – contract with the pirates. And now he had her word that she would take herself and her salamanders – and *him* – away from the impending battle if he did so. Assuming she would, again, stick to the strict letter of her word.

His people could withstand a normal siege. The Army, with its five thousand soldiers should be here sometime tomorrow. The next day at worst.

And something told him that *salamanders* were but the least of this sorceress's arsenal.

Damien pulled himself out of the embrasure.

"Genevieve. I *have* to do this."

"Damien, *no* – Tomas, Adam, Jason... *tell him...*"

But Jason was frozen in place. He only had eyes for the tall, pale-haired woman weeping in her husband's arms.

Megan looked up at last and saw him. "Oh, Jason, my sweet boy. I know you can never forgive me..."

Jason merely looked at her.

Adam spoke for him. "So, it's true? *You* are Jason's mother, *not* Alexa?"

Megan nodded, tears running silently down her cheeks as she met Jason's gaze hopelessly.

David spoke for *her*. "She was only fourteen when Jason was born. And Alexa had convinced both of them that they had shamed themselves and their families. She wed Evan herself – and she kept him in her bed. And then she sent Evan away in disgrace with her false accusations after Jason was born – she kept Megan in seclusion at one of their manor houses in the back of beyond at Brindlewell so no one would know. And then she set about brainwashing Megan to believe she had to accept those terrible stories as the only way they could move their lives forwards."

He shook his head sadly, his arms still tight around his weeping wife. "I don't know how much of that was at King Reginald's orders... and how much of it was her own vicious personality at work. Megan told *me* the truth... eventually. But only because things seemed *wrong* enough that I kept digging. And... she still bought into Alexa's stories about Evan until last week. I don't think she dared do otherwise."

Lord David focused on the new-made Duke and Prince. His... step-son. "I *did* do my best for you, Jason, poor little though it was."

"And now... now I have to *go*..." Megan said brokenly. "David... I don't want *him*... I don't want to leave *you*... but if it means you and the children will survive... *all* the children..."

Her eyes flickered to Jason, but wouldn't settle.

Damien pulled Genevieve close and kissed her over her protests. David, it seemed had run out of arguments sooner than Damien's Warrior-Queen.

Genevieve stopped protesting, and kissed him back, passionately as if by sheer force of will she could keep him there. He wrapped her in his love through the soul-bond, then gently disentangled himself from her arms and sank to one knee.

"I love you, too, little Giendra Marlerite," he said to her abdomen. "Be good to your mother."

He felt Adam start at hearing the names he and Genevieve had discussed. He didn't yet know that Queen Marian had told them it really was a girl. He didn't dare look at Adam's face.

The king stood up again and looked at Tomas. "Keep them safe, my friend. Keep them *all* safe." Tomas gripped his arm and pulled him into a rough embrace.

"My duty to the Realm," the duke muttered.

"Jason..." Damien looked at his oldest friend, but Jason seemed to have gone somewhere inside himself and didn't respond. "Adam... tell him..."

He threw his arms about his Champion. "*You* know."

The words he wanted to say to them – his *other* loves – he didn't dare. Genevieve and the baby would need every bit of legitimacy that he could leave them. Not scandal.

"Damien," Adam began, but still distracted by Jason's frozen state. "You can't..."

"I have to. Lady Megan." Damien started to hold out his hand, then stopped. "Damn. I almost forgot."

He unbuckled his swordbelt and handed Sword, belt, and scabbard to Genevieve. Or he tried. She just stood there, staring at him, her face blank with disbelief that he was really doing this. Always, always in their time together it had been *she* who took the physical risks, who put herself in the way of danger. If Damien had done so, it was by following her lead, as in the re-taking of the Castle.

He shook his head in mild exasperation and thrust the scabbarded Blade into Jason's hands.

Jason, who would no more let a weapon fall than speak an unkind word. To anyone, no matter how deserving.

The Crown Prince's hands automatically took it, not noticing what he accepted, his eyes still fixed on Megan.

Damien swallowed hard. "Lady Megan. It's time."

He held out his hand, and she took it, still not raising her eyes to Jason's. Lord David stood behind her, his arms crossed and his expression disapproving – but not trying to forbid his wife of a quarter-century the right to make her own decision. Or to follow her king's directive.

The king didn't try to meet Lord David's eyes.

"Damien, you are *not*–" Adam began, grabbing his shoulder as Genevieve cried out and Tomas held her back from reaching for her husband.

And then they were in the market square, on the far side of the moat.

Damien, Lady Megan... and Sir Adam Loveress Alsterling, the King's Champion.

"–facing pirates, that's my job," Adam finished. And shook his head. "Really? I thought we talked about thinking things through *first* and *then* acting. When you were *fifteen.*"

He stepped in front of the other two and drew his sword.

"Sixteen," Damien said weakly. "Adam, I'm sending you back–"

He hadn't expected Adam to touch him, hadn't specifically tried to exclude him from being carried along.

His eyes had been on Genevieve. He could never think straight when she was crying...

He couldn't do this to Jason...

"Don't you *dare*," Adam snarled over his shoulder. "This is my *job.* Your *Majesty.*"

"And who do you think *you* are?" Evan Alsterling glared at the Champion.

"Sir Adam Loveress, King's Champion," Adam growled. "You want His Majesty, you go through *me.*"

"He's also Prince Adam Alsterling, *Father,*" Jason called down, and the Pirate-King's eyes locked on the tall, golden-haired knight who looked so much like him. "And my beloved *husband.*"

Jason's voice was as calm as ever – as calm as the day he had offered to face all of Siovale's men-at-arms as Damien's Champion. The day he had only backed down because Damien ordered him to – and no matter that Harald's men had been torturing Adam before their very eyes.

The king was sure that only he and Adam and Genevieve could *feel* the naked fear in Jason's heart. He only felt a shadow of it himself, filtered through his awareness of the other two.

"I'd suggest that I'll come down there and skewer you myself if you harm so much as one hair of Adam's head," Jason continued, "*or my king's,*" he added as an afterthought, the hesitation almost enough to make Damien smile. "But since you face the finest swordsman in the Realm, I don't think I have anything to worry about."

The king could see the wry expression on his Champion's face as Jason verbally ceded that coveted title to his husband. Last he knew, Jason still won two bouts out of three with Adam. He wondered if Adam had won their last bout.

"So, Alexa let you live, boy." There was a hunger in the pirate-king's eyes that Damien knew only too well. From both sides of the equation, actually. He and Jason – and Evan – had grown up without their fathers. And now Damien was leaving his unborn daughter...

"If you want to call it that." It was the first trace of bitterness that Damien could recall hearing from his friend's mouth. "But you knew that. If you knew that Damien was crowned king, you certainly know all about *my* life."

The implicit challenge – why hadn't he ever come back? Or made contact with Jason in any way?

The pirate-king looked away from Jason's challenge and focused on his... son-in-law, standing with his blade naked between them.

"I'm not fighting you, Loveress." He looked past Adam. "I don't want your king anyways. Just his crown and his throne and his Sword. *She's* the one who wants the king."

Evan Alsterling gestured at the sorceress.

And then he grinned a broad, barbaric grin. "And I think he's decided to give himself up to her, regardless of what *you* may have to say about it. *I* just want my sweet Megan."

He glanced upwards again, but didn't add to that.

The sorceress still seemed diminutive, even at this closer range. Damien had barely been able to focus on the bluster between the pirate-king, Adam, and Jason for the sheer *presence* of her. She smiled at him, and he found he couldn't move. It was like he was a housecat and being regarded by an eagle – bigger, fiercer, and much more deadly, for all that he also was adept at catching mice.

For her part, Azella the Unpitying disregarded the others as well. It seemed that no one but Damien existed in this square for her anymore either.

"Come, my Sorcerer-King," the pale girl said in her honey-silk tones, and held out one fragile-looking hand. Reluctantly, but not unwillingly – he *had* agreed to this after all – Damien stepped forward, around Adam, to take it.

"Damie–" Adam's outraged cry was cutoff abruptly, and the king was startled out of his almost-daze enough to turn back. Adam was nowhere to be seen.

"I sent him back where he belongs," the white-gowned sorceress commented. "A King's Champion is all well and good for formal challenges and single combat. But quite useless when facing someone of *my* Power. No use in getting him killed by dear Evan for no purpose at all."

She smiled at the pirate-king. "Or making Evan face the question of whether to forever eliminate any chance of reconciling with his only child. May I suggest, O Captain of the Red Sails," she added with ancient amusement, "that abusing the city to which he has so recently been Bound – *or* attempting to usurp the Realm which is Bound to claim him if the king and queen should both die – will *also* not meet your heart's desire. Especially when he currently holds that Sword you've told me so *much* about. And which, I am given to understand, has spoken for him."

Evan stared at her, then up again at Jason – and Adam, secure in his husband's arms – then looked at Megan standing forlornly and abandoned on the spot to which Damien had brought them.

The king wanted to see how *that* reunion would turn out, but he was fated not to, for Azella took his hand and said again, "Come, my Sorcerer-King."

He felt the curl of her magick up his arm, Binding his will to her own. Not with enough Power that he could not break it... but as a test to whether he would hold to his word. And whether she needed to hold to hers.

"Damien! I *will* find you! And I *will* free you!"

Damien could not even turn for one last look at his raging, weeping wife as he followed Azella the Unpitying into a future he could not begin to imagine.

Did you miss the FIRST BOOK in this series?
Turn to page 183
(just past the MAPS)
to check out an exerpt from
The Rebel Duchess
Book One of the Chronicles of Ilseador!

MANGALA MCNAMARA

Alsterling Family Tree

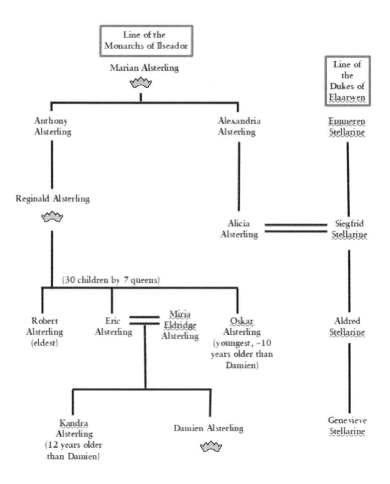

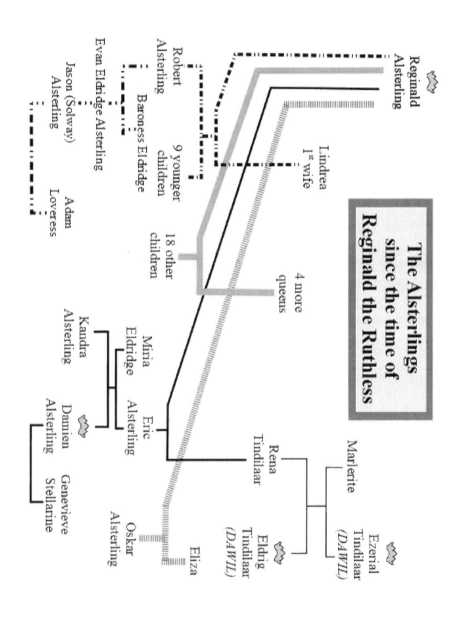

The Alsterlings
since the time of
Reginald the Ruthless

Index of Characters

Characters that appear in this book are <u>underlined.</u>
(Characters that are referenced, but do not actually appear are in plain type. Some additional characters are included who are not mentioned in this book to clarify relationships.)
Deceased characters are in *italics.*
Characters with speaking roles in this book are in **bold.**

The grandchildren of a reigning king or queen are officially grand dukes and grand duchesses in Ilseador, but are also referred to as princes and princesses when the question of their position in the line of succession is not in question.
Damien was Crown Prince after Oskar died.

Contents of the Index:
- Royal Family of Ilseador
- Provinces of Ilseador in order of precedence and relevant ruling family members
- Emeralsee contains the following fiefs named in the story: Seasbourne, Cedarwen, Eldyrwyld, Lynncrag, Elmirscroft, Ravenscroft
- Elaarwen contains the following fiefs named in the story: Brindlewell, Cloudcroft
- Siovale
- Reyensweir contains the following fiefs named in the story: Zialest
- Embervest contains the following fiefs named in the story: Minglemere, Everfields
- Alpinsward contains the following fiefs named in the story: Dalizell
- Dalzialest, duchy
- The Lost Provinces: Alpinsward, Minglemere, Elendria, Farivera, Everfields

169

Royal Family of Ilseador
(and noted individuals in the Royal City and Province)

- <u>**Damien Alsterling,**</u> King of Ilseador
  - <u>**Queen Genevieve (Stellarine) Alsterling**</u>, Duchess of Elaarwen (a.k.a. 'the Rebel Duchess'), King Damien's wife
  - *<u>Queen Marian Alsterling</u>* (a.k.a. 'Marian the merciful'), King Damien and Queen Genevieve's great-great-grandmother (common ancestress)
  - <u>**Crown Prince Jason (Solway) Alsterling,**</u> Duke of Emeralsee, son of Evan Eldridge Alsterling
  - <u>**Prince Adam (Loveress) Alsterling,**</u> husband of Prince Jason
    - *Eric Alsterling,* son of old king *Reginald Alsterling,* former Crown Prince, King Damien's father
      - » *Queen Rena (Tindilaar) Alsterling,* a princess from Dawil; mother of Prince Eric Alsterling; grandmother of King Damien; sister to *King Eldrig Tindilaar*
      - » *Miria (Eldridge) Alsterling,* King Damien's and *Princess Kandra's* mother; wife of *Prince Eric;* daughter of a minor noble family in the countryside of Emeralsee Province; oldest of seven children
        - * *Miria's father, David Eldridge,* was a failed squire, son of the former Baron of Elderwyld
        - * *Miria's mother, Alexa,* was a blacksmith's daughter
      - » *Grand Duchess (or Princess) Kandra 'Kandy' Alsterling,* King Damien's sister; Prince Eric and Lady Miria's daughter joined the army as a common foot- soldier at 18, worked her way up. Was to have married Lord Raphael Anvliyar of Cedarwen (love-match) and helped her parents and brother escape to the Rebellion in Elaarwen

    - *King Reginald Alsterling* (aka 'the old king' or 'Reginald the Ruthless'); King Damien's grandfather
      - » *'Lord' Prydeen*, his Apprentice Evil Wizard
      - » *7 wives*
      - » *1st Princess Lindrea Alsterling (died before he was crowned)*
      - » *2nd*
      - » *3rd*
      - » *4th*

- » *5th*
- » *6th Queen Rena (Tindilaar) Alsterling* of Dawil, *Prince Eric's* mother, King Damien's grandmother
- » *7th Eliza Alsterling* (Oskar's mother, married to *King Reginald* simultaneously with *Queen Rena*)
- » *Oskar Alsterling, the youngest son of Reginald.*
    - * <u>Sir Jason Solway</u>, *Prince Oskar's* bodyguard before he was Heir, his Champion while he was Heir
    - * <u>Sir Edmund Railston</u>, *Prince Oskar's* Champion and bodyguard at the time Ring was taken from *Prince Oskar (*also Adam Loveress' first lover)
- » Some 30 legitimate children (all dead), including the following:
- » *Crown Prince Robert Alsterling (son of Princess Lindrea)*
- » *Princess Selda Alsterling*
- » *Crown Prince Eric Alsterling (son of Queen Rena)*
- » *Crown Prince Oskar Alsterling (son of Queen Eliza)*
- » Some 100 grandchildren (all dead besides Damien and Evan) including the following:
    - * *Alric Alsterling*
    - * *Grand Duke Salleen Alsterling*
    - * *Grand Duchess Kandra Alsterling*
    - * Grand Duke Evan Eldridge Alsterling (son of Prince Robert)
    - * Crown Prince Damien Alsterling
- • **King Damien's Royal Guards**
- » **Champion: <u>Sir Adam Loveress</u>** (shield is puce with a rose, argent, crossed by a black sword), a close advisor of King Damien
    - * **Captain and Knight Commander of the Royal Guard: <u>Sir Timothy Ancellius</u>** (a.k.a. 'Tim'), Second-in-Command of the Royal Guard when Damien is crowned, marries Secret Cadre member Aryllis after Damien is crowned, has son Enrico (a.k.a. Rico)
- » **Original Guards**
    - * **Champion: <u>Sir Jason Solway</u>** (mother is Countess Alexa Solway), a close advisor of King Damien's.
    - * **Captain and Knight Commander of the Royal Guard: <u>Sir Adam Loveress</u>**
    - * **<u>Sir Timothy Ancellius</u>**

* Sir Leverett Childress (a.k.a. 'Lev'), marries
Secret Cadre member Terellie
* Sir Otto
* Sir Randolph
* (plus seven others not named)

- **Newer Guards members** (five years into Damien's reign)
  » <u>Sir Timothy Ancellius,</u> **(Captain and Knight-Commander)**
  » <u>Sir Marcus</u> (Second-in-Command)
  » <u>Sir Mikal</u> 'Mik'
  » <u>Sir Rodney</u>
  » Sir Everett Ladler
  » Sir Drake Milbourne
  » **<u>Sir Angelos Eldridge</u>**
  » (and five others not named)

- **The Secret Cadre of Royal Guards**
  » **Original twelve King's Ladies:** the Secret Cadre of Royal
  Guards (all but Lena and Ciriis marry one of Damien's
  original Royal Guards following his coronation)
    * Ciriis Celavell: Mistress of Protocol and
    Spymistress, Commander of the Secret Cadre
    under Adam Loveress, later King's Advisor
    and then Assistant to Duke Aldred
    * Lena Devergnon: Poisoner/anti-poisoner,
    later Assistant Royal Librarian
    * <u>Aryllis Ieldore</u>: marries Royal Guardsman Tim
    Ancellius; mother of Enrico Ancellius (a.k.a. Rico);
    becomes Mistress of Protocol and Spymistress and
    commander of the Secret Cadre under Adam Loveress
    * Felena
    * Terellie: marries Royal Guardsman Leverett Childress
    * Sasha
    * Elsa
    * Emerie

- * Thielda
- * Nalda
- * Kamauri
- * Licia
- * Mirabelle
  - » **Newer Secret Cadre** (five years into Damien's reign)
    - * <u>**Lady Alanna**</u>
    - * Lady Lisa
    - * Lord Aaron
    - * Lord Devin
    - * Master Xavier

- **Castle Personnel**
  - » <u>Elista</u>, senior maid, later Chatelaine. Began work the day *Prince Eric* and *Lady Miria* were killed, fed Damien until *Lady Theresa* discovered her. Married to *Robert*, Captain of the Castle Guard during the Usurpation
  - » *Captain Robert* of the Castle Guard, married to Elista, died during the Usurpation
  - » <u>Maree</u>, knife sharpener for the kitchen, had a huge infatuation with Damien

Provinces of Ilseador
in order of precedence and relevant ruling family members

- *Emeralsee,* duchy – Alsterling family, gold and turquoise (guards wear dark blue and black)
  - <u>**Duke Jason (Solway) Alsterling,**</u> Crown Prince of the Realm
  - <u>**Duke-Consort Adam (Loveress) Alsterling,**</u> husband of Jason
  - <u>**Damien Alsterling**</u> former duke
  - <u>**Genevieve (Stellarine) Alsterling,**</u> wife of Damien
  - *Ghost of Queen Marian Alsterling*, great-grandmother of Damien and Genevieve and great-great-grandmother of Jason
  - *Dead-and-gone:*
    - *Prince Anthony Alsterling*, eldest child of Queen Marian
    - *King Reginald Alsterling*, eldest child of Prince Anthony (see 'King Damien Alsterling' at top for details of *King Reginald's* offspring)

- *Other siblings of King Reginald* (and their families and Alsterling cousins)
- *Other siblings and half-siblings of Prince Anthony*
- *Princess Alexandria Alsterling,* youngest child of *Queen Marian* (fled Emeralsee with the Monarch's Blade shortly before *Queen Marian* was assassinated by Prince Reginald; played the role of 'Erawan the Kind Robber' while hiding out in the mountains of Elaarwen)
- *Grand Duchess Alicia Alsterling,* only child of *Princess Alexandria;* married *Siegfrid Stellarine,* Heir to the Province of Elaarwen, had one child, Aldred Stellarine

- **Others of note within Emeralsee** (see under 'King Damien Alsterling' at top)

- *Fiefs within Emeralsee*
  - *Seasbourne,* county – family Laidly
  - *Cedarwen, barony* – Anvliyar family
    - » Baron Raphael Anvliyar (intended husband of King Damien's sister, Princess Kandra)
      - * *Dowager Baroness Theresa Anvliyar,* mother of Baron Raphael, former Royal Librarian and guardian of King Damien as a child after his parents were slain; died a traitor's death for having conspired to betray *Crown Prince Eric, Lady Miria,* and *Princess Kandra,* as well as for Conspiracy Against the Crown due to her role during the Usurpation of *Harald Elsevier*
  - *Elderwyld,* barony – Eldridge family
    (Note: names in the Eldridge family aside from *Miria, Alexa,* Angelos, Eugenio, and Evan have not been given in the story yet; they are included here to make the family connections clear)
    - » <u>Baron Eugenio Eldridge</u>
      - * <u>Sir Angelos Eldridge,</u> one of Baron Eugenio's sons
      - * *Previous Baron Eldridge,* grandfather of the current Baron (Eugenio), father of *Baroness Dara* and *David*

* *Baroness Dara Eldridge*, mother of Baron Eugenio
* *David Eldridge,* Lord of Ravenscroft (gifted to *Prince Eric* and *Lady Miria* and deeded to her parents), younger son of the *former Baron,* a failed squire, husband of Alexa, father of seven (*Lady Miria* was his eldest)
* *Alexa Eldridge, David's* wife; a blacksmith's daughter, mother of seven
* *Lady Miria (Eldridge) Alsterling,* Damien's mother, eldest child of *David* and *Alexa Eldridge*
  » Unknown fate
  * Evan Eldridge, a cousin of *Lady Miria's,* son of *Baroness Dara Eldridge,* half-brother of Baron Eugenio
* **Lynncrag**, baronetcy – Loveress family
  » **Baronetta Linda Loveress**
  * Lord George Loveress, husband of Baronetta Linda
  * Their children (ages given for the 5th year of King Damien's reign)
  * **Sir Adam Loveress** – 34yo, Captain of the Royal Guard
  * Charles (a.k.a. 'Charley') Loveress – 32yo – a forest ranger
  * Lorenzo (a.k.a. 'Lorry') Loveress – 30yo – married and divorced twice
  * Desirée Loveress – 28yo
    * Desirée's 2 little boys (8yo and 10y o)
  * Fontaine Loveress – 24yo – priestess novitiate (but left before final vows)
  * Martin Loveress – 20yo - healer
  * **Marianna Loveress** – 18yo – lady-in-waiting applicant (Secret Cadre)
* *Elmirscroft*, property
* *Ravenscroft*, property
  » *David Eldridge*, grandfather of King Damien
  * *Alexa Eldridge*, grandmother of King Damien, wife of David

- *Elaarwen*, duchy – Stellarine family, violet and silver
  - <u>Duchess Genevieve (Stellarine) Alsterling</u>
    - <u>Duke-Consort Damien Alsterling,</u> husband of Genevieve
    - Lord Aldred Stellarine, widowed husband of Duchess-Consort *Giendra (Topasirre) Stellarine*, father of Duchess Genevieve, only child of Duke Siegfrid Stellarine and *Grand Duchess Alicia Alsterling*
    - *Duke Siegfrid Stellarine*, father of Duke Aldred, husband of *Grand Duchess Alicia Alsterling*, son of Duke Emmeren
      - » *Grand Duchess Alicia Alsterling*, wife of Duke Siegfrid Stellarine, mother of Duke Aldred
    - *Duke Emmeren Stellarine*, father of *Duke Siegfrid*
    - *Duchess Shalla (Elemandros) Stelarine*, wife of Duke Emmeren
    - Others of note in the duchy:
      - » Lord Adsel Topasirre, Chatelaine and Regent of Elaarwen, from Genevieve's mother's family

  - *Fiefs within Elaarwen*
    - *Brindlewell*, county – Solway family
      - » Countess Alexa Solway, mother of Megan and Jason
        - * <u>Lady Megan Solway</u>, Heir to Brindlewell, oldest child of Countess Alexa, wife of David
        - * <u>Lord David Solway</u> (a.k.a. Captain Daffyd Metreedi), husband of Lady Megan
        - * their children (ages given for the 5th year of King Damien's reign)
          - * <u>Elaina Solway</u> – 22yo
          - * *Rudolph Solway* (deceased) (would have been 19yo)
          - * Roger Solway – 13yo
          - * Esmerelda Solway – 11yo
        - * <u>Sir Jason Solway</u>, younger child of Countess Alexa
    - *Cloudcroft*, property – Stellarine family
      - » Lord Aldred Stellarine
        - * Lady Ciriis Celavell, Aldred's mistress

- *Siovale*, duchy – Elsevier family, forest green and silver (guards wear dark green and black)
  - <u>Duke Tomas Elsevier</u>
    - » Duchess-Consort Sildra (Miramar) Elsevier
    - » Their six children (ages given for the 5th year of Damien's reign, not all of their names have been given in the story as of yet)
      - * Mark Elsevier - 20yo
      - * Arabella Elsevier – 17yo
      - * Lorinda – 14yo
      - * Denis Elsevier – 12yo
      - * Gemma Elsevier – 10yo
      - * Gary Elsevier – 7yo
    - » *Duke Hector Elsevier,* father of Tomas, husband of *Lydia*
    - » *Dowager Duchess-Consort Lydia Elsevier*, mother of *Harald* and Tomas, died a traitor's death for Conspiracy Against the Crown for her role in the Usurpation by her son *Harald*
    - » *Harald Elsevier,* cuckoo's child of *Duchess Lydia* by *King Reginald*, died a traitor's death for Usurping the Throne after Damien was crowned... Genevieve Stellarine Alsterling's first husband

- *Reyensweir*, duchy – family Mirion
  - <u>Duke Quillian Mirion</u>

  - *Fiefs within Reyensweir*
    - *Zialest*, county – Teraseel family (adjacent to Dalizell, across some challenging mountain passes from Elaarwen; HOWEVER see also DALZIALEST below)
      - » <u>Countess Rosa Teraseel</u>
        - * *Gavin Teraseel,* Rosa's brother; he was to marry Ciriis Celavell

- *Embervest* duchy – family Eledor
  - Duchess Tariana Eledor
    - *Duke Istvan Eledor*, father of Tariana
    - Lord Robard Eledor, Tariana's older brother

  - *Fiefs within Embervest* The Lost Provinces of Minglemere (returned) and Everfields (still Lost to Vindalia) are part of Embervest
    - *Minglemere*, barony – family Krakenroost
      » Baron Densal Krakenroost
      » Lost to Vindalia some seventeen years before King Damien was Crowned
      » Regained in the 4th year of King Damien's reign
    - *Everfields*
      » Lost to Vindalia some fifty years before King Damien was crowned

- *Alpinsward*, duchy – family Marseill
  - The last of the Lost Provinces to defect (in their case to Mercasia after *Crown Prince Robert Alsterling's* negotiations failed following his murder by 'bandits')
  - The first of the Lost Provinces to return, following King Damien's coronation and negotiations with Queen Genevieve
  - Duchess Laura Marseill

  - *Fiefs within Alpinsward*
    - *Dalizell*, county – Miramar family; HOWEVER see also DALZIALEST below
      » Count Zachary Miramar
        * Sildra (Miramar) Elsevier, Zachary's next elder sister, was already married to Tomas Elsevier when *parents* and *Elsa* died
        * Zachary's *parents* (died of flux)
        * *Elsa*, eldest child and former Heir to Dallizell; Zachary and Sildra's older sister; died of the same flux as their parents

- *DALZIALEST*, duchy,
    combined of Dalizell and Zialest when Rosa Teraseel and Zachary Miramar married just after King Damien's coronation – the Miramar family was granted the promotion to a Duchy in recognition of their loyalty to the new king (the counties had been asking for royal permission to merge for several generations)
    - <u>Duchess Rosa (Teraseel) Miramar</u>
    - <u>Duke Zachary Miramar</u>
        - 2 children in the 5th year of King Damien's reign
            * Talia Miramar (a.k.a Tally), 3yo
            * Betha Miramar, newborn

- The Lost Provinces
    1. Alpinsward, duchy – family Marseill
        Duchess Laura Marseill
        - Lost to Mercasia some five years before King Damien was crowned
        - Regained in the 3rd year of King Damien's reign
    2. Minglemere, barony – family Krakenroost
        Baron Densal
        - Returned to Duchy Embervest
        - Lost to Vindalia some seventeen years before King Damien was Crowned
        - Regained in the 4th year of King Damien's reign
    3. Elendria, county – formerly part of Duchy Alpinsward
        Countess Miraly
        - Lost to Deltheran some twenty-five years before King Damien was crowned
        - negotiations begun to Restore Elendria to Ilseador in the 5th year of King Damien's reign
    4. Farivera – formerly part of Duchy Siovale
        - Lost to… Sindalla? Some forty years before King Damien was crowned
    5. Everfields – formerly part of Duchy Embervest
        - Lost to Vindalia some fifty years before King Damien was crowned

Others Mentioned

- *King Eldrig Tindilaar of Dawil*, brother of *Queen Rena* of Ilseador
- *Lady Giovalla Elemandros* of Wave (province in Dawil), mother of *Duchess Shalla* of Elaarwen

MAPS

Ilseador

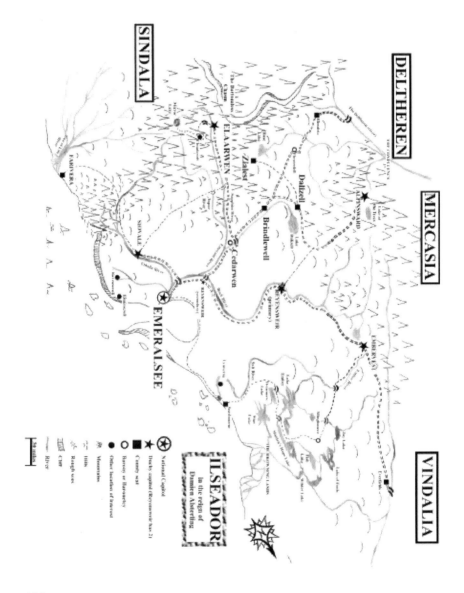

LANDS Around the MERUTIAN SEA

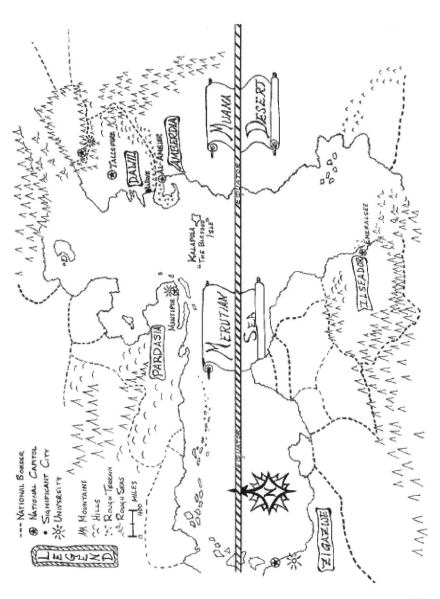

Mangala McNamara

*And now, for your delectation...
an excerpt from...*

MANGALA McNAMARA

Chapter ONE

Caught!

GENEVIEVE HAD NOT FORGOTTEN THE old king's pet sorcerer. She *had*, however, assumed he would not be a problem. This was clearly not the case.

She ducked into a rubbish-strewn alley and prayed that one of the doors leading off of it would open to somewhere that was not a dead-end. Unlike the alleyway itself. Genevieve really wasn't familiar enough with the layout of the capitol to be doing this sort of thing. As her advisors had repeatedly told her. Her chagrined memory replayed the scene of her tossing her head as she assured them that "the Rebel Duchess" could handle anything.

Not that she had *planned* to have to handle anything at all. She was just going to come in as part of the crowds hoping to get a glimpse of the new young king, on this last day of the coronation festivities. Just another gawker from the countryside. She still had no idea how Lord Prydeen had identified her.

The second door on the right opened at her frantic tug, and Genevieve hurried into darkness, pulling the door tightly shut behind her. She could hear people talking somewhere off to her right and the darkness seemed a little less dark in that direction. Perhaps there was a way through the building and back to the main street she had veered off of so abruptly. She needed to get back to the streets to complete her mission. The inhabitants of the room ahead would be startled, but if she could get past them quickly – before they decided to hold her for a thief – she might make it.

Just as the young woman started towards the sounds, the door behind her crashed open and the sorcerer stepped through.

Lord Prydeen was a master of dramatic effect, some odd corner of her mind noted absently. He stood framed in the doorway, too deeply cowled to see his face, his ankle-length black cloak flapping and curling about him in the sudden cross-currents of air between building and outside. The alley was brighter than the room – so perhaps he merely paused to let his eyes adjust – but in that moment he was more silhouette than shape, more demon than man.

Genevieve could not – *could not* – lead him towards those unsuspecting innocents in the room beyond. Perhaps the completely unexpected would gain her – well, *some*thing.

She took a deep breath, but carefully did not think too hard about what she was doing – though whether it was because Lord Prydeen was rumored to be able to pull one's thoughts from the air itself or because she wouldn't have the nerve if she did–

She spun on her heel and charged directly at the sorcerer, startling him sufficiently that she shoved past him and back out into the dead-end alley. Then to her left and back out to the main street – perhaps she could lose him in the crowd. She had to try.

In her haste, however, Genevieve's own hood was pushed back, exposing her signature red-gold hair – and confirming what had surely only been Lord Prydeen's guess about the identity of his quarry.

Fool that she was for not having dyed it.

Thrice a fool for deciding to skulk about the coronation festivities – like any small child playing "Erawan the Kind Robber" – instead of listening to the reports of her spies as the mature, careful, strategic leader of the rebellion should do. That stupid, romantic title – "Rebel Duchess" – really *had* gone to her head, as Rosa had accused her. She would do the Cause no good by being taken by the king's sorcerer. Even if the new young King Damien lived up to his month-old reputation for fairness, Lord Prydeen would never give her a chance to find out.

No time for this.

Genevieve jerked her hood back up and tried to blend into the crowded market square, trying to outguess Lord Prydeen. Which direction would the sorcerer be unlikely to go? – or which way would he be unlikely to follow? Surely the feared and hated Royal Sorcerer could not make his way through the crowd without causing an uproar that would let her dodge away... though he had before, when she first caught him following her. Could there be *any* safety for her here in the capitol, just six days after Damien's crowning? Surely the old guard was still in place and *no one* (not even the young king?) would dare to gainsay Lord Prydeen.

Abruptly, and entirely on instinct, not daring to look back to measure her pursuit, Genevieve swerved and tore for the royal viewing stand. Damien, if the stories were right – the stories that she had not believed and had come in person to verify – would merely have her executed for a traitor. Lord Prydeen – as she had reason to know – would sell her soul to demons and wring every last memory and secret from her shrieking heart.

The fine bright day taunted her travails, small poofy clouds ambling across a sky as blue as her own eyes. The market square – packed with a crowd of pleasantly frolicking merchants and peasants – impeded her swift progress. The swarms of children playing games of tag nearly tripped her up. The very *joy* of it all nearly derailed her thoughts, for such gaiety could never have been shown in the old king's rule, and part of her could not leave off trying to determine if there was still the undercurrent of desperation that she expected from her previous, and more successfully clandestine, visits to the capitol city.

But the Rebel Duchess knew exactly where the royal platform stood, both due to having marked it well when first she arrived and for the fact that it stood as tall any of the half-timbered two-story buildings surrounding the square. She had hoped to catch a glimpse of the young king from afar when first she arrived, and the royal platform had seemed like the right place to start. She had perhaps stayed still too long, staring too intently at the brilliantly bunting- and flower-clad structure, trying to discern which, if any, of the milling nobles on its three ornately decorated levels was the young king. Then, as now, the top level was empty, save for a matched pair of guards.

Part of her – the part that had insisted on this mad mission against all rational thought and advice – was certain that, if she could but look into his eyes, she would know if Damien was all that the reports claimed... or if he had been corrupted by his grandfather and Lord Prydeen.

Part of her – if she dared admit it – wanted to believe, even if it seemed beyond belief, that he could have been untouched. That the Cause was won, the need for a Rebel Duchess was done. That the Rebellion could quietly fold itself up and her folk could slip back to their homes, to their lives...

though perhaps not the Rebel Duchess herself, recognizable as she was as a symbol...

Yet – how could those two old, evil men *not* have insured that the crown prince was a "fit successor" to the king who had controlled a creature such as Lord Prydeen?

Genevieve had met the prince once, when they were both children. He had barely been of an age for his first pony, and she – a few years older – had just graduated to a mild-mannered horse... and her father's half-tamed, firebreathing mare that Duke Aldred had no idea she would even attempt to ride. Her father had brought her to Court to make her curtsy to the old king and see her named his Heir. Damien had been but one of a pack of the old king's grandchildren – a nondescript royal child, good-looking as they all had been, but special in no particular way. They had spent perhaps minutes in each other's presence, on separate ends of the audience hall that had seemed miles-long to her then.

Now those other siblings and cousins, aunts and uncles, were all gone and Damien – unremarked offspring of an unremarkable parent – had been named Crown Prince, and now King. For him to have inherited would seem to signal that he had done something to earn the old king's approval – perhaps by being ruthless enough to have ensured no other contenders were available. Certainly, he had made no mark by protesting his grandfather's policies while the old king lived, no mark of any kind, in fact. Despite all the time Genevieve had spent at Court, she did not recall ever noticing him again.

Yet she could still remember a certain clear-eyed gaze from that long-ago child. A gaze that seemed to recognize and promise to right all the wrongs that existed in the world. A gaze that had haunted her dreams since she had heard he had been crowned, and had kept her skepticism from becoming outright denial when rumors of the new king's beneficence came to her. And so, she had come to see for herself...

She had reached the royal platform at last, and hunted for a spot to clamber up. Not an easy endeavor, as it was so heavily be-ribboned – in every color, not merely royal gold and turquoise – with bright buntings stretched between triple rosettes made of actual rose petals. An elegantly illuminated sign noted that these were the coronation gifts of the Weavers' and Florists' Guilds – but the small barrel that the sign rested upon was of more interest to her, as it gave her a leg up to the first level, which was filled with younger noblemen. These young men were here to satisfy fathers and mothers who wanted them close to the source of power. They eyed her with interest – her cloak had of necessity been pushed aside to climb and she was dressed in hunting leathers fit tight to her athletic frame – and she in turn ignored them, using the spigoted ale kegs at which they were amusing themselves to give her a step up to the recessed second level.

The older noblemen and -women – and their maiden daughters – on this level looked at her quite askance. Genevieve hoped her hood shadowed her face enough to keep any of them from recognizing her, for she knew no few of them, though she did not recognize the barely-grown girls, nor more than a handful of the hardly-older lads below. These nobles had toadied up to the old king while Genevieve – and her father before her – had sought to protect their people. She knew all too well that they would as soon sell her out to Lord Prydeen as look at her. Even now they were trying to toady up to King Damien, bringing their marriageable daughters to parade before him – an array of maidens scarcely past puberty, for their elder ones had been taken to serve the old king and Lord Prydeen in years gone by, many never to be seen again. They, too, must surely be hoping for better from Damien, yet she saw nothing but avarice in the faces of even the children.

 A good-looking young man – unusual only for being the only *young* man on this level of the platform, did someone think the new king's taste ran to boys? – with very dark hair and clear grey eyes offered her a hand onto the level. Genevieve was not too proud to accept help, even from a scion of one of *these* families. They exchanged a startled look and nearly let go of each other as an electric spark seemed to jump between their hands. Surely it wasn't dry enough today for such things, and so close to the harbor besides.

Putting such irrelevant details aside, Genevieve brushed off her hands on her breeches as she looked up towards the highest level of the reviewing stand, but saw only the pair of Royal Guards – two blondely handsome men so perfectly matched as almost to be twins – decorating that august space. Knights chosen for their beauty, just as were the horses that pulled the royal carriage. She wondered who they were – might they have enough real skill at arms to have faced her in the Battle of Siovale seven years earlier? She'd caught no more than a glimpse of either of them so far, as they turned, watchfully, eyes raking the crowds. Perhaps they were more than merely decorative.

Hopefully the king himself was sitting down and merely out of view. Genevieve needed for him to be there, before Lord Prydeen caught up with her. It was a wild gambit – praise all the Gods at once that Rosa really could handle the Rebellion, since it looked like she was going to have to. Rosa – would never forgive her for getting herself captured and killed. The

Rebel Countess – surely that sounded just as impressive. They had known it couldn't last – this would free Rosa to wed and produce the Heir that she needed. Genevieve's own proper title – Lady Stellarine, Duchess of Elaarwen (she dared not think "Princess of the Realm", though her bloodlines were as good as the king's) – would pass to a collateral line…

No matter. The issue at hand was to get up there to the top level and there was no obvious stair or ladder.

Genevieve dropped her useless disguise of a cloak before it could hinder her further in climbing higher, ignoring the massed gasp from the gathered nobles, and looked for a convenient way to boost herself to the king's level. The balustrade of the king's level – still festooned with those slippery buntings and banners – was more than head-high to her. It was higher than she could hoist herself on arm-strength alone.

That young man was still watching her – looking slightly amused, damn him. Or maybe that was *be*mused. Surely, he had little idea what to make of her and her sudden arrival. But he seemed to come to a decision and wrenched a ring with a large grey pearl on it off his finger, thrusting it towards her. It was the sort of thing a nobleman might offer a noblewoman to indicate interest – a sort of "let's get to know each other" offer, not quite a tryst, but more than an offer of acquaintance. The ring would have a house sigil on it, perhaps even a personal seal – enough information for her to find him again later on. A crazy thing to hand to the highly recognizable Rebel Duchess as she attempted to single-handedly besiege the new king's festival viewing platform. The young man must be completely daft.

And then he bent and cupped his hands as a stablehand might do to help someone into the saddle. The sparkle in his eyes suggested he was prepared to toss her high enough to pull herself up over that balustrade.

Again, the gathered nobles gasped, but this time there were also mutters and a fearful eagerness… and she guessed someone had spotted Lord Prydeen approaching.

There was no time for this. Genevieve stuffed the ring onto her finger – her beltpouch would take too long to open – put her foot in his hands and leapt up in concert with his toss.

And got the – third? fourth? – shock of the day as her reaching hands were grasped from above and an all too familiar voice gruffly said "Young miss, this is the king's place, you can't be climbing… up… her–" The voice cut off as and the hands fumbled and nearly dropped her back down, as their owner peered over the edge and then grabbed her more securely and helped her over the balustrade.

The Royal Guard was looking at her in exasperation and some of the same confusion Genevieve was feeling. It was the strangest and least appropriate timing on anything ever – but the touch of his hands had inflamed her with desire. *Not now, not now!* The Rebel Duchess thought frantically. She'd heard of this, but thought it a fairytale... Rosa, *Rosa* was her love...

"Jason Solway?" she managed to gasp out.

"Genny?" He was as flabbergasted as he was, and if the blush rising in those perfect cheeks was anything to judge, he was suffering from the same reaction. Suffering...

"Here now," said the other Royal Guard, coming forward from his ceremonial position. "Jase, what's this all about?"

She looked almost gratefully at the other man, just as gratefully *not* recognizing him as yet another childhood friend. But his familiar behavior towards Jason – were they lovers? Why did that thought make her heart – or something lower than her heart – do flips? And why, oh, why, *was this all happening at once?*

"Stand back, gentlemen," growled a low, cultured voice.

Lord Prydeen.

Apparently, she wouldn't have to sort any of this out after all.

The two Guards obediently stepped aside, though she rather thought that Jason only reluctantly let go of her hands, and she could see that the sorcerer had come up a set of stairs at the back of the reviewing stand. A brief surge of wind whipped the cowled hood from off Lord Prydeen's spotty, balding head, and tossed his long, drooping mustaches. He had not aged well since the old king's death; his hair had been thinning, but was still full when last she had gotten a good look at him, some months earlier, and the lines around his mouth were graven deeply, where once they had been entirely masked by his whiskers. Genevieve had heard tell that evil sorcerers cast vile spells to keep themselves young – by sacrificing true youths and maidens to demons, some said. She had scoffed, even as she wondered. The old king had lived long past his age, and Lord Prydeen, some said, had not aged at all, even as those noble daughters came to serve them both and were rarely seen again.

"Lady Genevieve." Lord Prydeen greeted her, coldly, but not correctly. He needed nothing besides himself to emphasize his authority, but he had brought a squad of his personal guards up with him. They fanned out behind him, blocking the path, even to headstrong young women who might push past a sorcerer.

She tilted her chin up – her nose was too snub to properly glare down it, but she was tall enough to try... and the arrogance might mask the tremble that the tumult in her stomach had settled into. "The proper title is '*Your Grace*', messir." She was actually in line for the throne herself, with all of Damien's family gone, and 'Lord' Prydeen was, after all, a sorcerer of no particular breeding.

And if she told herself that a few more times, perhaps she could dare to face him.

A wintry smile passed over Lord Prydeen's lips – gone as quickly as snow in the Summer. "No longer, I fear. My former master stripped you of your titles for your treasonous activities."

Genevieve inclined her head. "So, I have heard. But even a Royal Decree does not make a thing reality. Even His – belated – Majesty never put it to the test in *Elaarwen*."

Something sparked in the sorcerer's eyes. Anger, perhaps? Could such a one as he even feel something as tender as grief? He gestured to his men. "Bind her and bring her."

Jason bestirred himself to protest, "My lord–!" but the other Guard pulled him back and Genevieve found herself being roughly seized and turned around by hands that made no pretense of not enjoying their task. Even the king's own Royal Guards, it seemed, dared not speak against the sorcerer. Not yet anyways. If only she had waited to see if the young king could consolidate his power; if, indeed, he would continue in the way he had begun!

"My Lord Prydeen! What passes here?" The mild voice interrupted from the direction of the stairs, but was no one Genevieve recognized. She had been turned to face outwards towards the square whilst they bound her, and could not see the speaker.

Lord Prydeen's voice was a curious mix of ingratiating and dismissive. "Nothing you need trouble yourself over, my lord. Some rabble found her way up here, clearly to cause some trouble to you. It is my task and my privilege to safeguard Your Highness. We'll be away momentarily."

Gentle hands cleared away the thongs that had begun to lash her wrists. "Surely you are mistaken, my Lord Prydeen. This is no rabble, but Her Grace, the Duchess Genevieve Stellarine of Elaarwen."

"Yes, my Lord, the so-called 'Rebel Duchess'," Lord Prydeen's voice was growing impatient. "I am taking her to the castle dungeons to have out of her what she knows. You can make an example of her later on – you must not detract from your coronation festivities."

"Nonsense, Lord Prydeen," the mild voice replied. "That isn't how we treat visiting royalty... not to mention that the people would rise in protest and not even you could put them *all* down at once."

He came around to Genevieve's right side, and before she could register that this was the same young man who had cupped his hands for her boot like any stableboy, he gave her that same enigmatic smile, and faced the crowd – who had begun to turn as they saw their king. Damien lifted Genevieve's right hand in his left, holding them high above their heads and called out, "I give you Genevieve Stellarine, the Rebel Duchess!"

It was the sort of moment a Duke's Heir is trained for and – bemused as she was at the turn of events – Genevieve flattened her palm against the king's and stood tall before the crowds, the errant breeze tossing her red-gold curls like a mane. She smiled fiercely, trying to think if this would be taken as some sort of inadvertent admission of surrender.

Even as the people roared their approval – and Lord Prydeen fumed behind them – a sudden, strange crackling noise erupted and ribbons of white fire fountained up between their pressed fingers. It wreathed down to wrap their hands and curl around their arms.

For all that she was the reigning duchess of a province, the leader of a rebellion against an unjust king and an evil sorcerer, and had spent most of her life in that struggle... Genevieve was tempted to faint right then and there. This was absolutely the *last* thing she had expected. If she hadn't seen this happen before, she would have thought it was some new and clever attack by Lord Prydeen.

But she *had* seen this before. And, likely, so had every member of the crowd below.

At least young King Damien looked nearly as befuddled as she felt.

He, however, recovered more quickly than she.

"And your future Queen!" he announced in what sounded like a calm voice.

He pulled her in and kissed her.

And the crowds went absolutely wild.

Read the rest of this exciting story of rebellion and romance!
The Rebel Duchess
now at your favorite online ebookseller in print or ebook!

Also by Mangala McNamara

Fantasy in the World of the Living Gods:

The Chronicles of Ilseador
> *The Rebel Duchess: Book One*
> *The King's Champion: Book Two*
> *The Pirate-King: Book Three*

The Prankster Prince
> *Thony and the Much-Anticipated Adventure: Book One of The Prankster Prince*
> *Thony Goes Astray! (in the Deep, Dark, and Dangerous Fairy Wood): Book Two of The Prankster Prince*
> *So You Want to Be a Hero? Book Three of the Prankster Prince*

Knightess of the Realm
> *A Not-So-Sacrificial Maiden*
> *Out of the Woods… Hopefully (a Prequel Novella)*
> *A Not-So-Simple Mission: Book One of the Heir's Journey*
> *An Entirely-Unexpected Revelation: Book Two of the Heir's Journey*

More Fantasy coming soon…
> *Turns of a Page (A Knightess of the Realm Prequel Novella)* (May 2024)
> *An All-Too-Surprising Homecoming: Book 3 of the Heir's Journey (A Knightess of the Realm Novel)* (June 2024)
> *How Thony Stopped a War (and Fixed a Friendship): Book Four of the Prankster Prince* (July 2024)
> *The Pale Sorceress: Book Four of the Chronicles of Ilseador* (August 2024)

Author's Note

So... for those of you who have been paying attention, you might have noticed some familiar themes showing up in this series.

Damien received the Monarch's Blade from a statue made of stone – who also happened to be a ghostly lady.

He and Genevieve are having trouble conceiving a child... and there a romance has brewed between the queen and their dearest friend and (former) Champion.

And now there's an evil sorceress who has Plans for Damien.

L'Morte d'Artur, anyone?

Before you ask, no, this wasn't something I'm shoehorning in and I'm not trying to re-write the legend of King Arthur. (I recommend the Legendborn series by Tracey Deonn if you are into that sort of thing. Which I am. Sometimes. Sort of.)

This is just the way the story is evolving... though you might find other stories that we know in our world making somewhat skewed appearances here and there in my writing. Not enough to call anything I do a 'fractured fairytale' but... you'll see bits and pieces.

I almost said stories from our world... but the World of the Living Gods (which will get a better I don't name... someday....) seems to be the world from which our stories come. They come to us a bit skewed, as I said.

For anyone who has studied folklore and mythology – which I have done in a desultory fashion since childhood as the daughter of a professional international folklorist and storyteller – you see patterns arising. The same stories told in different places – told differently, but with common threads that are identifiable.

Now that could be that there was transmission of these stories from culture to culture (though that isn't likely in a number of instances between, say, the Old and New Worlds). Or it could be – as Joseph Campbell opined – that these stories are derived from the common experience of being human;

that there are certain fundamental truths that all humans experience and therefore all cultures create the stories the same way.

Or... you could believe that there really is some place where the tales are true – in one sense or another – and some of us here on Earth simply have a connection to that other place. That the stories we tell each other (some anyways) are less our own fantastical creations, but are our fantastical interpretations of events happening in this other space. (Or spaces... I don't see why there couldn't be more than one.)

So, anyways... you can think of these tidbits in my stories as Easter eggs (in the movie sense) or just enjoy the ride as you go along. Like I said, these aren't meant to be re-tellings of fairytales... and the stories are going their own ways that may or may not follow the paths our familiar stories follow. But you may find extra flavor and interest in noticing where these connections fall.

Email me at RisingDragonBooks@gmail.com to let me know what other connections you find!

About the Author

MANGALA MCNAMARA LIVES IN FLYOVER Country (the far northern end of the US South) with her husband, The Professor, and four of her six children. The remaining children are in college — you can blame the oldest for the excessive amounts of math showing up in Mangala's fantasy novels, the second one for better attention to staging of scenes, the third for all the economics, and the fourth for great attention to history — and all of them for a focus on political science! Mangala is a former professional bellydance instructor, and used to enjoy knitting, crotchet and embroidering Temari balls but now is much more boring as she rarely does anything but write… although she also fences (the sport) and plays D&D with her kids. She owes her love of books and reading to her mother, who was a professional folklorist and could recite — from memory — stories from every nation in the United Nations.

Her Knightess of the Realm and Prankster Prince series occur in the same world as Damien and Genevieve's stories.

Learn about Mangala's upcoming projects (fiction and nonfiction both) and sign up for email updates at
https://www.RisingDragonBooks.com

Made in the USA
Columbia, SC
01 July 2024

212a51c1-e40c-4854-ad64-aa541c27ac27R03